PRAISE FOR THE FLAGLER HUNT :

"Combines history, secrets, and conspiracies in an entertaining and intriguing tale."
– Steve Berry, *New York Times* bestselling author of *The Malta Exchange*

"A treasure-hunter's dream read."
– Carter Wilson, *USA Today* bestselling author of *The Dead Girl in 2A*

AND FOR JEREMY BURNS'S PREVIOUS WORK:

"With *From the Ashes*, Jeremy Burns establishes himself among the best authors of taut, historical thrillers. In this gripping debut, Burns lays bare a fascinating conspiracy of deceit, full of action and twists. You'll find yourself rooting for his heroes, repulsed by his villains, and rethinking what you think you know about one of history's darkest times. Truly, a must-read for fans of suspense, action, and history."
– Robert Liparulo, bestselling author of *The 13th Tribe*, *Comes a Horseman*, and *The Dreamhouse Kings*

"*From the Ashes* is a thrilling race against time to expose a diabolical conspiracy that would shatter everything we think we know about the 20th century. With clever puzzles, enigmatic clues, and hidden secrets, Jeremy Burns re-imagines New York's landmarks so vividly that you will want to explore them all over again."
– Boyd Morrison, #1 *New York Times* bestselling author of *The Ark* and *The Vault*

"A book for fans of Steve Berry and Raymond Khoury, *From the Ashes* is well-written and impeccably researched with great characters and a conspiracy that is frightening in both its implications and plausibility. Jeremy Burns is an author to watch."
– Ethan Cross, international bestselling author of *The Shepherd*

"*National Treasure* meets *The Bourne Identity* in this riveting debut. Blending history, suspense, and adventure, Burns takes readers on a nonstop thrill ride through some of the country's most famous sites – and infamous periods of history – ensuring that you'll never look at New York City, the 1930s, or the name 'Rockefeller' the same again. Not to miss!"
– Jeremy Robinson, bestselling author of *Threshold* and *Secondworld* on *From the Ashes*

"Amazing historical research, very frightening agent-types and some people just trying to do the right thing and led into it quite nice by author Burns. Even if you don't believe in secrets, this is a story of the first-order and if you like mysteries pick it up. You won't be sorry."
– Cheryl's Book Nook on *From the Ashes*

"Start early as this is definitely an intriguing story that will have you muttering 'oh, no' as you are reading as fast as you can to get to the next page. For interesting plot and edge-of-your-seat, nail-biting suspense, *The Dubai Betrayal* is definitely the book for you."
– Vic's Media Room

"Will leave fans of Daniel Silva and Brad Thor breathless for more."
– Mark Greaney, #1 *New York Times* bestselling author of *Back Blast* on *The Dubai Betrayal*

THE FLAGLER HUNT

A Jonathan Rickner Thriller by

JEREMY BURNS

For Travis
The brother I never had, and the friend I always will

The Story Plant
Studio Digital CT, LLC
P.O. Box 4331
Stamford, CT 06907

Copyright @ 2019 by Jeremy Burns

Story Plant trade paperback ISBN-13: 978-1-61188-267-4
Story Plant mass market paperback ISBN-13: 978-1-61188-291-9
Fiction Studio Books E-book ISBN: 978-1-945839-31-3

Visit our website at www.TheStoryPlant.com

First Story Plant Printing: April 2019

Printed in the United States of America

0 9 8 7 6 5 4 3 2 1

ALSO BY JEREMY BURNS:

From the Ashes
The Dubai Betrayal
The Founding Treason

Prologue
October 12, 1565
Matanzas Bay, La Florida, New Spain

Father Francisco López de Mendoza Grajales felt his faith weakening with every headless, limbless soldier the admiral cast into the bay, each body part tossed into the saltwater inlet separately, dyeing the pristine cerulean waters a foreboding red.

This was not what he had signed up for. French heretics or not, this was not God's work.

This was a massacre. A vengeful message, written in blood.

Admiral Pedro Menéndez de Avilés was the commander of this heretic hunt. A favorite of King Philip, Menéndez had gained a reputation as a stalwart defender of God and country, a brave adventurer who defied the odds with his often-brash methods, seizing victory from the jaws of almost certain defeat. He had tangled with corsairs, pirates, privateers, and the mightiest warships France could muster, claiming goods, treasure, and ships for the crown. The Spanish empire was stronger, larger, and richer because of him.

But Father López couldn't imagine God smiling upon the scene before him now. Perhaps this was the strategic thing to do, but he could derive no solace from the thought.

Then again, this was why they had come, why Menéndez had founded St. Augustine after sighting land on the eponymous ancient church father's feast day. A group of French settlers—Huguenot Protestants, to be specific—had founded Fort Caroline just to the north, on territory claimed by the Spanish crown. The Gulf Stream made the region a perfect staging area for attacks on King Philip's Treasure Fleet laden with gold, silver, and jewels from Peru and the Yucatan en route to Spain. Furthermore, Fort Caroline was an unacceptable intrusion on New Spain, a blight ruled by an enemy king and a heretic god.

It would not stand.

To demonstrate his piety, Menéndez had called upon Father López to conduct mass shortly after landing at St. Augustine, calling on the Lord to bless their enterprise and claim this land for Spain.

God answered their prayers most spectacularly.

Menéndez's reputation as a bold mariner preceded him, such that any foe, including Fort Caroline's leader, the renowned French naval officer Jean Ribault, would expect a sea attack. So Menéndez attacked from the land.

Leading a contingent of soldiers overland under cover of a hurricane, Menéndez shocked the French with a surprise attack that led to the complete loss of the fort. The soldiers, farmers, and other Frenchmen were seized as prisoners and massacred. But one key threat remained.

While Menéndez was marching up the rugged Florida coastline, Ribault was launching his own assault toward the newly christened St. Augustine. But instead of catching the Spanish unawares, as his own countrymen had been farther north, the same hurricane that had masked Menéndez's approach shipwrecked Ribault's fleet miles below St. Augustine. All this on St. Michael's Day, a day celebrating the sword-wielding archangel of the church militant.

Further proof of Providence's blessing upon their mission.

Upon learning of the shipwrecks, Menéndez led his men, still high on the overwhelming victory at Fort Caroline, south through the swamplands and forests to capture Ribault and his soldiers. Menéndez had accepted their surrender, then put them to the sword. But this time, he went too far.

Ten at a time, the soldiers were blindfolded and brought overland to this spot on the banks of the inlet. Then, at a command from the admiral, Menéndez's soldiers slashed the necks of the kneeling prisoners. After decapitating the prisoners, Menéndez had his men hack off the dead men's arms and legs before tossing the dismembered bodies, piece by piece, into the river.

Father López had been hundreds of yards downstream from the massacre when it started. His first clue that something horrific was happening was the tinge of deepening red marring the river's waters. Then he saw the source, the desecrated heads, torsos, and limbs floating along like nightmare driftwood.

He had hurried to reach the site, the robes of his habit snagging on briars in his haste to witness the shocking massacre.

As he crested a low rise, he saw it was happening all over again, another ten Frenchmen, enemies of the true faith and of King Philip, slashed apart in a barbaric ritual of vengeance. But there was no reasonable purpose for the brutal posthumous butchery. This was the wilds of the New World, with no witnesses to teach a lesson. No more Huguenots to strike the fear of God into. No citizenry to illustrate the consequences of attempted treason. Such drastic acts may have been useful in medieval cities, scaring off future attempts at coups or other crimes against the crown. But the only witnesses to this horrific crime were its perpetrators.

And God Himself.

A plan began to formulate in López's mind. Perhaps it was a divine revelation. Or perhaps it was merely his heartfelt desire to see the natives of this New World brought into the Catholic fold. The one thing he was sure of was that it would equip the Church to do God's work like never before on this continent. And it wouldn't be possible without Admiral Menéndez.

That night, Father López visited the admiral in his quarters.

"God has seen what you have done, Don Menéndez," López said, adopting as piously stern a tone as he could muster. "He is not pleased."

Menéndez was taken aback. "I killed the Protestant heathens who would poison the peoples of this land with their pernicious influence. I would think God would be happy with such a result, especially since it was His hand that wrecked their ships and led them into our hands."

"True enough, but the manner of your posthumous desecration of the bodies—and of the river that flows here to the land I first blessed for us not six weeks ago—reveals the hidden darkness in your heart. As it says in the book of Ecclesiastes, 'For God will bring every act to judgment, everything which is hidden, whether it is good or evil.'"

It was unnerving to see the powerful admiral so stricken by his comments, but for all his bravado and vengeful actions earlier in the day, Menéndez was, in his heart, a devoted Catholic.

"What must I do to redeem myself in the eyes of the Lord?" Menéndez asked.

Father López smiled paternally. "Something that He has chosen you for. Something that can change the fate of the holy faith in this new land. But in this task for which He has called you, you must choose between two masters."

In a hushed voice, López quickly spelled out the overarching plan to ensure that the holy faith continued to strengthen and spread across the new continent long after he and Menéndez had departed this mortal coil. Shock and disgust took turns dancing across the admiral's face as López laid out what would be required of them both.

As soon as López finished speaking, Menéndez spat, "You speak of treason."

López took a deep breath. He was committed now. The Lord's will must prevail.

"I speak of reclamation, Don Menéndez. The King of Spain shall never know of our deeds. But the King of Heaven sees all. Your very soul is in peril. The Lord has offered you a path to redemption."

The admiral turned away, staring into the candlelight that dimly flickered on a table by his bed. He was clearly wrestling with the moral, legal, and spiritual ramifications of both options, while likely ruing his choice to dispatch of the French soldiers the way he had. López offered a prayer to heaven, for the admiral's soul, for his decision, and for the successful completion of the plan. Menéndez had built his career on risky gambles that had paid off, drawing King's Philip's favor even before he had ascended to the throne. Now perhaps his riskiest venture yet awaited. If only he would take the plunge. If not, Father López might find himself on that crimson-stained beach, kneeling in sand soaked with heretic blood and awaiting the sword's merciless blow.

Finally, after what seemed like an eternity of waiting on a knife's edge, Menéndez turned back to Father López.

"I am the Lord's servant first and foremost. If He commands it, I shall obey."

López smiled. "The Lord is pleased with your decision. If we are successful in our venture, it will change the fate of the New World."

Menéndez nodded, but he was already lost in thought, putting the pieces together for how he would pull off his most audacious mission yet. He was risking everything now. They both were. But if it worked as planned, no one would ever really know what they had done.

No one except God.

PART ONE

EDISON

Chapter 1
Mount Mansfield, Vermont
Present Day

Emerson Kirkheimer was overwhelmed with a deadly sense of irony. Ironic that this idyllic mountain forest should instill such fear in him. Ironic that the place he'd chosen as a refuge from his enemies might well become his grave.

Despite his need to keep moving, he was forced to stop again, hands on knees, trying to catch his breath in the thinning mountain air. A lifetime of studying rare manuscripts and artifacts had not prepared his body for arduous physical labor such as this. His tennis shoes, rarely used for aerobic activities in his sedentary lifestyle, were poor substitutes for the hiking boots he should have worn. More than once an ill-placed step had painfully turned his ankle.

Whoever decided that this hellish obstacle course should be designated a "trail" deserved to be slapped in the face with a dictionary. Trails were nice walking paths from which one could enjoy nature's beauty without getting lost in the woods. This was a series of crags and boulders perched over one precipitous drop after another, each yawning chasm deeper and wider than the last. If he managed to get out of here alive, he would have a serious talk with the park service about the dangers of false advertising.

As he rounded a corner, the canopy overhead opened up again, allowing him a view down the mountain. The blue sedan was still there, parked by the roadside thousands of feet below. Parked directly behind Kirkheimer's own rental. His pursuer wasn't being subtle. Out here, he could afford to be bold. And the overweight antiquities dealer was hardly a match for whatever the man in the blue sedan brought to bear.

It had started yesterday morning, when he discovered that his office in the St. Louis antiquities firm he co-owned had been ransacked. His office was his sacred space, the one place he felt completely empowered and in control. Now that was destroyed, ripped to shreds by some unknown enemy. Wondering how bad the overall damage was, he opened the office of his longtime friend and business partner, Geoff Vogt, and found an even more shocking scene. Not only was Geoff's office equally destroyed, with sheaves of paper and shards of priceless Ming vases strewn across a swath of broken furniture, but buried underneath a pile of bloodied documents and a toppled filing cabinet had lain the murdered body of his partner.

After vomiting profusely on his own shoes, Kirkheimer ran from the office, forgetting to lock up. He had never been one for spy thrillers or police procedurals, preferring to ferret out the mysteries of the past from the safety of his office, but he knew he had to learn how to go on the run very quickly. Someone was after him. Someone who wanted something he and Geoff had, some priceless artifact perhaps. Maybe they had already gotten what they wanted from one of their offices. Maybe they would leave him alone now. But no, people who did things like what had happened to Geoff didn't leave loose ends. And Kirkheimer was a loose end.

Tempted at first to go home and pack a bag, Kirkheimer realized that would be the next most obvious place for his faceless pursuers to look for him. He could buy more clothes when he got to wherever he was going.

He stopped by an ATM and withdrew as much as his bank would let him, then he used his smartphone to book the soonest flight out of state he could find. Burlington, Vermont. He'd always wanted to visit the Green Mountain State but had always been too preoccupied with work to find the time. Now all that had changed.

Hours later, he was on a plane to Burlington. He realized that Burlington was just a short drive from the Canadian border. He didn't have his passport with him, which had prohibited him from taking an international flight out of St. Louis, but perhaps he could sneak across the border with just his Missouri driver's license. He rented a car at the Burlington airport, then, choosing a route on his phone's maps app, he realized how many mistakes he had already made. Even if Canada would let him in with just his license, the authorities would surely make a record of his crossing. Just like his flight to Burlington and his car rental would show. Like bread crumbs for Geoff's murderers.

He powered down his phone—he vaguely recalled seeing a *60 Minutes* episode where a fugitive was tracked down using GPS data from his cell phone—and headed out of town and onto I-89 South, away from the Canadian border. Perhaps he could use Burlington's proximity to America's northern neighbor to bluff his pursuers into thinking he'd left the country. Regardless, heading north would eventually limit his options as he butted up against the border. His salvation, if it was to be had, lay to the south.

An hour later, he reached the turn-off for Waterbury Center and Stowe. His parents had gone on a ski trip to Stowe years before Kirkheimer was born. It was late October now, that dead time between the brilliant displays of fall foliage and the first snows of winter. An off-season resort town, miles off the highway and tucked between the state's highest mountains, could be just what he needed to hide long enough to figure all this out.

But it hadn't bought him nearly enough time. He'd spent the previous night at the cheapest motel he could find—paid for in cash—and returned after a walk this morning to find out that a man had been inquiring after him. Tall, solidly built, red hair, and driving a blue sedan was the only description the concierge could offer, but it didn't matter. They'd found him. He didn't know who the man was, but he knew his respite was over. Even this remote mountain town wasn't safe anymore. He had to hide. The man had apparently gone back into town to make further inquiries, and a rock slide had closed off the road through Smuggler's Notch, the narrow passage to the other side of the mountains that got its name from nineteenth-century fur traders who had used the isolated pass to circumvent tariffs on goods going to and from Canada. There was only one place to hide.

Up.

Kirkheimer drove to the base of Long Trail, a miles-long path that traced a circuitous route up the mountain—theoretically ideal since he wasn't so much focused on a particular destination as he was being inaccessible to bad guys—and began hiking. The hours drained away as he trudged up Mount Mansfield, the tallest peak in a state named for them. Fellow hikers passed him, many speaking Quebecois, offering the briefest of nods as they continued their ascent. Before long, most of his fellow travelers were coming down the mountain past him. And shortly thereafter, they dwindled down to nothing.

The sun was starting to dip behind the towering mountains above, and he had now left Long Trail for the aptly named Profanity Trail, a theoretical shortcut that seemed like less of a trail and more like a mostly dry waterfall. He had seen rock walls that were less arduous than that purported trail, and every time he slipped and banged his knee, hip, or elbow, he let loose with an increasingly vehement string of expletives.

It was then, lying on his rear after yet another tumble, that he caught his first glimpse of the blue sedan far below. How long had that been there? How long had his mysterious pursuer been following him? Was he still miles behind at the base of the mountain? Or was he right on his tail?

The gondola. That was Kirkheimer's only hope. According to the map he had seen miles back, he had to make his way to the top of the mountain, cross along Cliff Trail, and reach the gondolas that ran back to the base. Normally more active during the ski season, the gondolas gave visitors easy access to a mountaintop restaurant and a viewing station, but the dearth of tourists in late October meant the gondolas would be closing soon. And shortly thereafter, the cold dark of night. If he could pull an end run on his pursuer and get back to his car while the red-haired man was still ascending the mountain, Kirkheimer could leave town and find another hiding spot—or even turn himself in to the police and beg for protection. It was his best chance yet, and it had to work. If not...

Now clambering from rock to rock on the treacherous Cliff Trail, trying not to let fear or panic turn his exhausted limbs to rubber, Kirkheimer caught another glimpse of the red-haired man, ascending through switchbacks with a much easier gait than the rotund historian's own bedraggled pace. Kirkheimer had the lead, though. He just had to keep it.

Encountering another short slope far too steep to walk down without plummeting face-first off the mountain when reaching the end, Kirkheimer sat down and scooted along for a minute, his muscles grateful for the short break from stretching across chasm after chasm. Reaching the end of the

18

slope, he rounded a boulder to find another series of rock pillars floating over deep pits. Wonderful.

He took a moment to wipe the sweat from his face, cold and clammy in the alpine air as the sun continued to crawl behind the mountain, stealing its warmth and light with it. Not much farther, he told himself, though in reality he had no idea how far he still was from the gondola. He didn't know how much longer his aching muscles and screaming lungs could take.

Climbing across the first two boulders was tough, but nothing he hadn't done several times already since embarking on this ill-advised journey. But the gap between the second and third boulder was too far to just reach across. He would have to jump.

Planting his feet, he took a deep breath and leapt. His feet hit the other boulder, but his ankle buckled on the landing. Not good.

He could see it in slow motion, forced to experience it in excruciating detail while powerless to do anything to stop it. The pain shooting through his ankle. His body tilting to one side. His hands reaching, scrabbling for any sort of purchase against the rock. The world turning upside down, disappearing from view as he tumbled down into the crevice below. And then, the shockwave of all-consuming pain washing over every sinew of his being as he slammed into, then wedged against, the tight walls of the pit that might well become his tomb.

He was stuck lying at an angle, his girth pressed against the rocks on either side, with at least fifteen feet of tightening crevasse below him. His left arm was behind him, immovable other than his quickly numbing fingers. He tried to wriggle his other arm free, prying it from the rock. Immediately he started to slip farther down the chasm. He shoved his arm back against the wall. One thing was inexorably clear: he was in big trouble.

"Help!" he screamed, praying that one of the hikers he had seen earlier—or perhaps even one of the park rangers or staff operating the gondolas—would hear his cries and come to his rescue. He tried to control his breathing, feeling a panic attack coming on. And justifiably so, he reasoned subconsciously. He was going to die here.

He cried for help again and again, his pleas punctuated by sobs that racked his trapped body and sent new waves of pain through him. Surely someone would hear him. The gondolas couldn't be that far off. Darkness was fast engulfing the mountainside, with the temperatures dropping precipitously. He had no doubt that the combination of the elements and whatever injuries he'd sustained in his fall—not to mention whatever bears, wolves, or other predators that lived on the mountain—could very well mean he wouldn't live to see sunrise.

"Hello?" called a voice in the near distance.

Had he just imagined he'd heard it? Was his situation plunging him into delirium? Or was he about to be saved after all?

"Help! Down here!"

A few moments later, a silhouetted figure darkened the opening of the chasm twenty feet above.

"Are you okay down there?" the voice, a man's, asked.

"I'm not dead, but I hurt all over. And I'm stuck. Please, I need help to get out of here, and fast."

"All in good time, Mr. Kirkheimer."

A chill ran down Kirkheimer's spine. The red-haired man.

"Help!" he screamed, hoping someone, anyone, would show up and save him from his worsening predicament.

"No one can hear you, Mr. Kirkheimer. No one else is on the mountain. It's just you and me."

Kirkheimer swallowed, realizing how parched he had become. He had no idea if the man was telling the truth, but he suspected he was. The darkening skies told him all the sensible hikers—and the gondola operators—had long since gone home.

"Here's how this is going to work," the man said. "I'm going to ask you a few questions. You're going to answer them honestly and completely. And once I'm satisfied, I'll help you out of there. Heck, I'll even call the rangers to help you off the mountain."

"You killed Geoff, you monster."

"Your partner was more recalcitrant than he should have been. I hope you're smart enough to avoid the same mistake."

Kirkheimer said nothing, seething inside yet cognizant that he was out of options. He would do what he had to in order to get out of here. Otherwise, he would be dead before morning.

"Last week, you appraised a piece, a wooden container holding a wax cylinder. Who purchased that particular item?"

"I can't tell you that. Our clients' privacy is paramount in this trade."

The man laughed, a nasty, evil sound that made Kirkheimer's skin crawl.

"I'm sure even your most reclusive client would make an exception considering your current position. Who bought it, Mr. Kirkheimer?"

He had no choice. But wouldn't he be putting his client in danger? Could he really do that to another person?

"What do you want with the piece?" he asked.

"That's really of little concern to you. Suffice it to say that it's a piece I have a great deal of interest in. A very specific interest. And whoever your client is, I can offer him a great deal of money."

"Or you can just kill him, like you did Geoff."

"Again, Mr. Vogt brought his fate upon himself by being unnecessarily stubborn. He refused my offer of money, though I suspect your client will not. And, of course, I can offer you something far more important than money."

His freedom, of course. The only way out was through this murderous antiquities junkie. A devil's bargain. But the only bargain around.

"My patience is wearing thin," the man said. "And I'm pretty sure the wolves will want their evening meal soon enough. A terrible way to go, I'm told."

"Tristram Bouvier, in St. Augustine," Kirkheimer blurted out, the prospect of being devoured alive by wolves too much to bear. "Ancient City Antiques, on Aviles Street."

"St. Augustine, Florida?" the man said as though to himself. "Of course."

Kirkheimer felt his other arm growing numb. He had to extricate himself as soon as possible, lest he risk even worse long-term damage. "Now, please, let me out."

"One final question," the man said. "Did you listen to the wax cylinder? Did you hear what was on the recording?"

21

"No," Kirkheimer lied, suspecting he knew why the man was after the piece. It was bold and outrageous and exactly the kind of insanity treasure hunters like this monster would love to pursue. But telling him he'd listened to the recording would make him a liability. He had little doubt that the man would leave him here to rot if he knew Kirkheimer was onto his plan. "Geoff appraised the cylinder. I did the case."

"Good to hear," the man said. "I'll be back in a moment."

"Wait!" Kirkheimer yelled. But the man was gone. He thought he could hear the howl of a wolf carried by the wind, but he tried to convince himself it was just his over-active imagination. He had given the man the information he needed. Sold out Bouvier for his freedom. But he was still stuck. And night was falling.

Moments later, he heard footsteps above. A park ranger? Another hiker? Or the red-haired man?

"Hello?" Kirkheimer called. "Is someone up there?"

"Me again, Mr. Kirkheimer. Sorry to keep you waiting." The red-haired man's silhouette was less pronounced now as the light behind him had dwindled in the intervening minutes. But there was something different about it. Kirkheimer just couldn't say what.

"What took you so long?" Kirkheimer said. "Help me out of here already."

"You helped me out, so it's only fair that I return the favor, huh?"

"Exactly. Please, it's getting cold."

The moon must have come out from behind a cloud, because the man's face was suddenly bathed in pale illumination before the light dimmed once more.

"Wait a minute," Kirkheimer said. "I know you."

"Don't believe everything you read in the papers, Mr. Kirkheimer," the man said. "I'm not as bad as people say I am. I'm going to save you from a nasty death at the hands of a pack of wolves, after all."

Then the silhouette changed, and Kirkheimer saw the shape of something large and vaguely round lifted above the man's head.

"Know that your client and his recent acquisition are in good hands."

"Wait!" Kirkheimer yelled, realizing too late what was happening. "We had a deal! You—"

The last word was snuffed out as Kirkheimer's teeth, along with the rest of his face, were smashed in by the impact of the massive rock thrown from above. He was dead as soon as the stone struck his skull, unable to see his murderer skulk back down the moonlit mountain to his next victim, and his ultimate prize.

A treasure beyond imagination. Paid for in blood.

Chapter 2
St. Augustine, Florida

Jonathan Rickner was in heaven.

The room was built to be spacious, but it was packed to the brim with historical documents, antique books, and centuries-old curios that made Jon's heart thrum. Furthermore, he was in the oldest city in the United States, the Spanish-founded settlement that predated the Declaration of Independence by more than two centuries. Yet the cherry on top wasn't historical at all, rather a mere two years older than Jon's own twenty-one.

His brother, Michael.

It had been months since the two of them had spent much time together. Inseparable as youths, Michael was just starting in on his graduate program at Georgetown while Jon had taken a semester off from his studies at Harvard to backpack across Eastern Europe. This trip to St. Augustine wasn't just a vacation, but Jon found it hard not be excited by this abundance of history, especially stateside.

"Where do you think he is?" Jon asked.

"No idea," Michael said. "The door was open, and his 'Out to Lunch' sign isn't flipped around. I can't imagine he'd leave without a good reason. Especially with all this—"

A shadow crossed the glass of the entry door, then pushed its way into the shop.

"So sorry to keep you waiting... Michael! Jon!" Concern fell away from the man's face as he recognized his customers.

"How are you, Mr. Bouvier?" Jon asked as he and Michael shook the proprietor's hand.

"Please, call me Tristram," Bouvier said. "You're both grown now, after all."

Jon smiled at the request, knowing full well his father's aged friend would always be Mr. Bouvier, no matter how old the Rickner brothers were. He looked older than Jon remembered, his once salt-and-pepper hair having dispensed with the pepper altogether. But the passion that danced in the eyes behind that more wrinkled visage hadn't dulled a bit. If anything, it seemed even more fervent than before.

"How long has it been now?" Bouvier asked.

"Six years next month," Michael answered.

"That long already?" The antiquarian smiled wistfully off into the distance. "My how time flies."

"How is everything with you?"

"Great!" Bouvier said. "Well, almost. Been fending off a pair of shoplifters-in-training. Little scamps come in when I'm busy with another customer, grab whatever's handy, and make a break for it."

"Have you called the cops?" Jon asked.

"Twice. But it's a small force. And a couple of adolescent petty thieves aren't exactly their top priority."

"Is that where you were just a minute ago?"

"Heh." Bouvier wiped the back of his hand across his forehead. "Saw me panting, huh? They grabbed a couple of old comic books this time. Nothing too rare, thankfully."

"Sorry about that," Jon said.

"Eh, price of doing business these days," Bouvier said, moving toward a cabinet behind the counter. "Here, I've got something you'll absolutely love. Especially being here in St. Augustine."

The bell over the door jangled behind them. A pair of young towheaded boys darted into the shop, grabbed a pair of nineteenth-century hand-carved wooden toys off a shelf, and dashed back out the door.

"That's them! The little thieves!" Bouvier, still slightly winded from his last pursuit, moved to chase the boys.

"We'll get them, Mr. Bouvier," Jon said as he and Michael headed out the door. After blinking at the sudden burst of Florida sunshine, Jon saw that the boys were running in opposite directions down Aviles Street.

"You take that one," Michael shouted over his shoulder as he took off in pursuit. "This one's mine."

Anticipating his brother's plan before he'd even voiced it, Jon was already running after the other boy. The chase was on.

Chapter 3

Caeden Monk was not a patient man. If he were, he might still be enjoying the other half of his double life as a respected Cornell professor. Instead, he had been stripped of that honor, forced to dive headlong into his deeper, darker passions.

When he finally found a spot in the overpriced parking garage across from the St. Augustine Visitor Center, he meticulously wiped down the car. It was rented under a false name, as was his usual modus operandi, but he didn't want any trace hairs or other identifying marks to come back to haunt him. He wore black leather driving gloves, a strange fashion accessory despite the relative crispness of the autumn morning air. But this was Florida. Strangeness was so omnipresent here, they could write a book on it. Scratch that, he realized. They had written a book on it. Several, in fact. In theory, his gloves might bring some unwanted attention, but they were a necessary precaution. For now at least.

The fat bookworm in Vermont had given him what he needed. Monk had seen the desperation in the man's eyes, the fearful, pleading glimmer that almost always presaged the vomiting up of all one's deepest secrets. Anything to seize at the slimmest chance that Monk wouldn't kill him once he had given him what he wanted.

Monk found it surprising that, despite years of Hollywood indoctrinating people on how this was rarely the case, only a few of his victims had failed to grasp at that last desperate hope of survival. It was human nature. And, in Monk's experience, one of his greatest advantages.

Hope was one of mankind's great delusions. Hope in your fellow man, at least. All you had to do was turn on the evening news for a tiny sampling of the evils man would perpetrate upon his brother. A natural disaster hits, and more people are looting their local electronics store than helping their neighbor. Opportunism was what had ended his life in the Ivy League, but ultimately, his change in direction had been an opportunity in itself.

Monk believed in a different kind of hope. Hope in oneself, in a man's ability to shape his own world as he saw fit. To believe in oneself so strongly that anything was possible. Anything he wanted, he could possess. It was a mindset that had guided him for years, and it hadn't failed him yet. In this dog-eat-dog world, the strongest survived, but it was the smartest who thrived. And Caeden Monk was top dog in both of those fields.

He walked through the main gates of the city, which were constructed of the region's most distinctive building material: coquina. A soft limestone quarried in the area for centuries, the rock's most interesting aspect was the tiny seashells littered throughout its structure. Many of the city's most lasting landmarks, from the city gates to the seventeenth-century Spanish fort that guarded the bay to a host of old houses lining the cobbled streets, were made of the sturdy material, which had withstood centuries of hurricanes and invaders.

Funny, he thought. Nearly five centuries had passed since St. Augustine's founding, with these very city gates withstanding the advances of the mightiest armies of the world and the most infamous pirates of the Caribbean. But now, after nearly two centuries of peace, the greatest invader the city had ever seen was walking through its gates unmolested. Indeed, the artisans selling their wares and the restaurants luring customers with tantalizing aromas and free samples would welcome him more like a patriot returning from battle rather than a pirate seeking to steal the city's greatest riches.

But then, of course, they had no idea the treasure even existed. That was the point. Flagler had seen to that.

It had just been a rumor, a legend evanescent even in the company of myths. But in recent weeks, the mists of legend had begun to take shape in tangible, pursuable form. He was just a few days too late with Kirkheimer, but he was

catching up. Monk only hoped that the cylinder's new owner, this Tristram Bouvier, didn't already realize what he pos-
sessed. If he did, all bets were off.

Miriam was late, as usual, hung up in traffic en route from
Jacksonville, but she had assured him minutes earlier that she
would be arriving within the hour. Just like them to let him do
the heavy lifting, but then that was why he was the mastermind
behind this—and every—operation, and she was just the hired
help. She definitely earned her keep, however. If he could do
this without her, he wouldn't have contacted her in the first
place. But this was far too big a prize to let slip through his
fingers because he was too stingy to shell out for Miriam's invaluable services. After he was done here, money would never
again be a concern for him.

Monk walked down St. George Street, the main prom-
enade down the historical city center, dodging a mob of
field-tripping fourth graders and young couples falling in
love with the romance and mystique of a town that was already ancient before George Washington was born. Modern
additions to the cityscape like Kilwins and Madame Tussauds
clashed with signs advertising all sorts of "the country's oldest" sites. Despite the twenty-first-century elements that had
moved in to attract tourist dollars, most shops were locally
owned and operated, with store hours as nontraditional and
eccentric as their proprietors. And though commerce, local
and national, was front and center in the tourist town, the
city's bones oozed with history.

In keeping with the sixteenth-century Spanish civil engineer-
ing practices in vogue when the town was founded, the streets were
narrow, no more than two lanes, though most could only accom-
modate one car—or horse-drawn cart, as would have been the case
centuries before. One road, Treasury Street, was renowned for being the narrowest street in the country, scarcely wide enough for
two men to walk down shoulder to shoulder. It felt very much like
the conquistador-era outpost it was founded as.

The street names also commemorated its historical
roots. From Spanish cities like Avilés and Sevilla to sixteenth-century figures like Pedro Menéndez de Avilés and
Ponce de Leon, the coastal town wore its origins proudly.

Monk checked his watch. The diversion was set. In a few
moments, he would have his opening. He paused on King
Street, just a few paces from Aviles Street. Any second now…

A blond boy ran past the intersection, continuing down Aviles. He'd never taken the time to learn the boy's name. He didn't really care. He and his brother had apparently taken a liking to Bouvier's comic books. Miriam had offered them a hundred dollars apiece to do what they were already doing— steal from Bouvier's shop this morning. Get the old man out of his shop long enough for Monk to steal what he had come for. No more bodies. No witnesses. No more clues to lead to him. Or to what he was doing here.

Monk walked toward the intersection and turned onto Aviles in the direction from which the boy had come. As soon as he rounded the corner, a young man, early twenties perhaps, almost barreled into Monk, dodging at the last minute before continuing down the street, yelling a winded apology as he kept running. After the boy? Who was this guy? Hopefully the boy's brother had successfully gotten Bouvier to take the bait and give chase. Monk didn't have the luxury of waiting to find out, though. His diversion would only afford him so much time to get what he needed and disappear. And with each passing second, that window was closing.

A few moments later, he pushed through the front door of Ancient City Antiques. The bell that heralded his arrival was accompanied by the jarring realization that Bouvier hadn't taken the bait at all. He was still there, arranging items behind the counter. The proprietor wouldn't be one to sit idly by while Monk dug through his shop and took what he wanted. Time, also, was still a factor, since at least one Good Samaritan would likely be returning once he'd caught—or lost—Monk's decoys.

So, Plan B, then.

Chapter 4

The kid had a head start, but Jon was quickly closing the gap. Of course, in this day and age, chances were some misguided observer would decide that the man chasing the boy down the street must be a kidnapper and needed to be tackled. Glancing over his shoulder, Michael and the other boy were long gone, probably somewhere down a side street. He turned around and almost ran into a bicyclist coming the opposite direction. Side-stepping at the last second, he picked up the pace, closing the gap to his quarry to ten yards.

Just past 10 a.m., the morning air was growing warmer as the sun neared its apex, but the sea breeze off Matanzas Bay helped to keep him relatively cool. He dodged a store display of postcards and kitschy souvenirs, brushing past and sending it spinning on its axis.

The kid darted up Cadiz Street, heading toward the bay—and Avenida Menéndez. Jon wanted to catch the kid, put the fear of God into him, and recover Bouvier's goods, not chase him into traffic, but if he didn't catch him soon, something very bad could happen.

A gaggle of tourists in gaudy Hawaiian T-shirts poured out of a bed-and-breakfast into the street, oblivious to the chase they had just stumbled into. Not good. If the little scamp powered his way through the group, Jon would have little chance of catching him before he reached the main road.

But the boy stutter-stepped, caught off guard by his suddenly blocked path. It was just the delay Jon needed. A few bounding strides later, he snagged the boy's shirt collar and pulled him to the side of the road.

"Hey, you're not the police, are you?" the kid asked. "Undercover, like on TV?"

"What if I am?" Jon said.

"Look, I didn't do anything wrong, officer. Honest."

Jon thought it best to let the boy's assumption remain for now. Perhaps he'd be more likely to cooperate if he thought he was a cop. "I seriously doubt your parents would agree. Empty your pockets."

With a sour but defeated expression, the boy did as instructed. From one pocket came a Samsung flip phone and a Teenage Mutant Ninja Turtles wallet. From the other, the stolen antique toy. And a folded but otherwise crisp new one-hundred-dollar bill.

"Why on earth are you stealing when you've got a hundred dollars right here?" Jon asked, continuing to build his air of authority. This kid had tormented Mr. Bouvier enough. Jon was determined to not only retrieve the stolen toy but also to scare the kid straight for good. "Seems like you must really *want* to go to jail."

"No, no, no!" the kid said. "I wasn't stealing it. I was just supposed to get the old guy to chase me."

"What are you talking about? Why did you want him to chase you?"

"That's what the guy said. He gave me and my brother a hundred bucks each to get the old shopkeeper to chase us through the city for a while."

Jon shot a nervous glance back toward Bouvier's shop. "To get him out of his shop? Who gave you the money?"

"I dunno. Older guy, tall, kinda reddish hair. I don't know his name. All this was his idea. I didn't do anything wrong."

Jon grabbed Bouvier's toy and the hundred-dollar bill. "If you ever steal anything from his shop again, you'll spend the rest of your life in prison. Do you understand?"

"Yes, officer." The boy cocked his head. "Hey, that's my hundred-dollar bill, though."

"Crime doesn't pay, son," Jon said. The bill would help pay for some of Bouvier's losses from the kids' previous thefts. He was tempted to press the matter with the boy and attempt to retrieve the rest of the stolen goods. But this mysterious red-haired man's request set off alarm bells in Jon's head.

Something was very wrong in St. Augustine today. He began running toward Bouvier's shop, praying he wasn't too late.

Chapter 5

"Did you get them?" Bouvier asked, his back still to Monk. When he finally turned around, his face went white with shock, though whether it was from recognizing his interlocutor or reacting to the pistol that was now aimed at him, Monk couldn't tell just yet.

"You." A single word, spoken as an accusation.

"Me," Monk said. "I'm here for the piece Kirkheimer and Vogt sold you a few days ago. Give it to me, and I'll be out of your life forever."

"I'm not giving you anything," Bouvier said, though the defiance in his words were not accompanied by courage in his tone.

"Of course not. How silly of me. You're a businessman. I merely wish to purchase one of your wares." He laid a crisp one-hundred-dollar bill on the counter. "There you are. Payment for the piece. A bit under market value, perhaps, but can you really put a price on your own life?"

"I don't have it anymore. I'm sorry."

"Don't lie to me, Mr. Bouvier. I can become a very big problem for you."

The proprietor glanced at the cordless phone sitting in its cradle a few feet away. "I'll call the cops. Aren't you wanted for murder?"

"Not in this country. That can change in a hurry, though, if you're so intent on being obstinate."

"Like I said, I don't have it anymore. I sold it."

"To whom?" Monk asked.

Bouvier's eyes shifted to the left. "I can't help you. I'm sorry."

Monk grabbed the corner of a table and flipped it onto its side. Several complete sets of Gilded Age china crashed to the floor. Bouvier jumped at the violence of the destruction. He didn't have the stomach to hold out for long, Monk knew. The antiquarian would crack soon enough.

"The moment a would-be customer walks through that door, they get a bullet through the head. And then, so will you."

"You're nothing but a common thug. Get out of my shop, Dr. Monk."

Monk grabbed an illuminated medieval hymnal from a modern music stand, flicked a lighter, and touched the flame to the corner.

"No!" Bouvier's face wrenched in pain, as though the destruction of his pieces physically hurt him.

Monk stared at him over the growing flames. "Which hand do you like most, Mr. Bouvier?"

"What?"

"Unless you tell me where the cylinder is in the next ten seconds, you're going to permanently lose the use of one of your hands. I'm offering you the choice of which one. Or, of course, you can keep both of them and just tell me where the cylinder is."

"You'll never get it."

"Your shop is only so big, Mr. Bouvier. I think I'll find it soon enough. It's just a matter of how alive you want to be when I do."

Bouvier stared at him, his face reddening and fists clenched in seething fury.

"Or were you talking about something other than the cylinder, perhaps?"

Still silence.

"You've listened to the recording, haven't you?" Monk asked.

"There's nothing to find. Just delusions of grandeur even their architect distanced himself from."

"That only proves how real it is. He wouldn't have abandoned it otherwise."

"He abandoned the project because it was built on a lie."

"He abandoned it because the truth was far bigger than he'd realized."

Monk didn't realize that he'd been unconsciously closing the distance between him and the shopkeeper in his zeal to prove his point. Now they were just a few feet apart, only the low counter separating them. A noise from the back of the store, like the shifting of something heavy on shelves. Monk instinctively looked in that direction. He wasn't aware of his mistake until Bouvier made his move.

The proprietor leapt across the counter, grabbing for the gun. Monk pulled it back, but Bouvier already had a grip on it. Though several inches shorter than Monk, he was stronger than he looked. They were face-to-face now, wrestling for the weapon. This had already gone badly, but it could turn worse in the briefest of moments. Monk had to end this soon.

He brought his body low and drove his forehead into Bouvier's nose. Headbutts hurt like a beast even when done correctly, but Monk blinked through the pain, knowing the attack's recipient got the worse end of it. Bouvier staggered but failed to loosen his grip on the gun.

"The cylinder, and I'm gone," Monk grunted. It was a lie, of course. Bouvier knew who he was and what he was after.

He couldn't be allowed to live. But the man was clearly desperate. The shopkeeper had crossed a line when he attacked him, but if Monk was to get what he needed, he had to offer him a way back from the brink.

Bouvier didn't take the bait. He pressed upward on the barrel, attempting to turn the weapon back on Monk. Clearly he saw right through Monk's offer, realizing his life was forfeit if left in the disgraced archeologist's hands. Time to press the attack again.

Monk kicked out, sweeping Bouvier's ankle to the side. Bouvier stumbled, jarring his grip—and Monk's—on the pistol. The quick shift of their angles, coupled with the tight hold Monk had on the gun, made everything fall apart.

The bang echoed briefly off the walls, muffled somewhat by the preponderance of books lining the shelves. Bouvier's eyes went wide. His hands slipped off the gun entirely as his ankle finished buckling and he fell to the floor. He stared in disbelief at the expanding patch of crimson staining his shirt.

Monk crouched down next to him. "This doesn't have to be the end, Tristram. Tell me where the cylinder is, and I'll call an ambulance for you."

Bouvier's eyes darted to a cabinet across the room. His fear of death had betrayed his attempts to stop Monk. But nothing could stop Monk. Emerson Kirkheimer, Geoff Vogt, and countless others over the years could attest to that.

Monk walked to the cabinet and opened it. A wax cylinder, wrapped in standard Edison-branded paper, sat on the first shelf. The contents field was blank, but then, it would be. This was one of a kind, not a mass-produced recording. And as it was hidden away almost as soon as it had been created, it was understandable that no one had written down the contents.

Everything fit. This was it.

He walked back to where Bouvier lay dying on the floor. "Thanks for your assistance," Monk said, holding the cylinder so Bouvier could see it. "Sorry you chose to do this the hard way."

Monk considered finishing him off with a bullet in the brain, but the blood bubbling on Bouvier's lips and the wheezing and sucking sounds accompanying each labored inhalation told him his previous shot had punctured the man's lung. His fate was already sealed. Better to let him enjoy the fruit of his inaction in his dying moments.

He picked up the medieval hymnbook still smoldering on the floor where he had dropped it when Bouvier attacked him. Flicking his lighter, he lit the book in several more places until the flames took hold. Carefully holding one end of the burning book, he used the hymnal as a makeshift torch to set fire to a pair of intricately woven Regency-era curtains. Once the curtains had caught fire, Monk chucked the medieval artifact across the room into a wall-length bookcase filled to the brim with historical papers and rare books. That, too, quickly became consumed in flames.

Monk had watched the academic empire he had built crumble into ruin. Now Bouvier would be forced to do the same.

"Thanks for the memories, Mr. Bouvier," he said, pocketing his pistol and tucking the cylinder under his jacket. "Expect a five-star Yelp review from me."

His humor was lost on the proprietor, who was witnessing his life's work turning to ash as he lay drowning in his own blood. No matter.

Monk flipped the sign on the door from "Open" to "Out for lunch" and walked outside, leaving the dying man to his inferno. He would be dead in seconds. But what glorious final seconds they would be.

As for Monk, he had what he needed. Plus, the fire and subsequent investigation would help occupy the city's first responders while he chased down his objective.

A hard lesson he had learned years back, one he had never forgotten: for the man who was willing to do anything to achieve his goal, nothing was out of reach.

Caeden Monk was indisputably such a man. Nothing and no one would keep him from his prize.

Chapter 6

Jon got back to the shop first. As soon as he reached the door, he realized something was terribly wrong. Plumes of black smoke billowed from the far end of the shop, clouding the air with a thickening gray miasma. The flickering reflections of flames dancing somewhere in the shop played off the bookshelves behind the counter.

He pushed through the door, immediately hit with a wave of heat as his nostrils filled with acrid fumes. Straight ahead, a pair of ornate curtains were on fire, while the wooden wall behind them smoldered toward a flashpoint. A built-in bookcase across the shop was having its priceless contents devoured by flames, burning pages falling free like hellish autumn leaves and setting alight the contents of nearby tables and display cases. Both fires were accompanied by a dull crackling roar, one that seemed to be growing in intensity with each passing moment.

What had happened here?

And where was Mr. Bouvier?

Jon's second question was answered almost as quickly as it was posed when his eyes fell upon the proprietor's form lying on the floor, halfway hidden behind the front edge of the counter.

"Mr. Bouvier!" Jon shouted, running to the man and kneeling at his side. His foot slid as he crouched, and he realized that he had slipped in a widening pool of blood. The antiquarian had suffered at least one bullet wound and was bleeding profusely from his chest. Jon fought a sense of revulsion, but it was quickly replaced by concern for his father's old friend and vengeance upon whoever had done this.

Bouvier was staring at the ceiling, eyes fixed in a pained thousand-yard stare. Jon ripped off his jacket and pushed it against the wound. Bouvier let out a weak, gasping scream, but Jon held the jacket firm. He had to stop the bleeding.

"Can you hold this here?" Jon asked. He had to manually move the man's hand to the jacket covering the wound, placing it in the right spot and hoping his injuries hadn't completely sapped his strength. "Mr. Bouvier, I'm going to call for help. Hold this here to help stop the bleeding, and I'll call for an ambulance." He wondered if an ambulance could even get down the narrow, cobbled path of Aviles Street, but he had to try.

The entry door's bell jangled behind Jon. He turned around to see Michael standing in the doorway, his older brother's shocked expression matching what Jon imagined his face had looked like only moments earlier. In his right hand, Michael held the shirt collar of the boy he had caught, who looked equally astonished at the devastating transformation that had been visited upon the shop. Michael had brought him back to answer to Bouvier for his crimes, just as Jon would have done had his quarry not revealed that the most recent theft had been merely a ruse to get Bouvier to vacate his shop. Now Michael let his hand slip from the boy's neck as he took in the scene. The boy offered an exclamation that had no place in an eleven-year-old's mouth and took off down the street.

"Call nine-one-one!" Jon yelled at his brother. "He's bleeding out!"

Stirred out of his shock, Michael ran behind the counter and used the shop's phone to call for ambulance and fire services. Meanwhile, Jon put his free hand behind Bouvier's head, attempting to steady the man's neck and focus his attention.

"Mr. Bouvier, it's Jon. Jon Rickner. Hang in there for me. The ambulance is on its way."

"The phone line's dead," Michael said, hanging up. "Where's the fire extinguisher?"

"I don't know. Behind the counter maybe?"

Sounds of frenzied rummaging, thumping, and crashing as Michael shoved items to the side. "No fire extinguisher. Nothing except a bunch of old phone books and receipt registers. And this wooden box he was trying to show us earlier." Michael set the box on the counter, then hopped across to where Jon was tending to Bouvier.

"I'll check the back," Michael said.

"Should we try to move him outside?" Jon asked, though he feared the action might be too traumatic for the injured man. Of course, so would burning alive in his own shop.

Bouvier's eyes suddenly grew wide—in pain, surprise, or just some strange combination of dying synapses firing in tandem.

"Sil—" the proprietor rasped, meeting Jon's eyes for the first time.

"Don't try to talk, Mr. Bouvier," Jon said, hearing for the first time a slight sucking sound when the man inhaled. "Just hang on a little longer, and we'll get you the help you need."

"Cylin...der," Bouvier tried again, ignoring Jon's plea, trying to gesture toward something.

"What's he saying?" Michael asked, still moving toward the back of the shop, his body bowed to keep his head below most of the smoke.

"Flagler..." Bouvier wheezed.

Clearly the man would not be deterred. Jon moved his ear closer to Bouvier's mouth, straining to hear the proprietor's agonized gasps over the crackles and roars of the growing conflagration.

"Finish Flagler's hunt..." At least, those were the words he thought Bouvier was saying. "Don't let him win..."

"Let who win?" Jon asked. "Flagler?"

Bouvier jerked his head in what could be interpreted as a no. Then the light changed. Jon looked up to see that the flames had reached the top of the curtains and were beginning to lick their way along the support beams of the ceiling. It was only a matter of time now.

"Michael, the ceiling," Jon said, gesturing toward the flames with his head.

His brother turned and looked. Just as a woman moved out of the shadows of the shop's back storeroom. Swinging something heavy straight toward Michael's head.

Chapter 7

"Michael, behind you!" Jon shouted.

Michael spun around and half leapt, half fell out of the woman's path.

Jon jumped to his feet to help his brother, careful not to slip in the blood pool again. As he drew closer, though, the newcomer began to come into clearer focus. She was young, about Jon's age. And the weapon she had seemed to be aiming at Michael's head was the sought-after fire extinguisher.

"Move!" she yelled a second before loosing a long spray of white foam over the smoldering tatters of the curtains and up to the burning ceiling beams. The tongues of flame dampened in places but quickly scurried elsewhere, taking refuge from the fire-retardant foam by seizing yet another highly flammable section of the historic bookshop and setting it ablaze.

The store was a tinderbox. With each passing second, more bookcases, antique cabinets, and support beams caught fire. The woman's attempts to stem the flames were far too little, far too late. Jon could read the writing on the wall. Their only option now was escape.

"Come on!" he yelled, grabbing his brother's arm and gesturing to the woman. "It's too late! We've got to get out of here!"

"I can't let it burn down!" she yelled back.

He coughed. The acrid smoke stung his throat and stole precious oxygen from each breath. "Is there another fire extinguisher?"

She frowned and continued spraying at the growing inferno climbing the walls. Jon took that as a no.

They heard a groan from across the shop, followed by a crash. Jon saw that a chunk of nineteenth-century stucco, weakened by the flames, had fallen from the ceiling and crushed a table full of antique glassware. The building had been constructed decades before fire codes and sprinkler systems. It wouldn't be long before the whole place came toppling down on them.

Michael realized the immediacy of the threat as well, joining his brother in trying to get the young woman to leave with them. Whoever she was. Michael grabbed her shoulders and made her face him. The stream of foam weakened then stopped as the fire extinguisher ran dry.

"We have to go now!" he yelled over the infernal roars flooding the shop. "This whole place is about to collapse!"

Though the smoke stung his eyes, Jon could see the conflict in her face: to save herself from an almost certain fiery death, or to abandon the shop to which she apparently had some personal attachment. She looked over at Bouvier lying on the floor, and the color drained from her face.

"No!" she screamed, dropping the fire extinguisher and running to the shopkeeper's side.

"We'll take him with us!" Jon shouted. "But we've got to go now!"

The direness of their plight must have clicked for her, because she nodded once and grabbed Bouvier's arms. Michael grabbed the man's feet, and together they hefted the man aloft, staggering toward the entry door and the relative safety of the street beyond.

Jon grabbed the wooden box that Bouvier seemed to think was so important for them to have and ran for the door, holding it open as Michael and the woman carried Bouvier between them, she walking backward in front. They were just a few yards away now, the four of them almost out of the inferno for good.

A terrible groan birthed a deep cracking sound from above. Jon looked up to see one of the heavy timber support beams break loose from the ceiling and fall. Right toward Michael, Bouvier, and the mystery woman.

"Look out!" Jon yelled instinctively, but it was too late. The beam smashed into Bouvier's body, knocking him from their grasp and finishing off what the red-haired man had started. The esteemed antiquarian and longtime friend of their father was dead.

"No!" the woman wailed, dropping to the floor to try to pry Bouvier loose. But it was too late. The heavy beam was aflame and had crushed the man's chest, pinning him to the floor. The only hope now was for the three of them to escape.

Michael leapt over the flaming beam, grabbing the screaming woman and dragging her outside. As soon as they cleared the door, the three of them collapsed in a heap on the cobbles, the woman sobbing uncontrollably. Jon had to restrain her to keep her from trying to go back inside again.

"Who are you?" he asked.

Between sobs, the young woman looked up at him. Even in her sorrow, her face smudged with smoke, she was beautiful. Despite everything they had just been through, Jon couldn't help feeling a little stir of attraction within his chest.

"Elizabeth Bouvier. Liz. Tristram is... was my uncle."

Jon winced. No wonder she had wanted to save Mr. Bouvier. She wasn't just an employee or a loyal customer. She was family.

"I'm Jon. He's Michael. We're so sorry. Your uncle was a great man."

Almost immediately, he cursed himself for the clichéd vacuity of his words. She just shook her head slowly at the ground.

Part of him cursed his decision that morning to convince Michael to leave their cell phones in the hotel room, enjoying a day in the country's oldest city without modern society's newest distraction. If they had their phones, they could have called the authorities. As if they could do anything for Mr. Bouvier now.

Drawn by the raging inferno in the shop and the commotion caused by the trio tumbling onto the street, a crowd was beginning to gather, maintaining a cautious distance from the epicenter. Jon scanned the crowd, looking for a flash of red hair. He felt exposed out here, like a loose end that whoever had done this to Mr. Bouvier would be looking to cut off.

"Let's get out of here," Jon said. "Whoever did this might come back."

"No, Jon. We need to wait for the authorities," Michael said. "Give our statements."

Jon had seen the fear in Mr. Bouvier's eyes as he struggled to communicate on the floor of the burning shop. It wasn't fear of death—he had made his peace with God long ago. He was afraid of "him" winning. Something having to do with Flagler. Something that involved the wooden case Jon had saved from the shop.

"I agree with Jon," Liz said, her voice surprising Jon. He was about to defer to his older brother's judgement when she spoke up. "I don't feel safe out here, with all these people watching us. Let's go somewhere quiet. Somewhere with fewer people staring at us."

Outnumbered, Michael relented and helped Liz to her feet. Jon gripped the wooden case tight and stood. Finding a break in the crowd, he pushed through, leading the trio down the street and away from the gallery of judging eyes. Away from the funeral pyre of Tristram Bouvier.

Chapter 8

Caeden Monk opened the rear hatch of his rented Explorer and rifled through the suitcase. This level of the parking garage was already full of cars but fairly devoid of foot traffic, the vehicles' owners already enjoying a carefree day discovering the sights and sounds of the ancient city. Monk, meanwhile, was preparing to make a discovery of his own.

From the suitcase he pulled a century-old Edison Standard Phonograph. Looking around the garage, he grabbed the phonograph player and the cylinder he had stolen from Bouvier's shop, shut the hatch, and returned to the driver's seat. He'd need both privacy and acoustics for the next step.

Opening the phonograph's lid revealed the mechanized ironwork of Thomas Edison's invention. It was a brilliant creation, really. Translating all the audio varieties of speech and song into etchings in a hunk of wax, then playing them back with surprising faithfulness. Monk uncapped the cardboard tube and slid out the wax cylinder. After slipping the cylinder onto the phonograph and winding the crank, he affixed the audio horn to the stylus.

He took a deep breath. One final step. And then, at last, revelation.

Holding the horn in one hand, he carefully lifted and lowered the stylus with the other, gently touching down in the spinning groove. He was about to hear a voice from the dead, one of the oldest surviving examples of recorded sound.

The next piece of the puzzle. The final stretch to reach his prize.

But the sounds that came from the phonograph were not what he expected. The tinny yet melodious strains of Brahms's "Hungarian Dance No. 1" echoed through the horn. Not the voice Monk was looking for.

He waited, hoping against hope that this was just an introduction to the message he needed to hear, but with each passing note it became clear that he had been duped. Even in his dying moments, Tristram Bouvier had tricked him into taking the wrong cylinder.

Monk ripped the cylinder from the phonograph and smashed it against the dashboard over and over again until it was just a misshapen smear of wax. How could he have been so stupid? So incredibly shortsighted? Did he really think he was the only one capable of deception, particularly when it came to stakes this high?

The real cylinder, the one that would change Monk's fortunes forever, was still back at Bouvier's shop. And he had just burnt it to the ground.

Chapter 9

Miriam Caan was ready for her payday.

At twenty-six, she had already seen far too much of the world. Too much pain, too much death. Much of it at her hands, but that was irrelevant. The truth was, she was far too young to be as world-weary as she was. But that was about to change.

Driving across the Bridge of Lions from Anastasia Island, Miriam could see the ancient stonework of the Castillo de San Marcos defending the entrance to the Matanzas River she was crossing over. Terra cotta spires from Gilded Age churches and luxury hotels jutted above the low-slung skyline, Colonial-era buildings merging with the swampy forests of primeval Florida.

Somewhere in this city was the key to a new life for her and her sister. And Caeden Monk would soon show her the path.

She had worked with Monk on his globetrotting treasure hunts for nearly four years now. From Kenya to Germany to Nepal to Belize, she had helped share the dirty work that seemed to follow Monk in his profession. But there was too much blood on her hands for her to ignore anymore. And while her sister, Esther, had long wanted to follow in her footsteps, Miriam knew what a lifetime of murder and destruction would do to her. To them both.

Monk had assured her that this quest would be for the motherlode, with her cut alone being seven figures. Enough to forge a new life for her and Esther. Enough to stop running from her past.

Passing between the two stone lions for which the bridge was named, Miriam reached St. Augustine proper, turning right and heading for the parking garage that Monk had just texted her from. He was not happy. And not just with her tardiness. Something had gone horribly wrong with his plan.

Just before she reached the garage, she made a U-turn and headed back into town. She found a parallel parking spot, fed the meter, and took off on foot toward the shop where Monk had apparently been tricked by a dying antiquarian.

Maybe the fire hadn't taken hold quite like Monk had planned. Maybe the fire department had arrived in time to quell the blaze. A dozen maybes, one of which might yet hold the key to putting this mission back on track.

As she approached the shop's location, a crowd thronged the street, trying to catch a glimpse of the ruined store. Through the shattered windows, Miriam could see blackened timbers, hanging raw and broken from the ceiling. Bookshelves filled with ash and cinder. Tufts of charred paper floating on a ghostly breeze.

Nothing could have survived. Certainly not something made of wax.

"I wonder if they killed him," a middle-aged man next to her said.

"Henry, don't be so crass," his wife chided. "We're supposed to be on vacation, for crying out loud."

"Sorry, excuse me," Miriam said. "What happened here? Who killed whom?"

"Nobody killed anybody," the wife said. "This shop just burned up is all."

"And the owner is apparently dead inside," the man said. "Smashed by a wooden beam. Then burned alive."

"Honestly, Henry, I can't take you anywhere."

"Who were you referring to earlier, though?" Miriam pressed. "The people who might have killed him."

The man pointed to the shop. "Two young men and a woman ran out of there as the place was going up. One of them was carrying something wooden and old-looking, so maybe they stole it, murdered the owner, and burned the store to cover their tracks."

"One more remark like that and I'm heading back to the hotel," his wife threatened.

Miriam smiled. She had found their maybe. Monk would be pleased.

Chapter 10

Several blocks from the chaos surrounding the ruins of Ancient City Antiques, Jon finally stopped by a tree near the eastern end of the Plaza de la Constitucion, near a landmark that was now commonly called the "old slave market." In truth, the site had been used as a public market long before the African slave trade touched these shores, with only a handful of recorded instances of its being used to sell human beings. But when, in the peak of Henry Flagler's early tourism boom for St. Augustine, one account referred to it as the old slave market, the sensationalist name stuck. Filled with the controversial ghosts of the antebellum South, the plaza's new name drew tourists much like the history-laden rechristenings Flagler had given to other locales across the city.

A long masonry pavilion that once served as the town's primary marketplace dominated the end of the verdant square, with an array of towering trees filling the plaza with shade. In an adjacent park immediately to the east, abutting Avenida Menéndez and the Bridge of Lions spanning the Matanzas, a statue of Juan Ponce de Leon stared out to sea. Next to the statue, a plaque commemorated the Spanish explorer's connection to the area, reminding visitors that he had landed near that spot in 1513 on his legendary expedition.

"Who are you guys?" Liz asked when she had caught her breath from sobbing and running.

"Our dad was friends with your uncle," Michael said. "They studied together, years ago, and then kept in touch over their shared love of history. Dad's a professor and archeologist over in England."

If only for a moment, Jon was back in those halcyon days before tragedy had struck their family in Mexico a decade earlier. Back before Jon and Michael had been forced to rely on each other far more than any young adolescents should.

"They used to see each other a lot back before Mom died," Jon said. "They both loved trying to discover lost things from history, even if most of the time the pieces to the puzzle were long gone. It's a love Dad passed on to us. Even if he doesn't seem to care as much anymore."

The violent yet mysterious death of a man's wife would be enough to derail almost anyone's adventuring inclinations. Anna Rickner, a world-renowned linguist specializing in ancient languages, had gone missing in the Yucatan jungles on an expedition led by their father, Sir William Rickner, years before. Jon and Michael had been with them, as they were on nearly all of their expeditions over the years, but this one was different. Early one morning, Anna had gone with a small group of local guides to investigate some anomaly with a newly discovered set of ruins near Tulum, but only one member of the party came back, covered in blood and crazed with fear. William led a search party into the primeval rainforest to find his wife. All they ever found was a torn and bloody backpack. Her backpack.

But there was enough pain in the air right now. Jon didn't think disclosing the apparently violent nature of his mom's unsolved death would help with Liz's healing.

"Have we met before?" Michael asked. "Like maybe when we were visiting your uncle over the years?"

Liz smiled wistfully through a veil of pain. "Probably not. My dad and Uncle Tristram weren't close. I didn't even realize I had an uncle until a few weeks ago, when my dad died and my mom finally told me about him. Some stupid grudge my dad held over something that happened a long time ago. I took the semester off from college and came down to spend some time with him."

"And now, just as you're getting to get to know him, he's murdered." Jon immediately regretted saying it, even before Michael shot him a disapproving glare.

"Yeah," Liz said. "He taught me a little about historical manuscripts and artifacts, showed me the ropes about shop-keeping... If only I hadn't had my earbuds in while in the back. I could have helped him. I could have saved the shop. I could have saved his life."

"Liz, you can't blame yourself," Michael said. "Somebody else did this. And the cops will find them. Especially if you give them your statement."

"No!" she said, with an emphasis that surprised Jon. "I don't know anything that would help. But if they know I've been working there, off the books... I mean, come on, his long-lost niece, who may well stand to inherit some of the insurance money, shows up a few weeks before he's murdered and his business is burned down? And she's the only one who can be placed at the scene of the crime when it happened? I'd be suspect number one, and the cops would completely stop looking for his real killer."

Despite her grief and fear, Jon was struck by how attractive he found her. He hadn't really been able to see her face through the smoking panic of the burning shop or his sub-sequently burning eyes, but now, in this sun-dappled square with the cool sea breeze blowing, he was able to take in her features. Shoulder-length brown hair pulled up in a short ponytail, soft brown eyes reddened by sorrow and smoke, and a face that looked as though it would be breathtaking if she smiled. Considering everything that had just happened, he didn't particularly think that would happen anytime soon. But that was no reason not to try.

"What about this?" Jon asked, holding up the wooden container he'd saved from the conflagration. "Your uncle seemed to think it was important. He implored me to 'finish' something before he died. Did he mention anything about it?"

Liz looked at it thoughtfully. "Nothing specific. He had just acquired it the other day. He was really excited about it and kept mentioning... well, come to think of it, I guess it was your dad. 'The old days with William' or something like that."

Jon felt his skin tingle with excitement. Michael's eyes lit up, too. "The old days" meant adventure, discovery, the kind that their dad had cast aside since Anna's death but that Jon and Michael still thoroughly embraced.

Turning the container over in his hands, Jon found a recessed button in the housing and pressed it. With a solitary click, the case opened a fraction of an inch. He lifted the lid to reveal a cardboard tube spanning the length of the case. In a blocky but stylized font Jon fondly thought of as "old-timey," the words *Edison Records* were emblazoned across the tube's label.

"Whoa," Jon said, carefully removing the tube from the case. Michael and Liz leaned closer to get a good look at it. On the opposite side of the label was a handwritten message.

Dear Henry,

I hope you'll be pleased with the record-ing we've made. Good luck with your new venture, and be sure to tell your guests that their experience began with a high-quality Edison Phonograph record-ing.

Yours in progress,
Thomas A. Edison

"Edison actually made this recording?" Michael asked.

Jon knew that Edison Records came into being in the mid-1880s, about a decade after Thomas Edison's 1877 invention of the phonograph sent shockwaves through the world and led to Alexander Graham Bell's own patented Graphophone wax cylinder recordings. Edison would shortly afterward tweak Bell's version to create his "Perfect Phonograph" line, the first of several wax cylinder models marketed through Edison Records. But, while it paled in comparison to the record giants of later decades, the company mass-produced popular recordings—three-minute snippets of famous speeches, songs, and nursery rhymes. This, however, looked to be an original, a special order recorded and delivered by Thomas Edison himself.

"Who's 'Henry'?" Liz asked.

"Flagler," Jon said.

"What?"

"When he was dying, your uncle told me to finish Flagler's hunt and pointed to this. Henry Morrison Flagler."

"The oil baron and railroad magnate," Michael said. "In the late nineteenth century, he was instrumental in transforming St. Augustine into a tourist destination for the rich and famous."

"I've definitely seen his name around town. But what guest experience is Edison referring to?" Liz asked. "What does an Edison wax cylinder recording have to do with Flagler's tourism plans?"

Jon could hazard a guess, but he kept it to himself, afraid it was more his own wishful thinking than an actual reflection of the facts.

"Do you know of anywhere in town that has a phonograph player?" Jon asked. "One that plays cylinders like this?"

"I think we may have had one in the shop," Liz said, "but it's too late for that." She started getting misty-eyed again.

"Maybe a museum?" Michael prompted, trying to steer her away from her grief.

"Ripley's?" Liz wiped a hand across her eyes. "We've got a Ripley's here. I'm sure they would have something like that there."

"Perfect," Jon said. If his hunch was correct, Bouvier's claims about a return to "the old days" would soon prove prophetic in more ways than one.

Chapter 11

Caeden Monk had disposed of the wax cylinder he'd destroyed and was standing just inside the garage entrance when Miriam Caan pulled alongside.

"You want a lift?" she asked through the open window.

Without responding, Monk climbed into the passenger seat. Miriam started driving toward the ramps leading to the upper levels.

"What took you so long?" Monk asked, trying to tamp down his persistent fury at being duped by a dying old bookseller. He had a temper. He had a reputation for having a temper. But he still viewed publicly losing his temper as an admission of weakness. And weak he was not.

"Traffic," she said.

"Traffic?" he asked, fighting the rage rising again. "The archeological discovery of the decade could now be jeopardized because you got stuck in traffic?"

"Relax, Monk. We've got another lead."

Only Miriam could speak to him like that and get away with it. She was his hired help, yes, but over the years she had gained his trust. She had been one of his graduate students when he had made the fateful choice that had kicked him out of academia and into the shadows. She had stuck with him then, and though her historical knowledge and strategic planning paled in comparison to his own, she had proven invaluable on many occasions through the years.

"What's that, then?" Monk asked.

"You weren't the last one to exit the shop."

"Bouvier lived?"

"No, but three others did. They were seen leaving the shop. And they were carrying something."

A spark. "Something cylindrical?" he asked as a hopeful grin crawled across his face.

"It sounds like it could be."

The wheels in Monk's head began working overtime. Could this be the real cylinder, the one Bouvier had hidden from him? And these newcomers, were they associates of the antiquarian, perhaps even the ones who had taken the bait he'd set with the two young thieves and left Bouvier alone to contend with Monk?

Whoever had taken the real cylinder, the one that should have been his, would be limited by their own technological resources. And unless they too had come to St. Augustine specifically seeking the cylinder and the secrets it held, they wouldn't have brought their own antique phonograph player like Monk had. So they'd need one.

And that was how he would trap them and recover what was rightfully his.

"You're right, Miriam," he finally said. "This is very good news."

Chapter 12

The imposing gray stone castle now housing the St. Augustine location of Ripley's Believe It or Not! rose before Jon as he, Michael, and Liz approached. Unlike many of the kitschy over-the-top buildings created for Ripley's and other such tourist museums across the country, this location had a history that predated even Robert Ripley himself.

Long before the globetrotting cartoonist had established "Believe It or Not!" as a classic tagline for the bizarre and astounding, the Moorish Revival castle had been built as a winter home for oil magnate and Flagler business partner William G. Warden in 1887. In 1941, Warden Castle was purchased by *The Yearling* author Marjorie Kinnan Rawlings and remodeled as the Castle Warden Hotel, playing host to numerous renowned guests, including Zora Neale Hurston, Wendell Willkie, and Robert Ripley. A 1944 fire in the hotel claimed the lives of two women, the ghosts of whom are still rumored to haunt the building, which only added to the mystique. After Ripley's death in 1949, his estate purchased the building to serve as the home of the very first permanent Odditorium, gathering and displaying hundreds of the most intriguing artifacts the amateur adventurer had acquired, a collection that grew substantially in the following decades.

Surely there had to be an antique phonograph capable of playing vintage Edison wax-cylinder recordings within Ripley's premier collection. Even if it wouldn't have been quite so "unbelievable" back in 1950, modern visitors would have found the old device fascinating, a seeming shoe-in for a more recent acquisition.

At least, that's what Jon was counting on.

They crossed to the side of the building and walked through what was now the main entrance. Flanking the door inside, a statue of Jack Sparrow constructed of old car parts and a working turn-of-the-century scale model of a carousel greeted them. Already, Ripley's love for the bizarre and unbelievable oddities of invention, nature, and culture were on full display. A two-headed cow, a gleaming set of samurai armor, a collection of Zulu tribal masks, and a portrait of Elvis made entirely of jelly beans also adorned the lobby, presaging the menagerie of the weird and macabre that awaited inside.

Michael paid the entrance fee for the three of them, then asked the representative at the desk—Jadena, according to her name badge—if they could speak with the curator. When she politely refused, he told her to mention that his father was Sir William Rickner and that they had something that would pique the curator's interest. With a resigned shrug, clearly fully expecting a confirmation of the denial she had started with, Jadena picked up the handset from the desk and punched in a four-digit internal extension. After relaying Michael's request and name-dropping the Rickner family patriarch, her expression changed to disbelief, then became mildly simpering. Though Ripley's wasn't quite the intellectual and cultural bastion of the Smithsonian or the British Museum, it was clear that, with this curator at least, Sir William's name still carried some weight.

"Renée will be down in a moment," Jadena said in a placating tone. "If you'd like to browse the lobby in the meantime, I'll send her over to you when she arrives."

Michael thanked her, with Jon and Liz joining in. Then the trio moved through the entrance gate to browse the collections of the entrance hall.

"Are we going to let her listen to the recording?" Jon asked, referring to the curator.

"I don't see why not," Michael asked. "She may be able to provide some insight. Besides, it's not like we can use her phonograph and then kick her out of the room while we listen to it."

Jon chuckled uncomfortably, giving his brother a wry grin. "Sure we could."

False mirth aside, Jon didn't like the way this was starting to go. It was too fast, and the more people in the know, the more likely whoever had killed Mr. Bouvier and set fire to his shop would find them. If the cylinder was as significant as Bouvier had intimated, if finishing "Flagler's hunt" was crucial enough to implore Jon to do so with his dying breath, it seemed likely that the murderer was also after the Edison relic. Which meant the clock was already ticking, even if none of them understood what they were up against.

Still, Michael's judgement had gotten them through more than their fair share of scrapes over the years. Jon couldn't imagine his big brother steering them wrong here.

Liz was standing in one corner, biting at a fingernail and taking an inordinate amount of interest in a pair of six-shooters purported to have belonged to Wyatt Earp. Jon walked over and put a hand on her shoulder. She jumped.

"Sorry," he said. "How are you holding up?"

"I'm here." She looked up at him. Her eyes were red with the ghosts of recently fallen tears, but there was a determination behind them that Jon recognized.

"You're going to get through this," he said, laying his hand on her shoulder again. This time, she didn't jump. "Michael and I have seen our share of loss in our time. But it gets better. You just have to keep living, even when it feels like it's all crashing down."

She gave him a half-hearted smile.

"You lean on him, or the other way around?"

"Mainly the former," Jon said, looking across the atrium at Michael, who was studying a display of samurai swords. "But I like to think I've helped him out once or twice."

"I'm sure you have. It must be nice to have someone like him around." She began to look misty-eyed again. "I just lost my dad, then I dropped everything to come down here and connect with my long-lost uncle. And now that he's gone, I feel so alone."

"Hey, hey, you're not alone. I'm here for you. Michael is too."

"Thanks," she said, offering him a more genuine-looking smile that seemed to push back the impending tears. "I think having something to do here is helping, too. If there's a chance we can use that cylinder to catch whoever is responsible for killing Uncle Tristram and destroying his legacy, I'm all in."

"I think whoever did this is probably after this cylinder, too." He waggled the case in his hand. "So it stands to reason our paths might cross again."

"I won't have my iPod on full-blast this time." She clenched her fists, the knuckles going red, then white. "This time, I'll be ready for him."

Jon started wondering if he should have sided with Michael in calling the cops when they'd first exited the burning shop. It was too late now, of course. They had left a crime scene, a dead body, and a burning building without so much as calling for an ambulance or fire truck. There would undoubtedly be consequences, likely starting with a long-term stay in a holding cell. Without another suspect, without the mysterious stranger who had actually committed the crimes, Liz, Jon, and Michael were the cops' best bet. The only way to discover the real perpetrator would be for the three of them to keep chasing whatever it was that both Bouvier and his murderer were so interested in. Whatever Thomas Edison had recorded on this cylinder.

Jon glanced over at the reception desk just in time to see Jadena speaking with a thirty-something woman in a sharp black pantsuit and pointing in their direction. The woman thanked her and headed their way.

"You look like him," she said, approaching Michael. Jon and Liz walked over to meet her. "I'm Renée Strickland, the curator here at Ripley's."

Michael introduced himself, shaking her proffered hand. Then, pointing to his cohorts in turn, "My brother, Jon, and our friend Liz."

Jon glanced at Liz, who seemed to blush a bit at Michael's already claiming her as a friend. Maybe she was finally starting to feel not so alone.

"Admiring my outfit?" Renée asked, catching Liz's undisguised stare.

"I was just expecting something a little more... eclectic."

"Ah. Because we're Ripley's rather than a 'serious' museum?"

Liz looked like she wanted to melt into the floor and disappear. "Something like that."

"To be honest, this isn't my normal attire. I'm much more of a business-casual type, but we have an investors' meeting this afternoon. They're looking at converting a nineteenth-century mansion in Cincinnati into a Ripley's property, so with this being the flagship Odditorium as well as a repurposed historic home, corporate felt an in-depth tour of our fine facility here would be helpful in their decision-making process.

"As such," she said, turning back to Michael, "I don't have a lot of time, but I wanted to come down and meet with you. Your parents' early work inspired me to become a cultural anthropologist, which led me here." A brief but awkward pause, then, "Sorry about what happened to your mother."

"Us too," Jon said.

All things considered, it made sense for Anna to have been the one to have been such an inspiration when it came to anthropology. Her passion for discovering and studying people's cultures, languages, and values was the driving force behind many of their forays outside of Europe and the Middle East. The cultures they visited across sub-Saharan Africa, Siberia, the Amazon—all had little in the way of traditionally recorded history but were rife with unique mindsets to tap into. Meanwhile William rarely cared a whit about anyone who hadn't been dead at least a century, which, ever since Anna died, had largely included his own sons.

"We recently stumbled across an old Edison wax cylinder," Michael said, "and we were hoping you had a phonograph we could use to play it."

"Can I see it?" Renée asked.

Jon depressed the wooden case's hidden button again and opened it up. He uncapped the cardboard tube and showed her the cylinder.

"Yes, I think I can help you out. Follow me, please." Renée started up the stairs, at one point unlatching a gate to take them through a shortcut. They meandered through the exhibits, ducking through a screening room showing vintage footage of Robert Ripley's own anthropological expeditions across the globe, past a holographic leprechaun taunting visitors with bad puns, and into a dark gallery full of medieval torture instruments and vampire-hunting kits. In the shadows between a collection of thumbscrews and an iron maiden, Renée used a cleverly disguised keypad to enter a code, then pushed through the adjacent door subtly marked "Employees Only" and into a hallway that looked like they had stepped right into the Castle Warden Hotel, circa 1946.

"Nice digs," Jon said, marveling at the crown molding overhead and the ornate wall sconces fitted with electric lighting.

"That's where one of the ghosts usually appears," Renée said, pointing to a doorway at the end of the hall. "Miss Nelly. Died in the fire back in forty-four. I've never seen her myself, but plenty of my staff has."

Jon couldn't think of a reply to that, which was just as well since Renée stopped at the next door they reached.

"My office is right through here, next to our archives," she said, leading them inside. The office was decently sized, seemingly a lightly remodeled hotel room. A desk sat against the far end of the space, framed by period windows on either side. In the center of the room was a circular conference table surrounded by a half dozen chairs.

"Please, have a seat," she said, gesturing to the conference table. "I'll be right back."

Once Renée had disappeared through the side door to the archives, the trio sat down. The ticking of a clock somewhere in the office was the only sound until Jon unlatched the wooden case once more and extracted the cardboard tube. Staring at the cryptic note penned by Thomas Edison, Jon rolled the tube back and forth in his fingers, subconsciously hoping that the motion would cause the message to become seasick and let loose its secrets. By the time Renée returned less than a minute later, he had gleaned nothing.

"I think this model is the one we need," she said, now wearing white linen gloves and carrying a heavy wooden case bearing an "Edison Perfect Phonograph" plaque on its base. She placed the case on the table, opened the lid, and set up the device. Then she looked at Jon.

"May I?" she asked, hand outstretched. Still not comfortable with adding more unknowns to their circle of trust,

Jon reluctantly handed the tube over. It was her phonograph, after all. He hoped she would excuse herself, or at the very least ask if they wanted some privacy, but he had a feeling curiosity was now driving their meeting more than any sense of duty to the memory of Jon's dead mother. Renée removed the phonograph from the tube and carefully slid it onto the assembly.

Now or never, Jon thought as Renée affixed the horn to the stylus assemblage and wound the phonograph. *Either she offers us privacy, I make things awkward, or we open up our little circle to someone who will likely have her own agenda...*

The intercom on the curator's desk bleated twice, followed by a female voice.

"Dr. Strickland, Mr. Schaeffer is here to see you."

Renée carefully set down the stylus in its cradle as the Edison cylinder continued to spin soundlessly. "I'll be right down, Jadena. Thank you."

A click, as Jadena disconnected the line.

"I'm sorry about this. Mr. Schaeffer is one of the investors for the Cincinnati project." She checked her watch. "And he's about thirty-nine minutes early. Unfortunately for our little concert from the past, I'll have to go meet with him now." She pulled a BlackBerry from a jacket pocket and typed for a moment. "I'll have Kamlesh see you out once you've finished. Don't worry about disassembling the phonograph. I'll take care of it this afternoon after the tour."

"Thank you so much, Dr. Strickland," Michael said, rising.

"The pleasure is mine, Michael, Jon, Liz," she said, nodding to each in turn. "It was so great meeting you finally. Give your father my best. And, please," she added, offering Michael a business card, "let me know what you find on there. Especially, as you can imagine, if it's bizarre, wondrous, or unbelievable."

With that, she turned and left, shutting the door behind them. For a moment, all Jon could hear was the ticking clock, her receding footsteps, and the phonograph spinning, waiting.

"Well, that solves that problem," Jon said.

"She still could be useful," Michael countered.

"Come on," Liz said. "Let's see what's on here already."

Michael, still standing, carefully lifted the stylus and placed it at the start of the cylinder's recording.

Seconds later, a voice long dead floated out of the horn. But none of them were prepared for what it had to say.

Chapter 13

The stink of smoke and ash still hung thick in the air—a wet, pungent stench when mixed with the water the fire department had used to drench the antique shop. Detective Audrey Yang stepped across the blackened, waterlogged floorboards, careful not to disturb any of the tables, shelves, or anything else at the scene. Not that there was much to disturb anymore. The fire department had done plenty to contaminate whatever the inferno itself hadn't already taken care of.

She stared up at the melted remains of a camera that once stood sentinel over this humble emporium of antiquity. In the rear storeroom, the hard drive that could have provided her with the video to piece together what had happened here was a charred husk of plastic and metal, its memory wiped clean by heat and flame.

Still, what remained told a story. Backtracking past the damage, from both the fire and the water, a crime was committed here. Several, most likely. And as an arson-trained investigator, it was her job to uncover the truth.

"Insurance money."

She turned to see Chuck Pryor, a bullheaded cop whom she'd worked alongside for six years. He was good at his job, but an ace investigator he was not. Which was why she wore the detective badge and he was tasked with securing the scene.

"How's that?" she asked, humoring him.

"The way I see it, the owner sets fire to his shop—probably after inflating the value of his inventory—and tries to escape to claim the insurance money. He's getting old, but maybe business is bad, so he can't exactly retire. Place goes up and boom, instant millionaire. But on his way out, he gets clocked by this falling beam and he becomes a victim in his own insurance fraud."

"Poetic justice, huh?"

"Exactly," he said, grinning at the prospect of having solved the crime before Yang.

"And you've checked Mr. Bouvier's financial records to verify his net worth and his insurance policies?"

"Well, no, but it's just a theory at this point."

"Ah." She pointed toward the back of the shop. "And that fire extinguisher? Pin pulled, completely empty. I guess he used that to buttress his claim of innocence in the arson? That he tried to stop the fire but was unable to do so?"

"Yeah, I guess. That fits, doesn't it?"

"Theoretically." Yang gestured toward where the body lay, still underneath the fallen ceiling beam. "But did he fall facing away from the door?"

"Maybe he forgot something important he didn't want to leave behind. A memento or something."

"Or his watch?" She pointed to where a man's wrist-watch lay, next to where he had fallen.

"Firefighters yank it off trying to pull him free?" Pryor asked.

"Not according to them."

"Maybe he was trying to put it on when the timber came down."

He was defending this theory to death. That was the thing about crime-scene investigations and detective work in general. Hunches were all well and good, but if the facts changed, your theory had to change with it. Otherwise, you risked forcing your theory to supplant the truth. And then nothing ever got solved.

"A stretch, but sure, perhaps. But here's the kicker for me. If he's got this big plan to burn his shop to the ground, defraud his insurance company, and retire to an island somewhere, why did he shoot himself in the chest first?"

"What?" Pryor bent down close to the body. "Well, crap."

"Crap indeed," she said. "This is a good old-fashioned homicide. And somebody wanted to cover their tracks."

Kyle Weiss opened the door and entered from the street. Weiss had been her partner ever since she had made detective three months ago. He did his best to keep her level-headed, which was useful. She was ambitious, passionate about her craft. But she still had a lot to learn, as Weiss reminded her often.

"Just finished talking to some witnesses," he said, thumbing toward the lingering crowd outside. "Multiple accounts corroborate that three people ran out of the shop while it was ablaze."

Yang gave Pryor a smug grin. *Told you so.*

"You get descriptions of our suspects?" Yang asked.

"That's just the thing. They may not be suspects at all. At least two of them, both young men, were seen entering the shop while it was already on fire."

"Good Samaritans with a death wish?" Pryor said, throwing his hat in the ring, hoping for a second chance at solving this curious crime.

"Maybe."

Pryor waggled his eyebrows at Yang in premature triumph.

"But if so," Weiss continued, "they may also be opportunists. One of them was carrying some sort of wooden case or something when he left that witnesses swear he wasn't carrying when he went in."

Yang crinkled her nose, the way she always did when she was thinking hard. It was a habit, one that had been cute when she was little, but now that she was trying to be taken seriously, she found it less appealing.

"So they went in to try to help, maybe tried to carry the victim outside." She walked over and squatted next to Bouvier's body. "But then the falling beam knocks him to the ground and crushes him, the impact of which causes whoever's carrying his arms to accidentally yank off his wristwatch."

"And then they grab the first pricey antique they see and run off," Pryor said, trying to reclaim his narrative.

"But why? Mr. Bouvier had been shot and was weak enough to need to be carried. If they were merely opportunistic thieves, they would have just grabbed what they could and leave, instead of stopping to help out the guy they were trying to rob."

"Therein lies the mystery," Weiss said. "That, and who actually killed him and started the fire."

Murder, theft, arson, a trio of purported Good Samaritans, and a mysterious fourth entity, likely the killer. Something big was afoot here. Something much bigger than St. Augustine had seen in a long time. And three months into her career as detective, it had fallen into Yang's lap.

It was a tremendous opportunity. A potential career maker. She just had to be careful not to screw it up.

Chapter 14

"**T**his is Henry Flagler, welcoming you to sunny St. Augustine."

Jon leaned forward, as did Liz and Michael. It was surreal, hearing the famous magnate's voice emanating out of the horn. The sound quality was somewhat scratchy, as would be expected of this first generation of recorded media, but Flagler's voice was clear enough.

"While the natural beauty and pleasant weather of Florida is abundant here, St. Augustine has something even more fascinating: ancient history. This fascinating city was founded more than two centuries before our own great nation came into being. Kings warred over the city, pirates sacked it, and Spanish adventurers ferried through golden treasures from Mexico and Peru."

Not quite true, Jon thought. St. Augustine had been an important city to protect the Spanish treasure fleet traveling from Central and South America en route to Cádiz, but the galleons laden with gold and silver didn't load or unload at St. Augustine. In fact, most of them didn't even moor there, unless they needed refuge from the storm or to replenish lost supplies for the voyage back to Spain. Still, Flagler was playing the role of an entertainer, impressing his guests with tales of wonder. He wasn't offering a dissertation on the subject.

"Today, I invite you to embark upon a treasure hunt for a priceless artifact from the city's ancient past. The hunt will not only introduce you to some of the wonders of St. Augustine, but will also stimulate your mind as you puzzle your way to victory. Your first clue stands alone, but the following three will require your own observations at the previous location. Ready? Here is your first clue:

"This house of God has recently found a new home, but its location is not the only thing altered. Look to the Lord to see if you can see the first part of an ancient cross beneath Christ's.

"Your clue to the second artifact is: Here on the idyllic shores of sunny Florida, health is important for all our guests. At the former site of your previous destination, look within the pipes of a technologically marvelous, modern influencer to see a reminder of the greatest therapeutic power of all.

"The third clue is: All of us, including titans of industry, must bow before Almighty God. This game's founder is no different. Beneath his seat under heaven, an ancient secret awaits.

"And finally, my friends, your last clue: Even here in St. Augustine, where ages past merge with modern marvels and the worries of New York's busy schedules melt away, it sometimes pays to discover how time flows. Even our city's legendary explorers took note of the tolls life's years took on them. Look deep within the face of time to reveal the final artifact and complete your journey through the mists of yore.

"Remember, you're looking for unique artifacts from this majestic city's ancient past, something that has been hidden in our modern establishments but clearly belongs to that legendary age. Good luck to you all, and no matter what, enjoy yourselves and enjoy St. Augustine!"

The sound stopped as the stylus hit the end of the cylinder.

"A treasure hunt?" Jon asked, his pulse accelerating at the thought. "Have you ever heard of Flagler holding a treasure hunt for his guests?"

Michael shook his head. "Never. Something like that would have made headlines for sure. And Flagler knew how to make headlines, so he wouldn't have missed such an opportunity."

"I've heard of it." Liz shifted in her seat as Jon and Michael looked at her.

"You have?" Jon asked.

"From Uncle Tristram. According to local legend, Henry Flagler had planned a city-wide treasure hunt as a big draw for his St. Augustine hotel guests."

"He'd planned it. But he didn't actually hold the hunt?"

"Apparently not. Again, this is all just hearsay on my part, but supposedly Flagler had already taken out advertisements in *The New York Times,* the *Boston Herald, Harper's,* all the major publications read by the nation's well-heeled blue bloods and nouveau riche alike. Business had been great, but Flagler was looking to take things to the next level. The treasure hunt was his gimmick for the 1891 season. But then, the day before the advertisements were set to go to press and announce his big plans, he pulled the plug on everything. The press releases were scrapped, and all traces of the inaugural Flagler hunt were destroyed."

"Not all of them," Jon said, gesturing to the wax cylinder Thomas Edison had recorded for the hunt.

"So this is it, then," Michael said. "Whoever killed Mr. Bouvier and burned his shop is trying to solve Flagler's treasure hunt, more than a century after it was abandoned."

"What was the 'treasure' in the Flagler hunt?" Jon asked.

"No idea," Liz said. "But it must have been worth a lot."

Jon agreed. Whatever Flagler had hidden back in 1891 was clearly valuable enough to kill for more than a hundred years later. A treasure like that didn't belong in the hands of a murderer and arsonist.

Assuming Bouvier's killer was also searching for the treasure, following Flagler's trail of clues could also help Jon, Michael, and Liz ferret out the culprit and clear their names. Or bring them directly into the sights of a deadly adversary.

Chapter 15

For the first time since losing his tenured post at Cornell, Caeden Monk was on the cusp of making a world-changing discovery. But this time, instead of going to inflate the salaries and prestige of the overstuffed suits who fired him after his expedition in Turkey, the fame and fortune would be his and his alone.

Today was the day he would shift the course of his life once more. To justify his methods, to prove how wrong they had been to toss him out like a puppy that chewed the furniture. Dogs chew. Archeologists discover. Unlike what the self-aggrandizing ivory-tower idiots believed, true historical discoveries happen in the field, not arguing over theories postulated by other pompous buffoons enamored of their own purported intelligence.

Certainly there were exceptions, but even the men and women he had worked alongside on digs in Syria, Lebanon, and Iraq had not come to his defense that fateful day four years ago outside of Cappadocia. All his colleagues, their local sponsors, and especially his dean had turned their backs on him when everything went wrong. Everyone except Miriam Caan.

The point of no return had come on Day 39 of a planned six-week dig. *His* dig. Cornell was partnering with the University of Ankara to excavate the site just east of the ancient anthill city of Cappadocia.

Months earlier, in a shady shop on the backstreets of Damascus, Professor Caeden Monk had discovered a cracked second-century vase. Along the edge of the vase was a rough map depicting a Roman temple and the unmistakable Swiss-cheese rock formations that he instantly recognized as Cappadocia. There was only one problem. No ruins of the sort were near the underground city. After haggling for the vase, he had shown his discovery to Ted Karlsson, who greenlit an expedition to Turkey to search for and unearth the long-lost temple.

Using the natural landmarks depicted on the vase, Professor Monk had narrowed the search grid to a square mile, which allowed the geeks back at Cornell and Ankara to use infrared-detecting drones to find the anomaly. The ruins of a massive ancient Roman temple dedicated to Mars, god of war. Forgotten by time, buried for centuries under several feet of hard-packed earth, the temple was to have been the crowning jewel in Monk's professional résumé. Rumors had floated throughout the archeological community for years about the unorthodox or unethical methods Monk used in the field, from using bribery to gain exclusive permits, using black-market dealers to unload purloined relics acquired from his dig sites, skirting local and international antiquities laws, and even physically and psychologically intimidating area experts and authorities to gain an edge. It was all true, of course. There wasn't enough evidence for anyone to ever bring charges against him, and the fear factor also kept his detractors from getting too bold. But the archeological community was relatively small and interconnected, and despite all he had done for the discipline, he was still tainted by the rumors about how he had gained his impressive results.

That all changed on the thirty-sixth night of the Mars temple dig. Though most of the pillars had fallen long ago and been carted away to be repurposed for masonry in other projects, the temple's sizable footprint remained. Most notable, however, was what one of Professor Monk's students, the beautiful, young Miriam Caan, had discovered on Day 37. A magnificent mosaic, perfectly preserved from centuries of war and the elements by the foot-thick earthen cover that had hidden it from the world until now. The mosaic's size and artistry rivaled those of Madaba, Jordan—another shining example of the intricate tilework from the Roman Empire's far reaches. It was a major find. Monk couldn't have been prouder.

That night, in his hotel room, he made love to his student, raw and passionate, though for Monk, he wasn't celebrating Miriam so much as how her discovery increased the significance of his own find. It was clear she looked up to him, and in a world where the whispers behind his back had grown ever louder, Monk was glad to have a stalwart supporter, naive though she may have been.

Two nights later, alone in his bed, Monk had awoken with a start. Looking around the darkened hotel room as the fan-blown ripples in his curtains cast ethereal dancing shadows across the walls, he couldn't see or hear any reason he should have awoken. Bad dreams again, perhaps. But Monk had a gnawing feeling that something wasn't right with the dig site. And his instincts were rarely wrong.

Quickly dressing in dark clothing and grabbing his illegal Desert Eagle pistol, Monk slipped out of the peaceful confines of the archeological team's hotel and into the night. He stalked the five-minute trek to the dig site in darkness, the only sounds his footsteps on the rock-strewn path.

The headlights were the first clue that something was amiss. That and the silhouetted figures moving through the truck's low beams. His first impulse was to drop low, observe, but he could already see what was going on. The pick axes. The laden pick-up truck. The three men working under cover of night. At the dig site. His site.

They were trying to steal his discovery.

He drew his pistol and approached, stealthily silent, tempering his rage into productivity. As he approached, he could see his targets more clearly. Two of them were young, mid-twenties, while the third was older, early forties, perhaps. All three looked fairly well kempt, and two wore wedding bands. Did they have wives waiting back at home? Families who depended on them? Monk didn't care. All he saw was red. And then, so did the men, spilling from their wounds.

Monk shot the first man in the cheek, the bullet shattering his jaw, teeth, and hard palate before shredding through his brain. The next two, startled by the sudden gunfire, he shot in the torso, the shock and impacts knocking them to the ground. They attempted to crawl to safety, but Monk was quickly upon them. One, he flipped over to face while he emptied two rounds into the man's forehead. The second, the older man who now had managed to haul himself halfway into the truck, Monk impaled with his own pickax before delivering another double-tap, hitman style.

Monk was a mafia of one. Don and enforcer, all wrapped up together. Nobody messed with what was his.

Cornell didn't see it that way. Neither did the government of Turkey. Owing to the importance of the find, Turkey accepted the university's request for simple deportation rather than a full-blown murder trial. Ankara University would take primary credit for discovering the lost temple ruins, with support from visiting researchers from Cornell. Caeden Monk's name would be nowhere near the find. And though he protested every step of the way, no one cared what he had to say about any of it. It was out of his hands now.

Upon arriving back stateside, Monk was met at the Ithaca airport by Karlsson and two campus police officers. The trio escorted the professor back to campus, with the dean informing Monk that he would be cleaning out his office immediately and was henceforth banned from all Cornell events, campuses, and communities in perpetuity. Again, Monk's vehement arguments fell on deaf ears.

Under the watchful eyes of the campus police officers, Monk was seething as he packed up a lifetime's work. Award-winning published papers, mementos of acclaimed discoveries, photographs with local leaders and university presidents from across the globe all went into the box. The archeology department was world-renowned today because of him and his work. And now they were kicking him out for protecting a fantastic discovery. The men were thieves who came in the night to reap the rewards of his efforts. They deserved to die, no matter what the Turkish authorities or Dean Karlsson said.

With one last frustrated look around his office, Monk hefted one box of his personal belongings as the two officers gathered the others. He ignored the looks from students and colleagues alike, the stares of disbelief and judgment, of indignation and shock—pretty much the same gamut of emotions Monk himself felt, though targeted at a very different individual.

When he left the archeology building and passed through the Arts Quad, he saw a gaggle of students and reporters gathered in front of Uris Library. The oldest library building on campus, its iconic McGraw clock tower stabbing boldly into the sky, Uris occupied a prominent hilltop spot that had long been used for photo ops and press conferences. At the front of this press conference, in the center of everyone's attention, was Dean Karlsson.

Monk's fingers dug into the box, poking holes in the cardboard. This should have been Monk's press conference. Words floated across the quad to his ears—*Turkey*, *Cappadocia*, *mosaic*, and worst of all, *discovered*.

He dropped the box and broke into a run, hoping the element of surprise would give him a head start on his equally burdened police chaperones. They were probably shouting at him to stop, possibly even throwing his possessions to the ground as they began pursuit. But he didn't hear anything but Karlsson's words, burning holes in his ears. They were his words, his announcement, his discovery. And like the nocturnal thieves in Turkey, he was trying to steal what should have been Monk's.

Within moments, he had crossed the quad and was shoving his way to the front of the crowd. Numb to the protests of reporters as he knocked them and their equipment to the ground, he finally reached the podium, where Dean Karlsson wore an expression of undisguised fury. *Funny*, Monk thought, *since I'm the only one with the right to be furious. Or, for that matter, the right to be making this announcement.*

Shoving Karlsson to the side, Monk wrenched away the microphone and began to tell the gathered crowd how it was he and he alone who had discovered the site, how Cornell and Karlsson were attempting to steal his find and push him out the door. In his mind's eye, he heard the crowd boo Karlsson, saw them pick him up and throw him in the nearby fountain before singing the persecuted Monk's praises and asking him fawning questions about his discovery. But instead, they reacted with confusion and horror at—as the *New York Times* editorial the next day called it—a "shameless display by an uncouth and ego-maniacal academic hack." He stared into the crowd, demanding the credit and attention he deserved, but instead of hoisting him onto their shoulders while singing "For He's a Jolly Good Fellow," he was seized by the police officers, handcuffed, and led away, raining down verbal hellfire on Karlsson and Cornell until long after he had been shoved unceremoniously into the back of the cruiser.

In the coming days, the outburst received a decent amount of play on cable news networks and a handful of on-line publications, giving Monk his fifteen minutes of infamy. Across the archeological and academic communities, however, the story had a more lasting impact, offering validity to all the rumors levied against him over the years.

For Cornell, the situation was highly embarrassing, with the university trying to downplay it and move on as quickly as possible. Again criminal charges were not pursued save for the issuing of a permanent protection order against Monk, preventing him from being within a thousand feet of Karlsson or the Cornell campus. To date, there was no provable violation of the injunction, but somehow, a week after Monk was dragged away from his academic career in handcuffs, Ted Karlsson's body was found with a pair of bullet holes in his forehead, just off the wooded path he used for early morning jogs. The dean's wallet was missing, so a robbery gone wrong was theoretically a plausible scenario, though Cornell staff and Ithaca police weren't shy about their alternate suspicions.

For his part, Monk realized that his time in academia was done. Calls to other universities and institutions across the United States, Western Europe, and Canada revealed he had been virtually blacklisted from the field he had been instrumental in shaping over the past two decades. Left with no choice, he decided it was time for a change.

With his small retribution visited upon his former dean, Monk sold his two-hundred-year-old Federal-style house in Ithaca and his Mercedes to start over. If the world thought him a villain, he would give in to that fully. Academia had closed the door on the more respectable aspects of his career, so he was now forced to focus on the more nefarious aspects of his professional life—black market dealers, bribery, theft, and murder... whatever it took to score the next big find.

Having liquidated his ties to Ithaca, he caught a flight back overseas, spending a few weeks in Ireland, visiting his parents' graves and clearing his head of the wreck that his life had become. Over the next six months, Monk traveled from one black market antiquities hot spot to another, from Iraq to Peru to Romania to India, rebuilding his networks of informants and illicit business partners.

It was in Egypt that Miriam finally caught up with him, seven months after their first night together in Turkey. How she found him she never did reveal, but it was clear that she was resourceful. And in love. She had dropped out of Cornell as soon as she heard about what had happened with him. After all, it was her discovery of the mosaic that had made the site so valuable. In her mind, he had been protecting her find just as much as she had his. Thus, they were bound by the same fate, to leave the ivory towers from which he had been cast and wander the earth together, pursuing their mutual passion in whatever way they saw fit.

At his hotel in Heliopolis on the outskirts of Cairo, they re-consummated their dedication to one another, this time not as professor and student but as master and apprentice. No longer were they bound to the rules and rigors of academia, pursuing abstract pipe dreams like the betterment of human understanding. They were treasure hunters, pursuing lost antiquities with high-dollar resale values and qualms about little else. The next few years had taken them to the far corners of the earth, scoring a number of lucrative finds that had not only funded their next excursions but allowed them to indulge in some of the finer things in life. Things an honest professor's salary could never touch.

But this—this was different. What Flagler had discovered, what he had hidden, made everything else Monk had done look like peanuts. When he finally completed the eccentric tycoon's treasure hunt and revealed the truth, it would solidify Monk's place in the history books at last. And then he would sell everything to the highest bidder, the betterment of humanity be damned.

He was so close now. The three newcomers had thrown a monkey wrench in his plans, but they were pawns, soon to be swept from the chessboard.

Barring the forgotten inventory of an antique shop that he had missed, there were only two logical places in town for the new players to go with their purloined wax cylinder, and both were museums. Of course, he assumed that the newcomers hadn't brought their own phonograph, as Monk had, but if they had been well-informed enough to realize the importance of the recording before entering Bouvier's shop this morning, they never would have taken the bait and run after the young shoplifters. Monk held on to that reasoning, because if his unknown adversaries were as prepared as he was and were now in possession of the recording, he had already all but lost.

Two museums meant he and Caan needed to split up. He had sent her to cover the Lightner Museum on the other side of the city's historic district, while Monk was heading to Ripley's. Normally, he'd have taken the Lightner himself, since the museum's period collection was more likely to have the right model of phonograph to play the cylinder. And they did have one, but he had done his homework beforehand: the Lightner's piece was on loan to the Alexander Graham Bell National Historic Site museum in Nova Scotia. So no matter where the thieves went first, eventually they would be coming to him.

And this time, Monk would be ready.

Chapter 16

A treasure hunt. It was the last thing Jon would have expected, and yet, despite the obvious danger, the prospect lit a spark of excitement in Jon's belly. It would be like old times, before Michael had gone off to college, before Jon's world shifted ever so subtly off its axis.

As Renée had promised, Kamlesh had emerged from the archives shortly after Jon, Michael, and Liz had agreed upon a course of action. Following a curt introduction, Kamlesh took them back the way they had come, padding down the preserved hotel hallway, through the secret door, and back into the darkened torture chamber exhibit.

History, Jon reflected as the trio meandered through the exhibits toward the exit. History was rich in St. Augustine, the oldest continually inhabited European settlement in the United States. And history had been his and Michael's greatest passion as long as he could remember. It was hard not to become engrossed in the subject, growing up with parents who lived and breathed it. Not only that, but they made it fun. The stuffy atmosphere of his father's university classroom may not have been the ideal place for a pair of energetic young boys to fall in love with a subject, but when complemented with international family vacations and field research trips, Jon and Michael found it impossible not to become enamored of it.

Further, their common interest had made the Rickner brothers inseparable. On family excursions, they would often go off exploring together, making their own adventures walking through crumbling ruins and ancient fortresses. Michael was their fearless leader, and Jon admired him for it. They occasionally ran afoul with the local authorities or gangs in the area, but even through their mishaps they had managed to make a few minor historical discoveries themselves.

After their mom died, their father had dialed back on the family trips, becoming somewhat reclusive and burying himself in research. Jon and Michael, however, would not be deterred. In fact, their joint adventuring helped with the healing process, in some way honoring their mother's legacy by continuing to do what she loved. In recent years, with Michael away at college, the brothers hadn't been able to indulge in their favorite pastime together nearly as much as Jon would have liked. But what had started out as a simple journey to explore a centuries-old city they had loved visiting in their youth had turned into a deadly hunt for something long hidden. Already a family friend had been murdered and a shop full of historical documents and other relics had been destroyed. Now they had uncovered a double mystery that neither he nor Michael had ever heard anything about.

What was this treasure hunt Flagler had created? And why had he abandoned it on the eve of its announcement?

Jon was still pondering both questions, fully cognizant of the fact that someone believed at least one of the answers was worth killing over. He clutched the wooden case containing the Flagler cylinder more tightly now as they finally reached the central stairwell that would take them back down to the atrium.

"Have you figured it out yet?" Michael asked.

"The first clue?" Jon replied, grateful for all those summertime trips they had taken to the city while visiting their mom's family in Jacksonville. "I have a pretty good idea where to start."

"Grace?"

"That's what I'm thinking."

"You've figured it out?" Liz asked, excited.

"Maybe," Jon said. "In theory, an event like this would have taken about a week or so, allowing visitors to explore the city, share ideas with one another, and puzzle out each clue. Unfortunately, it will be significantly harder for us."

"How so?"

"Four reasons I can see. First, we're doing this more than a century late, after decades of new developments have changed the cityscape. Second, considering how we're kind of fugitives for leaving the scene at your uncle's shop, we'll have to finish this in a matter of hours, not days. Third, there's no guarantee Flagler wouldn't have hidden away the markers or whatever for subsequent clues when he decided to can the hunt, meaning the whole thing might now be unsolvable."

Jon nodded at Jadena as they passed through the entrance gate. She nodded back, saying nothing but wearing an expression of disbelief that they hadn't continued through the rest of the exhibits and exited through the gift shop. Jon understood. Ripley's was certainly full of curiosities that were right up his alley. But at the same time, they had just uncovered something far more interesting and stimulating than any of the bizarre oddities housed in this collection.

"And the fourth thing?" Liz asked as they left the building and turned toward the street.

Jon saw him first. A mane of red hair complemented by a full red beard. He had been cleanshaven during his more respected days, but Jon recognized him just the same. And with a twinge of fear, he realized that the man's presence in this city at the same time as Bouvier's murder and the discovery of the Flagler cylinder was no coincidence.

"Him."

"That can't be..." Michael said. "I thought he was operating out of Brazil these days."

"Who?" Liz asked.

"Caeden Monk," Jon said. "Once a respected archeologist, now wanted for antiquities crimes, theft, assault, and murder in nineteen countries at last count."

"And he sees us," Michael added.

Monk started coming their way, his eyes fixed on the case Jon carried. Jon quickly formulated a plan of action, then just as quickly abandoned it upon seeing the bulge in Monk's jacket.

Gun. Likely the very weapon used to murder Mr. Bouvier.

Jon looked behind him, away from the street, but it was a dead end. A high fence blocked their way to the left, the stonework of Ripley's to the right. There was no way out but through. Ultimately, unmasking Bouvier's murderer had been their goal before discovering what was on the cylinder. But now, this was far bigger than a simple case of clearing their identity and bringing a killer to justice. Caeden Monk was a man of much avarice and few scruples. Whatever historical mystery they'd run across with Flagler's abandoned treasure hunt would be forever lost if Monk completed it first.

Finish Flagler's hunt, Bouvier had implored with his dying breath. *Don't let him win.* In Dr. Strickland's office moments earlier, they had discovered what Flagler's hunt meant. Now it was clear who *him* was. Which left only one other participating team.

"I'd prefer not making a scene," Monk said, a hint of a musical Irish lilt in his voice. "But you've taken something of mine, and I'd like it back." The former professor had left his homeland decades before, but traces of his origins remained in his inflection. Although Jon often loved the sound of Irish accents, he couldn't get the image of a leprechaun out of his head. Not because of Monk's flaming red hair or

Hibernian accent. Because leprechauns prize gold. And they are marked by deception.

"I think you've mistaken us for someone else," Michael said.

Monk was a few yards away now. Jon's fingers started to ache from his death grip on the wooden case. *Think, Jon, think!*

The disgraced archeologist cocked his head, studying Michael. "Hmm..." he intoned absentmindedly. Then, more purposefully, "No, I don't think I have. That"—he pointed at Jon's case—"is mine."

"How do you figure that?" Jon asked, trying to buy some time as he scrambled to figure out something, anything, to get them out of this mess.

"I purchased it from an antiques dealer earlier today. Unfortunately, there was a mix-up and I left with the wrong item." He pulled out the pistol, careful to keep it close to his body. "Again, I don't want to make a scene."

They were trapped. Monk had already proven his willingness to kill over the cylinder. And though the Irishman probably didn't want to draw undue attention to himself by murdering them in the middle of the Ripley's parking lot, Jon wouldn't put it past him if he felt there were no other way.

"Fine," Jon said, unlatching the case and slowly hinging it open. "We never even got to listen to it anyway. What's so important on there?"

"Just an old folk tune my grandmother used to sing," Monk said. "Purely sentimental value to me, but I don't like being swindled."

"I'll bet," Jon said, uncapping the cardboard tube and sliding out the wax cylinder.

"What are... no, just leave it in the tube." Monk reached forward. Jon caught his brother's expression, wondering, then recognizing what his younger sibling was doing. Almost imperceptibly, Michael nodded.

"It's all yours," Jon said, throwing the cylinder in a high arc to the left. Monk's face blanched with terror, his eyes locked on the fragile recording as it sailed overhead. Jon chucked the wooden case at the distracted Monk, then ran for the street, Michael and Liz close behind.

The professor instantly took off, scrambling for the falling cylinder. Jon prayed it smashed on the pavement, that it would break into a million pieces, forever obscuring the secrets Monk would exploit for his own wicked purposes. But as they reached the street, Jon saw that Monk was close enough. The cylinder might be damaged on impact, but Monk would likely catch it.

Jon had bought them an escape and a slight head start, but neither would last long. Now, even more than before, time was against them. The Flagler hunt had just turned into a race.

PART TWO

FLAGLER

Chapter 17

Audrey Yang blinked at the sudden burst of sunlight assaulting her pupils as she exited the burned antique shop. A dwindling crowd of passersby still clogged the street outside, but Weiss had already taken statements from everyone who had witnessed the trio of unidentified suspects tumbling out of the door. No one claimed to have noticed anything prior to the two males in the group entering the already burning shop. So either the young woman had set the fire and stuck around to burn up herself, or, more likely, the murder and arson had been perpetrated by a fourth person, who left undetected before the fire caused people to take notice.

For nearly an hour she had poked and prodded, studying the crime scene and entreating it to give up its secrets. But whoever had set that fire had done irreparable damage to the story the evidence could have told. The lab techs had collected samples and taken a flurry of pictures, but she felt there wouldn't be much for them to find anymore. Even worse, her gut told her that this was bigger than a simple crime of opportunity. The fire wouldn't cover up the fact that Bouvier was murdered. But it would cover up the theft of some uniquely valuable item. With so much destroyed, it would be impossible for insurance adjusters or anyone else to authoritatively verify what, if anything, might have been stolen.

"You get anything?" Weiss asked, leaving his most recent interviewee.

"I don't like this," she said.

"It's a homicide, Yang. You're not supposed to like it."

"No, not that," she said, giving him a look. "The whole thing smells wrong."

77

"How so?"

"We're focused on the murder and the arson, both major crimes that were obviously committed. But I get the feeling there's something more."

"Like another victim?"

"Like another crime. What if all this—the arson and the murder—are just to distract us from the culprit's real goal. Like if they stole something from the shop."

"You don't kill someone and burn down their shop just to get some antique tea set or old book, Yang."

"You do if the item is rare and valuable enough."

Weiss put a hand on her shoulder. Yang tried not to cringe and turn away. She knew he was trying to look out for her as her partner, particularly as new as she was to the detective role. But she still felt belittled by his action.

"Pretty soon you'll learn not to make things more complicated than they are," Weiss said, affecting an avuncular smile. "Already we're dealing with two major crimes that will make the front page of tomorrow's *Herald* and maybe even the *Times-Union*. We don't need to go adding an art theft when there wasn't one. More times than not, Occam's razor will cut to the truth of our cases, despite the convoluted conspiracies Hollywood movies and primetime TV churn out."

"But arson wouldn't cover up bullet slugs in the victim. It would, however, cover up the theft of a particular item."

Weiss laughed. "This isn't the Louvre, Yang. It's a small-town antique shop. Yes, Bouvier was a presence in town for going on thirty years, but he didn't have any million-dollar pieces worth killing over."

"But how else do you explain—"

"Audrey, look," he said, lowering his voice. Glancing at the staring crowd, Yang suddenly realized that she had been talking far too loudly. Rookie mistake. And another reason why Weiss wouldn't take her theory seriously. "Big takeaway: most criminals aren't that smart. If they were, they wouldn't be criminals. Our suspect here probably just panicked after shooting the victim and tried to cover his tracks. The murder is the main thing here. Figure out the motive for that, and we can find our suspect."

She wasn't going to win this argument. In fact, she had already lost, though her mind was not changed. As Weiss walked to talk with one of the lab techs leaving the scene, she realized that all she had accomplished was making her partner think she was an idiot or an attention hog—neither of which, at least in her mind, was a fitting description. But she was undeterred from her theory.

Audrey Yang had grown up down the coast in Cocoa Beach, then had moved to St. Augustine for college. After double-majoring in criminology and history at Flagler College, she decided to join the local police force, aiming to make her way up to detective and then, hopefully, launch her way into the FBI. Her father had been the chief of police for Cocoa Beach before getting gunned down on the job her sophomore year of high school. Gone were her dreams of becoming a marine biologist. All she could think of now was making her father proud by continuing his work.

Now, twelve years later, she had finally made detective after realizing that one problem with small police departments was the relatively limited advancement opportunities. And in the first big case of her detective career—one that could make a name for herself and get the FBI recruiters' attention—she was all alone. Her more experienced colleagues were adamant that she was wrong. And, to an impartial observer, her theory was more convoluted and complicated than the obvious solution at which Weiss had arrived. But that was what detectives did, wasn't it? Tried to look through the fog and noise to discover the truth buried underneath it all? Her father had done that, even to the point of uncovering and exposing a drug ring helmed by a popular city commissioner.

And look where it got him. The voice, unbidden as always, had plagued her ever since her father's death. It sounded like her mother, who had died of breast cancer two weeks before her only daughter graduated from college. She had never approved of little Audrey giving up the hard sciences for a gun and a badge. And every time Yang felt plagued by doubt, she heard her mother's voice, telling her how she didn't belong in law enforcement at all, much less arguing far-fetched theories with veteran detectives.

Yang tamped down the voice, trying to ignore the confusion and self-doubt it always brought. She had earned a spot at the table. Summa cum laude with honors from Flagler, top in her class at the academy, and the youngest woman detective on the force in two decades. No matter how small her mother's voice or Weiss's patronizing guidance could make her feel, she deserved her detective's badge.

Slipping a hand into her breast pocket, she stroked the worn metal surface of her father's badge, a totem she had carried since moving to St. Augustine. He hadn't been afraid of unorthodox theories when they were right. And, initially at least, where it had gotten him was the chief's office. People noticed when you put yourself out there and thought outside the box. And sometimes, when no one else would listen, the only way to pursue those theories was by yourself.

Which was exactly what she would do.

Chapter 18

Jon finally allowed himself to stop running once he saw the majestic terra cotta spire of Grace United Methodist Church. As he, Michael, and Liz approached the church from Cordova Street, Jon tried to imagine what this treasure hunt's intended participants would have seen more than a century ago. It wasn't hard. Only two blocks from the twenty-first-century tourist trappings of St. George Street and the main historic shopping district, the church was surrounded by quiet homes and sleepy side streets. With no cars on the road at the moment, it wasn't hard to picture a fancy nineteenth-century horse-drawn carriage driving down the avenue, gossamer curtains pulled aside to let its Yankee occupants gaze wide-eyed at the sunshine-drenched ancient Spanish city—or Henry Flagler's invented vision of it at least.

The warm Florida weather and sea breeze off the coast had made St. Augustine an ideal winter home for many of Gilded Age New York's elite, from tobacco kingpin George L. Lorillard to shipping titan William Henry Aspinwall to legendary architect James Renwick. Even Astor family scion William Astor Jr. found the town fascinating, investing in railroad lines in the early 1880s and spending weeks yachting along the Florida coastline. But while the natural beauty of the town was appealing to visitors, its location on the far-flung outskirts of the country and its lack of any major port or other commercial draw meant it remained in many ways a backwater community, devoid of the amenities, facilities, and entertainment that contemporaneous high society had come to expect of resorts. Even President Grant's two-week stay in the city in 1880 didn't change the fact that, in many ways, St. Augustine was ill-equipped to support the lifestyle demands of the era's rich and famous. And without a major investment in capital and resources, it would perpetually lag behind other existing resort communities dotting the Atlantic coast.

Enter Henry Flagler.

Flagler had made his fortune years before he set his sights on St. Augustine, co-founding the multinational behemoth Standard Oil in 1870 with his more famous business partner John D. Rockefeller Sr.—father of Rockefeller Center–creator John D. Rockefeller Jr. and patriarch of the Rockefeller dynasty. Even in that era of robber barons and industrial titans, Flagler was a figure to behold, wealthy beyond measure with a reputation to match. He had put his oil wealth to use building his own railroad empire, not just for ferrying goods and supplies across the country but with a particular focus on luxury cars for his wealthy contemporaries. And one of the best ways to spur demand for travel on those luxury rail lines? Create a new, exclusive resort destination.

When Flagler first made his mark on St. Augustine, the city had been in American hands for more than half a century. Much of the town's Spanish influence had been anglicized, reflected in the English street names and the Castillo itself being rechristened as Fort Marion. But when Flagler came to town, he saw the value in tapping into the city's exotic history, even if his own interpretation of that history was an idealized one.

He changed street names from English descriptors like Bay Street to more grand ones like Avenida Menéndez, paying homage to explorers and key figures from Florida's Spanish past. He promulgated myths about Ponce de Leon and other famous conquistadors to drum up the wonder of the city's heritage. And, most of all, he used his own significant architectural contributions to transform St. Augustine into the idyllic Spanish paradise he imagined it once had been.

Grace United Methodist Church was a fine example. The original Olivet Methodist Church in town was on the site that Flagler desired for his Hotel Alcazar, itself a masterpiece of Moorish Revival architecture. In his deal for the land, Flagler offered to build the congregation a larger, better house of worship elsewhere within the city, an offer the church leadership accepted. Commissioning the famed New York architectural firm Carrère and Hastings, the same architects who were building his landmark hotels in the city, Flagler followed through on his promise, constructing a basilican church made of coquina and terra-cotta. The overall design as well as the details were meant to evoke the image of a seventeenth-century Mediterranean Spanish church, another artificial throwback to the grand conquistador-era city that St. Augustine never was. Even in his philanthropy, Flagler had seized another opportunity to remake the city to suit his needs.

Jon led the trio into the entry pavilion of Grace, a low-walled concrete wedge surrounded by the church's otherwise verdant grounds. Though the church's front doors were only a few dozen feet from the street, the relative quiet of this area of town allowed the nature-rimmed cloister to provide a brief retreat from the bustle of man's world and into the sanctity of God's. Passing beneath a terra-cotta rose window, he entered the church through the massive red doors.

"So let me in on the clue here, guys," Liz said. "What are we looking for?"

"When planning his luxury hotels," Jon said, "Flagler wanted to put one on the land occupied by the local Methodist church. He offered to build them a magnificent new church on another plot in the city if they would sell him their land. They agreed, and this is the church he constructed." He held a hand aloft, gesturing to the chandelier that resembled an upside-down golden sieve above their heads. Exposed wooden beams and carved archways adorned the nave, straddling the line between high ecclesiastical architecture and an open-plan beach style more akin to Caribbean missions. "Welcome to Grace United Methodist."

"According to the clue, we're looking for something that's been altered," Michael said.

"Wait, so Flagler didn't build this place from scratch?" Liz asked.

"No, he did," Jon said.

"Then how could something be altered if it was brand new at the time?"

Jon looked around. Besides the seemingly strange dimensions—the width of the shallow sanctuary far exceeded its depth—the interior décor was fairly traditional, stalwart but rather simple compared to some of Flagler's more luxuriant creations. But Flagler hadn't been building this for himself or to impress his guests. It was for the congregation he had uprooted, an existing body of believers that simply wanted a new home to continue their worship of God. Four sections of wooden pews spanned the sanctuary, all eyes facing the cross at the far end.

"Oh wow," he finally said. "He thought he was so clever."

"What do you see?" Michael asked.

Jon pointed toward the apse. "Flagler fancied himself a punster. 'Alter,' to change, versus 'altar,' like in a church."

"Of course." Michael led the way across the sanctuary, Jon and Liz right behind.

The altar was positioned in front of an alcove housing the choir loft, the people's lectern to the right, the high pulpit to the left. Above the choir loomed a wooden cross set against a latticed arch. Carved of wood and solid-looking, the altar was draped with a white cloth, topped with a stand displaying a large Bible opened to the Gospel of John.

Michael stood back and studied the altar and its surroundings. "So for the lay people visiting the church—Flagler's guests who would be participating in this hunt—the altar would have appeared to be beneath the main cross there."

"So we follow the altar crossways to..." Liz drifted off as she raised her finger, tracing an imaginary line from one end of the altar to the far window.

"You're making it too complicated, Liz," Jon said, stealing a quick look around. He only saw two staff members, both of whom were busy with parishioners at the far end of the church. "Flagler wanted to challenge and entertain his guests, not infuriate them with overly obtuse clues. The clue mentions the altar and beneath the cross. So let's try

Occam's razor first." He crouched down in front of the altar, checked the sanctuary once more, and lifted the cloth.

Set into the wood at the front of the altar was a gleaming golden shaft. Ornately detailed in the old manner that bespoke guilds and apprentices, where becoming a skilled craftsman was one of the highest professional aspirations of someone not born into nobility, the curious artifact was jagged at one end, as though it had been broken off from a larger whole.

"What in the world is that?" Liz asked.

"'The first part of an ancient cross,' I'd wager," Michael said, staring at the piece.

"So what do we do now? We found it. But what's the point?"

Jon studied the artifact. "Maybe the original plan was to pass out some sort of card where participants could write down the location of where they found the pieces, verifying that they solved the clues and discovered the hiding spots."

"This is bigger than that now, though," Michael said. "Caeden Monk didn't murder Mr. Bouvier and torch his shop just to check a few tourist destinations off a list and win a garden-party prize."

"If this is the first 'piece' of an ancient cross, then perhaps the whole cross is worth something? Like the Cross of Coronado?"

Michael chuckled at his brother's passing reference to Indiana Jones lore, but nodded. "Maybe so."

Liz reached out and gripped the piece. Slipping the blade of a Swiss army knife behind the artifact, she pried it free with a soft pop, century-old adhesive finally loosing its bonds.

"What are you doing?" Michael asked, astonished.

She met him head-on. "If Monk's really after this, we need to make sure he can't get his hands on it, right?" She placed the pilfered piece in Michael's hand. "Well, now he can't."

"Good Lord, is she for real?" Michael asked his brother.

Jon let go of the altar cloth, allowing it to fall back into place and conceal the theft. "She makes a good point." It was perhaps more audacious than his initial impulse, but stealing the piece may well have been the best option. She just got there faster than he or Michael had. Already he was starting to see reflections of her uncle's love of adventure in Liz. Just like their father and her uncle, they were setting out on a new quest together. It was almost poetic. Rickner and Bouvier, the next generation.

He glanced down the central aisle where one of the staffers had just finished conversing with a parishioner and was now heading their way. "Time to go."

Michael saw the man coming and slipped the golden artifact into his backpack. Then, as reverently as they could, the trio made for the doors, leaving behind the desecrated sanctum and breaking into the bright Florida sunshine.

One down, three to go.

Chapter 19

Caeden Monk's hands worked furiously over the wax, picking the last few pieces of debris from the cylinder. Like an idiot, he had let his goal quite literally slip through his fingers. As he dove for it at the last second, the cylinder landed in his outstretched hand, only to bounce upon impact and roll onto the asphalt of Ripley's parking lot.

So the cylinder was damaged. But not destroyed.

He had texted Miriam immediately afterward to meet him at his Explorer, ready to try the Edison phonograph player on the correct cylinder. Monk had studied it while walking back to the parking garage. Most of the damage was minimal, but pebble-sized indentions marred the surface in places. He had carefully brushed away the dirt and grass that stubbornly clung to the wax in the cloying humidity. It had to be enough. After all this work, untold research, three murders, arson, and a poorly executed theft, he finally had the Flagler cylinder in his hands. If, because of his clumsiness, he came up empty now, he would never forgive himself. Or those who had come between him and his discovery.

"What happened to it?" Miriam asked as he neared the Explorer.

"Don't ask," he said, unlocking the vehicle. They climbed into the backseat, where he set up the phonograph player and turned the crank. Holding his breath, he carefully positioned the stylus at the beginning of the recording.

Silence.

Monk felt an acidic pain melting his chest. It was too much to bear. All this work, for nothing? For more than twelve decades this cylinder had survived, one of the oldest of its kind and certainly the most valuable. And then, thanks to one sloppy incident of butterfingers—*poof*.

In an instant all his fears dissolved into nothingness. Out of the ether, from across the bounds of time, Henry Flagler was talking to him. The cylinder's message had survived his mistake after all.

Miriam's eyes lit up as the recording played. She gazed at him with unmitigated excitement, a combination of eagerness, relief, joy, and desire. There would be time for celebration and lovemaking soon enough, but this signified only the next step of their journey—the beginning of the hunt itself. Though he tried not to show it, he was heartened by the turn of events. They were so much closer than ever before.

As he listened, Monk was overwhelmed with the realization that no one had listened to this for more than a century. No one alive, at least. Unless...

Flagler was offering the first clue now. Monk only had to ponder for a moment before he knew the hiding spot. When the recording reached the second and third clues, Monk had good general guesses for those, too, though he would need to be on-site to pin down the exact location.

Suddenly, Flagler's voice stopped. Monk looked at the machine. The stylus had fallen into one of the indentions and was now dragging its own rut across the aged wax. He lifted the stylus and studied the spinning cylinder, looking for the next undamaged section. Finding it, he replaced the stylus.

"...to you all," the recording began midsentence, "and no matter what, enjoy yourselves and enjoy St. Augustine!"

No!

"Where's the rest of it?" Miriam asked. "What was the fourth clue?"

"We don't have it," Monk said, forlorn. He double-checked the cylinder to see if he had missed anything, but he hadn't. The impact with the ground had obliterated the waxen grooves that preserved the only copy of Flagler's fourth clue. Without it...

"Can we still solve it?" she asked. "Can we still finish the hunt?"

Monk thought back to the young man who had caused all this trouble in the first place by throwing the priceless artifact and damaging it. He had thought he and the other guy looked familiar, but suddenly it dawned on him. He didn't know them, but if family resemblance was anything, he definitely knew their father. He'd bet money that they were William Rickner's kids, and if that was the case, then they never would have destroyed something like that cylinder without good cause.

Like not wanting Monk to have it. Because they already knew what the recording contained.

"Yes," he finally said, exiting the Explorer and motioning for Miriam to do the same. "I definitely think we can."

Chapter 20

J on bit off the interminable string of cheese tracing its way back to his slice of pepperoni pizza. It was past one in the afternoon, and after their hasty departure from Grace UMC, Liz was complaining of hunger. Considering the day they'd already had, and how the rest of their day looked, Michael agreed that they should grab a bite to eat.

Pizzalley's was an ideal place to lunch today. Its main entrance on St. George Street opened into a narrow New York–style pizzeria, complete with open kitchen and brick oven. But while the pizza hit the spot, the location's real lure for them lay in the second part of its portmanteau name. The back entrance of the pizzeria led to a secluded courtyard, at the other end of which was the back entrance for Pizzalley's Chianti Room, a full-service Italian restaurant that also served the establishment's namesake dish. The dual-faced restaurant and the adjoining courtyard essentially encompassed an alley, with two entrances on two separate streets. Jon, Michael, and Liz were the only diners in the courtyard, hidden from anyone looking in the windows of either eatery. But even if Monk were to somehow find them, they could simply exit through the opposite entrance and disappear into the street.

Jon hoped it wouldn't come to that. They were all scarfing down their food as quickly as their stomachs allowed, ready to get back into the hunt. Jon still didn't know for sure if Monk had managed to save the cylinder, but if he had, they surely would have some competition on their hands shortly. So all in all, that was a big reason to be grateful for Liz's seemingly impulsive extraction of the artifact. On the other hand, the church's rector would surely discover the vandalism before long. Yet another reason for the cops to be after them today.

Wiping his hands, he used a second napkin to pick up the gold object and study it.

"So the second clue refers to something at the hotel Flagler built on the old Methodist church's lot?" Liz asked in between bites of pizza.

"Exactly," Michael said. "He must have hidden the next piece at his Hotel Alcazar."

"Is the hotel still there?"

"Yes and no."

"Guys," Jon said, "there's something written here."

Michael and Liz leaned in close, trying to see what Jon was talking about. Pointing without touching, Jon used a finger to trace a line of writing inscribed along the periphery of the intricately carved artifact.

"Latin?" Michael asked.

"It looks like it," Jon said. "But it's cut off on both ends."

"Meaning the rest of the message is on the other pieces of it?"

"Four clues, four pieces..."

"So there's a message at the end of the hunt for Flagler's guests?" Liz asked.

As Jon studied the inscription, a chill went down his spine. "No, I don't think Flagler wrote this message. I think it's much, much older than that."

Chapter 21

When Caeden Monk arrived at Grace United Methodist Church, the staff was already in a tizzy. Passing through the portal and into the normally placid sanctuary revealed that something awful had just happened. Monk had a guess what that might be.

"Don't tell me they were already here," Miriam Caan said in a hushed tone.

"Fine, I won't tell you," Monk said.

"Smart-ass."

Monk approached the altar, which seemed to be the epicenter of the commotion.

"What happened here?" he asked, adopting an official tone.

"It's gone!" wailed one of the staff, a young man whose tortured facial features were obscured by an unkempt beard more befitting the hermitic desert fathers of the early church than a modern-day ecclesiastical representative, but then Monk had never been much for religion.

"What's gone?" Monk already knew the answer, but he wanted to know how much they knew.

"A historic piece of a golden cross. One discovered and gifted to this congregation by Henry Flagler. And now it's gone!"

Monk forced himself not to roll his eyes at the man's theatrics. The guy was acting like he'd just been excommunicated or the church itself had burned down. Sure, damaging an altar might be viewed as desecration, but he was acting as though it was a physical wound, a personal offense against his very soul.

"Did you see who took it?"

"No. But God knows. And His vengeance will be swift."

So they didn't see the Rickner party. Which meant the cops wouldn't be sniffing up that tree either. Monk still had control of the chase. He left the distraught man to his pious sorrows and walked back toward Miriam without a word. He had never announced his presence, nor his alleged purpose. If the young man remembered being questioned, he wouldn't be sure if it was a cop, a coworker, a parishioner, or a tourist, seeding further confusion. Especially since Monk was none of the above.

The man was right about one thing, though. Vengeance would be swift. It just wouldn't be God who was doling out the wrath.

"They took it," he said between his teeth as he reached Miriam's side, grabbing her arm and leading her outside.

"You don't think they already understand its importance, do you?"

Monk thought for a moment. "No. They're coming into this blind. They're ahead of us, but we've got the roadmap and the endgame. They're probably just trying to pull in the rope so we can't follow them."

"They can try."

"Indeed. A false sense of security won't do them much good, but there's still the matter of them collecting the pieces. Not only does that prevent us from studying them ourselves, but if they get enough of them, they may realize what's really at stake here. And then all bets are off."

Miriam nodded. "Then let's get ahead of them before they do."

Chapter 22

In its heyday in the decades before and after the turn of the twentieth century, the Hotel Alcazar was one of the premier hotels in St. Augustine. Built on land previously occupied by the Olivet Methodist Church, the Alcazar's beautiful stonework and Moorish architecture attempted to draw guests into another world, one theoretically harkening back to the city's mythologized Spanish origins. Named after the famed Alcazar castles in southern Spain, the magnificent edifice was dripping in its Arabesque and Mediterranean influences.

Though, like most of Flagler's lavish hotels, the Alcazar was no longer serving its original purpose, the new tenants did their luxurious and storied surroundings justice. The

building had been home to St. Augustine's City Hall offices for decades, while a number of boutique shops lined the
palatial complex's open courtyards and plazas, much as their
forbears had in the 1890s. But the most famous of the Alcazar's current residents was the Lightner Museum.

Jon and Liz followed Michael through a maze of concrete sidewalks and low bushes that made up the main plaza.
Passing through a pointed archway in a wide arcade, they
entered a fairytale courtyard, with antique lampposts and
palm trees lining curved walkways. The focal point of the
scene was a beautiful stone footbridge that rose over a fish-
pond, where the bride and groom usually stood during the
site's regular use as a wedding pavilion. Yet another fanciful
Flagler creation harkening to another age and another continent. But the second clue was clearly something of a more
modern bent—in the late nineteenth century at least—than
this whimsical throwback to a storybook past. If it still existed, the next piece of the puzzle would be farther on, in the
heart of the former hotel—the Lightner Museum.

The museum was founded in 1948 by Chicago publisher
Otto C. Lightner and was mostly comprised of his personal ac-
quisitions. The collection was an impressive representation of
Gilded Age treasures and curiosities, from vintage player pianos
and original stained-glass creations by Louis Comfort Tiffany
himself to stuffed exotic birds and an Egyptian mummy. It felt
like a collection of museum exhibits that tourists from a century
ago would have experienced. *Mysteries of the Orient*, *Wonders of
the Modern Age*, and *Treasures of the Renaissance* would have been
emblazoned across each collection, as cultured blue bloods and
curious blue-collar patrons held nickel tickets in hand to see the
eclectic assortment of pieces.

Leaving the courtyard behind, Jon, Michael, and Liz
entered a glass atrium filled with small exhibits teasing the
treasures within, alongside historical displays showcasing
the site's transformation from church and skating rink to
hotel to museum. This part of the hotel once housed two of
the most renowned of the Alcazar's public guest features—
its state-of-the-art health facilities, including a massive
Turkish bath, and its three-story ballroom. By all accounts,
the museum had put the spaces to good use. Jon just hoped
they had preserved whatever Flagler had used as his second
hiding place.

The trio paid the entrance fee and walked into the museum proper. Even judging from the signs directing them to key exhibits, Jon could see the collection was as eclectic as he had heard. A massive desk commissioned for Louis Bonaparte, one-time King of Holland and brother of Napoleon, graced the third floor, while shrunken heads from Papua New Guinea and arrowheads from Montana were but samples of the first floor's wide-ranging offerings. What they sought would be newer. And hopefully still there.

"A modern influencer of the era would have been hypnotism, maybe?" Liz asked as they passed an array of antique typewriters and a collection of early twentieth-century hooked rugs.

"Perhaps," Michael said. "Spiritualism was also on the rise, so there might have been an aspect of that there."

"Yeah, but spiritualism was hardly 'technologically marvelous,'" Jon said. "Flagler clearly references technology, so perhaps some sort of invention?" The hotel would have been full of the latest and greatest technologies in its heyday, many of which would have been provided by Flagler's friend Thomas Edison.

"Good point," Michael conceded. "And he references health, so logic would dictate that we're in the right place. Built on the site of the original home of the local Methodist congregation prior to moving to Grace. Flagler's hotel was most renowned for its cutting-edge health services."

"The problem is," Liz said, "if it was modern a century ago, it's completely outdated now. Plus, this place isn't exactly a health spa anymore."

Jon grinned. "Ah, but that's where we may find ourselves a break. Separately, either issue would have likely left us dead in the water. But together... I mean, look around. This place is full of old things that have been replaced by newer technology in the real world. But in here, they're preserved and revered long after they would have otherwise outlived their usefulness."

"So Flagler's hiding place in the original hotel might have been repurposed as a museum piece now," Liz said, slowly nodding as the pieces fit into place. "With the Lightner unwittingly preserving Flagler's secret more than a century after the fact."

"Either that or Flagler built it into the walls or something," Michael said. "Barring those scenarios, we may be out of luck."

"What do you mean?" Liz asked.

"The Alcazar still operated as a hotel for nineteen years after Flagler's death in 1913, and then another fifteen years passed until Lightner purchased it in 1947. Three different eras, spanning more than a century, without Flagler to ensure the continued survival of the hiding place. If this 'modern influencer' was removed from the hotel at any point in there, which seems likely considering how quickly technology evolved even then, the second piece of the puzzle is probably lost forever. The treasure hunt would be a wash."

"But it would also be a lost cause for that Monk guy, right?" Liz asked.

"Yeah," Jon said, though he doubted that would stop someone like Caeden Monk from tearing the city apart in his attempt to find what he was looking for. "But I'm feeling hopeful."

"Why's that?"

"Because if this hiding place was important and prominent enough for Flagler to use it to showcase the majesty of his St. Augustine creations, it would likely have been interesting enough for posterity to preserve it in a museum. And where better to display it than here, in its original home?"

"Here's hoping, bud," Michael said, clapping his brother on the back. "All right, let's make this quick. If Monk was able to get the cylinder working, he won't be far behind us. Why don't we spread out and triple our efforts?"

They split up, all remaining within sight of one another, weaving through the collection and scouring each item's description for any indication it was tied to the original hotel. There were a few false alarms, but nothing fit Flagler's description. Agreeing that their solution was not on the first floor, they took an elevator to the second.

Splitting up again, they explored the next phase of the collection, navigating through a gorgeous assortment of glass-blown art and Victorian-era furniture. After a few minutes of fruitless searching, Jon noticed a large item sitting in the middle of the floor. Framed in wood and concealed in a glass case, the device consisted of five massive glass discs held vertically on a horizontal spindle, with rods and pipes zigzagging around and underneath.

He moved to read the plaque adorning the case.

> Morton-Wimshurst-Holtz Influence Machine

Bingo.

"Guys, I found it!" he shouted. A moment later, Liz and Michael had joined him.

"What is this?" Liz asked, eyes wide.

"It would have used some sort of static electricity generated by these discs to provide a rudimentary electrotherapy for guests back in the hotel's heyday," Jon said. "According to this diagram, a platform would have been set up here. You would sit on it and *voilà*, your typhoid is cured."

Michael suppressed a laugh. "So the next piece is hidden somewhere in this contraption?"

"But where?" Liz asked.

Jon tapped on the glass. "Back when he was devising this treasure hunt, Flagler intended for his guests to be able to see that they had solved the clue and move on. It would need to be in plain sight. So, theoretically, it should be visible somewhere on here."

They worked in silence for a few moments, scouring the nooks and crannies of the machine, looking between the discs and from every angle that the glass display case would allow them.

"I've got nothing," Michael said.

"Me neither," Liz echoed.

Jon frowned. "O for three."

"So if it was visible all this time, maybe somebody took it," Michael said. "This thing's been here for more than a century, and I can't imagine that a hunk of gold stuck to the side of this thing wouldn't have attracted attention from someone with sticky fingers."

"But then—" Jon paused, his attention suddenly caught by something anomalous in the otherwise pristine invention.

"What?" Liz asked.

"The hunt's participants needed to see the cross piece, not actually touch it or anything, right?"

"Sure, but this case would have prevented that," Liz said.

"This thing wouldn't have been in the case while it was in use. It would have been in the open air, allowing the static electricity to flow more freely."

As usual, Michael was picking up on his brother's line of thought. "So in order to be both visible and physically inaccessible, the cross piece would have to be enclosed in something transparent. A glass chamber or something."

"But we've looked all over this thing," Liz said. "There's nothing like that here."

Jon held up a finger. "There's nothing up here *now*."

He pointed to a section of copper pipe at the bottom of the device. "See those scratch marks? And how the pipe pieces are slightly different in color? That section was added later."

Liz's eyes lit up. "Replacing an old glass version with the cross in it."

"But would Flagler have put the cross piece into the new pipe?" Michael asked. "Or would he have hidden it elsewhere after abandoning the treasure hunt idea?"

"Only one way to find out." Jon tugged on the small cabinet knobs in what looked like a door in the case. Unsurprisingly, they didn't budge.

"Hang on a second." Jon leaned close to the door, trying to spy whatever locking mechanism was holding it closed. "Maybe I can jimmy it or something. But I can't see how it's locking..."

"Is it stuck into the wood or something?"

"I hope not. I won't be able to crack the lock if that's the case."

"Move!" Liz said. Jon looked up to see her running at him with a brass stanchion she'd picked up nearby. He dove out of the way just as she smashed the base into the glass display case. The glass shattered and fell away, creating a massive hole that allowed Jon access to the questionable pipe.

But the cacophonous shattering of glass was immediately joined by another, more ominous sound.

Alarm bells.

Chapter 23

Jon plunged his hand into the hole, trying to ignore the alarms. He gripped the scoured pipe in one hand and yanked on the adjacent piece with the other. It didn't budge.

"This is a crazy long shot, Jon," Michael said, anxiety clear in his voice. "We've got to get out of here."

"We've come this far," Jon said. "And those alarms won't go away just because we change our minds. I can finish it. Just keep an eye out."

Liz and Michael moved to watch for attendants or guards, adjusting their sight lines while remaining close to the case. Jon felt the tension rising. The fuse had been lit the moment the alarms went off. Though he didn't know how long until the authorities arrived, he knew they were coming, and getting closer with every second.

He adjusted his grip and tugged again. Nothing.

"Come on, Jon," Michael said. "They're gonna be on us any second."

Liz was even less successful in keeping the worry out of her voice. "If the guards show up, we're screwed."

A light bulb flicked on in Jon's brain. That was it. It had to be. Putting his hands back in their original positions and gripping the pipes tightly, he twisted the pieces in opposite directions, hoping against hope that the reason they wouldn't separate by tugging was that they were screwed into each other.

The pieces started to loosen. It was working.

A few twists later, Jon had freed the scoured pipe. He tilted it so the newly opened end was pointing down.

Out slid the most beautiful chunk of gold he had ever seen. The second piece of the cross.

"Got it!" he shouted over the alarms.

"None too soon," Michael said, backing toward Jon. "Guards found us."

"Over there!" Jon heard one of the guards yell to his partner, who quickly came into view. Going back out the way they came was no longer an option. If they were going to escape, they had to find another route.

"Come on!" Liz yelled, heading farther into the museum.

Jon shoved the golden cross piece into his pocket and ran after her, Michael running alongside. They reached a stairwell and started descending back toward the first floor. Only a few steps down, another guard turned the corner coming up toward them.

"Back!" Michael shouted, and the trio retreated from the new pursuer. The original pair of guards was less than twenty yards away now. Trapped. There was no other option.

Jon bounded up the stairs to the third floor, his brother and Liz close behind. They still had to get to ground level, but it wouldn't be via that stairwell. And now, they were even further away from their goal. But at least they were still free. For the moment, at least.

The third floor was flush with Renaissance sculptures in marble, oil canvases painted by minor American masters in the late nineteenth and early twentieth centuries, and ornate vases, furniture, and other items crafted by European artisans more than a century ago. One thing it did not have was an exit.

However, Jon knew that Flagler's designs for his resorts were always a far cry from the one-entrance, one-exit setups found in many modern hotels. For his St. Augustine guests, the outdoors was just as much of an attraction as anything inside the luxuriantly appointed interiors. Guests could be found roaming the grounds throughout the day, exploring any of the courtyards, plazas, or lawns that made up the resort complex, partaking in the archery ranges and tennis courts, or merely strolling a few blocks east to the cerulean waters of the Atlantic. As such, numerous entry portals would have been built into the structure from all sides. Jon just needed to find one.

They left the exhibit hall they were in and entered the vast open chamber of the ballroom. A truly unique room, the three-story structure had, in fact, only been a ballroom during special events hosted at the hotel. Normally, it held a palatial swimming pool, the largest indoor one in the world at the time, with curving staircases at the corners leading from the water to the second floor. Now drained, as it would have been for its preparation to host Gilded Age extravaganzas, the bottom floor was filled with seating for a cafe, with half a dozen diners enjoying a midafternoon treat.

But only one thought truly resonated with Jon's current circumstances as he glanced over the edge of the stone banister while running alongside: it was a long way down.

From a door across the open center of the room, yet another guard emerged to join his colleagues' pursuit. *Wonderful.* Their options were quickly narrowing down to nil.

Jon continued running, stepping back from the banister and toward the middle of the balcony. He weaved around a Regency-era chaise lounge and a malachite urn from Tsarist Russia to the echoing cadence of a flurry of footsteps—his,

Michael's, and Liz's loudest, though those of the growing contingent of guards were steadily getting closer.

Once the accidental treasure hunters reached the far end of the chamber, yet another guard appeared from a door directly in their path if they were to continue running around the periphery. He was quickly joined by the other guard. Jon looked behind him to see the three guards from below emerge from the previous exhibit hall and sight their targets. Five guards were moving on them now—two on one side, three on the other—with a forty-foot drop to a stone floor in between.

"Through here!" Michael said, grabbing his brother's arm. Jon turned to see a wooden door with a large window in its center. And on the other side, Jon could see the edge of the rooftop of the historic hotel complex they'd just traversed. Below the window, a series of boards had been nailed across the door, preventing them from opening it.

The window above, however, was fair game.

Hating himself for what he was about to do, Jon grabbed a hefty marble bust from a nearby display and chucked it through the window. The glass shattered cleanly, with only a few shards still clinging to the left edge. Michael kicked those out as he dove through the newly formed exit. Liz went next, followed by Jon. But just as Jon was almost through the window—one foot on the ground, torso and head safely through—one of the guards grabbed his hind foot.

"You're not getting away that easily, you filthy vandal," the guard growled. Jon resisted the urge to glance back. If he got out of this, he didn't want to give the guard a good look at his face that would help the authorities track them down. He pulled and twisted his foot, but the guard held on. Hoping to throw his captor off balance, Jon kicked backward, hitting the guard in the center of his chest and causing him to lose his grip on Jon's foot. Seizing the opportunity, Jon pulled his leg through and ran.

When he caught up with Michael and Liz, they were beating on a locked door. This one was solid, with no window for breaking. Jon stole a look behind him and saw a guard climbing through the window after them.

They were trapped.

"Can we climb up here?" Liz asked, attempting to scrabble up the steeply pitched terra-cotta tiles to the left. After gaining a few feet, she slipped back down. "Guess not."

The only other way out was to the right, a three-story drop to the ground. Jon peered over the edge.

"We've got to jump."

"Are you crazy?" Liz asked.

Michael looked over and saw what Jon had seen. "The bushes?"

"It's our only chance," Jon said.

Liz edged over to see. "What bushes?"

Jon pointed. "If we land just right, those should break our fall."

"They'll break *something*," she said.

"If you've got a better idea, now's the time for it."

Liz glanced around Jon at the guard who was now running in their direction, with another almost through the window they'd broken.

"Fine." The fear in her voice said she wasn't fine, but they were out of options. "On three?"

Jon looked to their right again. The guard was less than fifteen yards away. "No time. Jump!"

They leapt as one, free-falling for a couple of seconds before crashing into the large cluster of bushes at the edge of the building.

"You guys okay?" Michael asked.

"Fine," Jon said as he half crawled, half rolled out of the foliage.

"A few scratches, but nothing broken," Liz echoed.

Within a few moments of being trapped on the roof, the three amateur adventurers were running across the lawn, down the street, and out of sight, leaving the less-daring guards trapped three stories above with no easy avenue of pursuit. And safe in Michael's backpack was the second piece of Flagler's puzzle.

Chapter 24

Miriam Caan hated Caeden Monk.

There were mistakes people made in their youth that had a small impact on their later life—

sleeping in through an important test, flubbing a promising job interview, opening too many college credit cards. Other errors in judgment had a more lasting impact—getting pregnant out of wedlock, dropping out of high school, getting a DUI. But some mistakes irrevocably destroyed the course of a life. Aligning herself with Monk all those years ago had been one of those.

She had been young and stupid, she realized that now. Actually, she had realized it some time ago. Throwing away her promising archeological career and casting her lot with Caeden Monk had ruined all her academic achievements. All the years spent sacrificing her social life in pursuit of a respected career in academia had been for naught, tossed aside in a moment of lustful passion and professional excitement. Even her virginity, preserved largely because of an almost exclusive dedication to her studies rather than due to religious or ideological values, had been given away the night after her first major discovery. She could have been an esteemed archeologist, teaching at Cambridge or Tel Aviv and making a great name for herself. Instead, she had impulsively chosen to forsake it all to be Monk's lackey.

Given, she had grown in her own ways in the years since leaving Cornell. She was skilled with a number of firearms and in hand-to-hand combat. She had traveled to dozens of countries and made significant discoveries like she'd always dreamed, though the circumstances were far removed from her original plans. She was living a life on the edge, full of adventure and wonder. But it was also full of Monk. And that made it a nightmare.

During their relationship, it had always been clear that she was the lesser partner. Though their first sexual experience together in Turkey and their reunion in Cairo had seemed mutually enjoyable, it had since devolved into a power trip for Monk. Miriam was a brilliant, capable woman, so using her for his own pleasure only served to increase his egotism. He enjoyed lording his power over her, how he had made her into who she was today. And she hated him for it. Not only for the control he exercised over her life, but also for how he had twisted her lifelong dream into a dark and shameful mockery of its former self.

But apart from Monk, she was all alone. During her senior year of undergraduate studies, her parents had died on a pilgrimage to Israel when a Hezbollah suicide bomber blew up a Tel Aviv cafe. Her younger sister, Esther, had taken the news very hard, on the cusp of adulthood with suddenly no parents to usher her through the gates. But Miriam had all but abandoned her sister, instead burying herself in her studies to avoid confronting the painful truth. Weeks later, Miriam was in Turkey, and shortly thereafter, she had left behind all vestiges of her former life. Including her sister.

No more.

This discovery Monk had caught wind of was bigger than anything they'd done before. Much bigger. The prize at the end of the rainbow here was enough to build a new life, making up for lost time with Esther, redeeming herself after years of tainted dreams and regret. The prize Flagler had hidden—the treasure behind the treasure—was worth enough to buy new identities, to wash away all the blood and guilt that working with Monk had poisoned her with. But the share that Monk was offering was a pittance, as usual. He had enough dirt on her to send her to prison for the rest of her life—or worse. Even if she were able to make her share stretch far enough for a new beginning, Monk would never let her go. In his mind, she was his greatest discovery, one that was his and his alone to keep. Without this treasure—all of it—she would never be able to disappear, to fully start over.

Yet that prospect looked dire at present. Entering through the courtyard of the former Hotel Alcazar, Miriam already sensed that something was wrong. The old health facilities would now be housed in the Lightner Museum, so she headed there, only to be told by the woman in the gift shop at the museum's entrance that it was temporarily closed due to vandalism.

They had already been here. She was too late.

Miriam pleaded with the attendant to simply gain admittance to the rest of the exhibits, as she was from out of town and had long wanted to visit the museum. But the woman refused, saying the decision came from the museum's administrator himself. Looking suitably frustrated, Miriam thanked her anyway—no sense in burning too many bridges or drawing undue attention to herself—and left the shop.

Back in the foyer outside, she realized that she still had a chance to get ahead of them. While Monk had figured out most of the third clue and was already headed to that location, the fourth clue remained a mystery. However, she knew enough about Flagler and the previous three locations to know that there was only one place he would hide that final piece of the artifact. And she would definitely be able to get there well before they did.

If Monk failed to stop them at the third site, the initiative would be hers and—soon enough—so would the treasure. And her freedom.

Chapter 25

Scarlett O'Hara's seemed to be the only place in the area that didn't have *Old* or *Oldest* in the title. After making their escape from the Lightner Museum, Jon, Michael, and Liz had braved one of the tourist shops to purchase a change of clothes for each of them in order to throw off the guards' descriptions. They changed in the public bathrooms off St. George Street before seeking a new refuge to plan their next move. Privacy, however, was at a premium in the historic district. The streets were clogged with tourists, and most of the establishments were either small shops with intrusively attentive shopkeepers or museums with effusive welcoming staff in the tiny lobbies. The Oldest House, the Oldest Wooden Schoolhouse, the Pirate and Treasure Museum, the Oldest Drug Store, and the Colonial Quarter Museum were all crammed within a few blocks, while signs on passing tourist trolleys advertised the Oldest Store and the Old Jail museums not far away. But Scarlett O'Hara's was a place where they could be invisible for a few minutes, disappear into the crowd of other conversations and figure out the next clue and what to do next.

Scarlett's was a famous restaurant and watering hole just a stone's throw from the old city gates. The establishment had been a popular attraction with tourists and locals alike for nearly four decades, but its history—like most everything in St. Augustine—extended far earlier. Before it was a restaurant, the building was actually two separate houses, both built in 1879. The spirit of one of the original homeowners was still said to haunt the martini bar on the second floor, earning Scarlett's a spot on the city's many ghost tours. Jon didn't know if the back corner Michael had chosen to regroup and plan was haunted or not, but it was at least quiet and secluded enough for their purposes.

"All these cryptic clues," Jon said. Liz had ducked into the back to use the restroom, so Jon was enjoying being with just his brother again. "It's like Flagler fancied himself a pirate or something ever since he came down to Florida."

"I know, right?" Michael said. "It's hard to believe he was such a serious New York businessman. I mean, can you imagine a Rockefeller leaving clues like this all over the city?"

Jon laughed. "Never."

"So what do you think? Did he hide a real treasure somewhere in town?"

"Wouldn't that be something? Remember Vienna?"

"The cemetery?" Michael chuckled. "Who could forget? The look on your face when that mausoleum wall gave way and you found yourself face-to-face with a pyramid of gilded human skulls. Priceless."

Jon gave his brother a playful slug on the shoulder. "I happen to remember a certain girlish shriek coming from your direction right about then."

"Me, scared? Never. I'm a paragon of courage. The shriek must've been from one of those ghosts you let out."

The brothers laughed for a moment, keeping their voices down but unable to stem the mirthful tears. Jon was in his happy place. Adventuring with his best friend. It was almost enough to make him forget about the murderous maniac on their tail.

"Oh, man," Michael said, wiping at his eyes as his laughter subsided. "So you like her, huh?"

"Who?" Jon asked, playing dumb.

"Queen Elizabeth. Who do you think?" Michael nodded toward the restrooms.

"Liz?"

Michael stared at him, a cocked grin on his face. One that said, *You forget how well I know you.*

Jon shrugged. "She's all right, I guess."

"She's cute. And Uncle Tristram wasn't a real relative, so it's not like you two are cousins or anything."

Jon rolled his eyes. "We just met, okay? Oh wait, you were there. You know, this morning?"

"I do. But I also know how hard and how fast you can fall for the ladies. Especially if they like history and exploring."

"Yeah, I guess."

"Just be careful, bud. I don't want you to get hurt again."

Jon nodded. His brother was right. But he had to get one last rib in there. "Are you afraid she might step in and break up the Rickner brothers' adventure team?"

Michael smiled. "Like that would ever happen. Nothing and no one will ever mess that up. Rickner brothers for life, little bro."

"Darn tootin'," Jon said, fist-bumping his brother.

"What did I miss?" Liz said as she returned to the table.

Michael winked at his brother. "Nothing much." He pulled his backpack from beneath the chair and slid out the second artifact.

"Does this one have a Latin message too?" she asked, leaning forward to get a better look.

He studied it briefly as Jon scooted closer to get a look for himself. "Yeah. It does."

Jon read silently for a moment. One phrase in particular caught his attention. "'*Aerario secreto*'? That means..."

"Secret treasury," Michael said, finishing his brother's thought. "But there was no major treasury here. Florida was a strategic colony, but hardly a rich one. Most of their funds had to come from elsewhere in the Spanish Empire, often from Cuba or Puerto Rico."

"Maybe that's why history doesn't record it," Jon said. "It was secret."

"Yeah, but that doesn't even fit with the events that *were* recorded. Certainly not in the early days. St. Augustine was an outpost that barely had the money to pay its soldiers half the time. If they had some massive treasure trove established in the Spanish colonial period, from which this cross seems to date, they would have used it to fund the city's fortifications earlier in its history."

"Hey, I'm not arguing with you. But it's written right there."

Michael chewed at his cheek while he read the Latin again. "So it is."

"So there's some sort of treasury hidden somewhere in the town?" Liz asked, excitement amplifying her voice more than Jon was comfortable with in public. "Like pirate gold or something?"

"Highly doubtful," Michael said.

Jon had to agree. "Pirates usually didn't call their hiding spots 'treasuries,' and the Spanish presence here meant they would use the city for sacking rather than hiding their existing hoards."

"And even if the Spanish did establish some sort of treasury here centuries ago, they would have exhausted it long before the city fell into British hands in 1763."

"Or taken it with them," Jon added.

Liz slumped in her seat, the wind knocked out of her sails at the sudden dashing of her hopes for undiscovered pirate treasure.

"Even this is something incredible, though," Jon said, trying to make her feel better. "And who knows, when we collect the final pieces of the cross, maybe the complete message will reveal something really cool."

"Yeah, maybe so," she said, seeming to brighten a little.

"The third clue, though," Michael said, steering the conversation back toward their most pressing objective.

"A 'titan of industry' who is 'this game's founder'?" Jon said. "I think we can agree that's Flagler, right?"

"Sure," his brother said. "So we're looking for his seat under heaven."

"His tomb?" Liz ventured.

"Flagler was still alive and well when he devised this treasure hunt, so I'd imagine not."

"He may have been alive, but his daughter, granddaughter, and first wife weren't," Jon said. "Remember the church Mom took us to? The one with the mausoleum inside?"

"Memorial Presbyterian. That's where he attended church when he was in town, too."

"And with the first clue being a church, it stands to reason that the church he personally attended would be a place he'd want to share with his guests."

"Great," Liz said. "How far away is it?"

Michael looked at a tourist map he had procured from a brochure stand in the lobby. "Just a few blocks."

"Let's get going," Jon said, rising from his seat. "Don't forget that whether or not he was able to save the cylinder, Caeden Monk's still in the city somewhere looking for us and this cross."

"Yeah," Liz said as a pair of uniformed officers passed by the window just feet from their table. "And so are the police."

Chapter 26

Detective Audrey Yang couldn't believe her ears. Her hunch now seemed even more prescient than she'd expected.

"A second one?" she asked into her phone as she walked down Cordova Street.

"Sounds that way."

Yang had told her source, a dispatcher whom she had helped out with a family matter several months back, to let her know if any crimes related to historic artifacts or antiquities popped up. Almost all the sites in town and even the streets themselves were full of their own long histories. But antiquities theft, vandalism, or other crimes directly tied to the city's past would be given priority. And in the hours since Bouvier's murder, at least two more had been committed.

"The piece dates back to the original hotel," her source continued. "Some primitive health spa sort of contraption or something."

"The hotel being the Alcazar."

"Yeah."

Yang knew the Alcazar was one of Henry Flagler's premier hotels in the city's Gilded Age revitalization. Flagler was almost singlehandedly responsible for the birth of Florida's east-coast tourism industry, from the modern railroad lines that brought people south through the state to the amenities, entertainment, and infrastructure that transformed cities, St. Augustine included. If Admiral Menéndez had been the city's founder, Flagler was its father, building it from a pioneer outpost into an elite destination and ushering it into the future. He had built hotels and plazas, churches and roads. Even the first Edison power plants that brought electricity to the city were Flagler's doing.

He was also one of the era's richest men, with a fortune that would easily put him on an inflation-adjusted Forbes list today. Was that a factor with the recent crimes? Or was she grasping at straws? A Flagler connection between the Bouvier murder/arson and the apparent spate of historic vandalism would make a great Hollywood plot, but this was real life. Was Weiss right? Was she sensationalizing her detective work, letting her imagination and desire for a career-making case weave a fantastic conspiracy that now involved one of the richest and most powerful men in American history?

Yang entered the grounds of Grace United Methodist and stopped at the door. She glanced to her right, fully realizing she was stalling. A large green marker had been erected at the corner of the lot, created to honor the church's listing on the National Register of Historic Places. If her theory was that the city's history was somehow involved in the trio of crime scenes erupting across her adopted hometown today, she would be remiss to not check it out. Maybe that would also give her time to work up the courage she needed for the next step.

Leaving the church's portico, she crossed the courtyard to the sign. The markers were ubiquitous in St. Augustine, with dozens of sites and several entire districts nationally designated as having historic importance. This church was among the more impressive sites on the list. She began to read.

Grace United Methodist Church is a reminder of the tremendous physical impact Henry M. Flagler had on St. Augustine. This complex of structures resulted from a compromise between Flagler and the congregation of Olivet Church. That group of northern Methodists agreed to exchange the land on which their church and parsonage stood for a new complex designed by John M. Carrère and Thomas Hastings. Flagler, in turn, employed the same architects in designing his Alcazar Hotel, which rose on the former Olivet site. Construction began in 1886 and was dedicated in January 1888. The church and parsonage are excellent examples of the Spanish Renaissance Revival style of architecture, and the decision to execute the design in poured concrete resulted in unusual and aesthetically pleasing structures, which have stood the tests of time and the elements.

And yet, it couldn't survive these vandals. Or whatever they were.

It was time. She turned and faced the church's entrance. A faithful churchgoer throughout her youth, she hadn't set foot in a church since her father's memorial service. Her mother's funeral had been a graveside affair, so she hadn't been forced to darken the doorway of the sanctuary of a God she'd felt had abandoned her father. In the years since, she had realized the grief-fueled youthful foolishness of her anger. She had even begun praying again on occasion, particularly when confronted with major decisions or potentially dangerous situations on the job. She was facing both now, so it was surely not mere coincidence that had led her to a house of God. But for years she had avoided stepping foot in a church, any church. In some convoluted leap of logic she had subconsciously arrived at years before, she felt that the life she had built in the years since her father's murder would come crashing down, reverting some part of her to that scared and vulnerable teenage girl sitting in a darkened sanctuary at her father's wake.

See, you weren't cut out for this, her mother's voice arose from the depths of her subconscious. *You should have worked hard on your science classes, found yourself a nice man, and settled down with a prosperous, safe life. If you had used your brain, you would be married, with a nice house and beautiful children. Instead, you're chasing ghosts and conspiracies that even the real cops don't believe. You should never have tried to become something you're not.*

Yang clamped her eyes shut, trying to squeeze her mother's voice from her mind. She focused on her father's face, his benevolent gaze, and eventually his wife's deprecatory voice faded away, though the fresh wave of doubt it brought remained.

What would he do?

She knew the answer. He had lived it his whole career. Yes, eventually it had also claimed his life, but the legacy he had left—obvious from the standing-room-only wake crammed with those who had been touched by his dedication and integrity—spoke for the power of the choices he had made. It was a choice she had to make as well. No matter the cost.

She took a deep breath and opened the door. Her heart clenched with illogical fear, then released as the sanctuary welcomed her. She had made it. She was still a cop, still a detective, following proudly in her father's honorable footsteps. Her faith in God may have fallen away, but even that could be rebuilt. She wasn't reduced to a sniveling mess, transported backward in time to the darkest day of her young life. She was instead brought back even further in time, to an era when robber barons built monopolies and then assuaged their consciences and their public personas with philanthropy.

She turned and saw a pair of church employees hovering near the altar. She headed that way and introduced herself.

"I'm Sandra, and this is Josh," one of the employees said, shaking Yang's hand.

"So can you tell me what happened here?"

"Sure," Josh said, nervously stroking an overgrown hipster beard. "I was preparing the altar for this evening's service when I noticed something weird about the way the altar cloth was lying on the mensa. That's the top of the altar, in case you didn't know. Part of it was folded over, but it shouldn't be like that. Smooth lines, cleanly draped—that's how it's supposed to be—so I figured someone had just messed up, that whoever had most recently set the cloth had just been hurrying. But when I tried to adjust the cloth, I discovered this."

He lifted the cloth to reveal a shallow alcove set into the front of the altar. Yang knelt to inspect the small recess. The remnants of some material that could have been an adhesive of sorts was stuck in a few places to the back of the wood, but other than that, it was empty.

"What am I looking at here, Sandra?"

"A theft, that's what!" Josh jumped in. "A theft of a holy relic, from God's holy church!"

"The altar was given to the congregation by Henry Flagler shortly after this building's completion," Sandra said. "The alcove there held a fragment of an old golden cross. It was a beautiful piece, not too dissimilar in its artistry with some late medieval crosses and reliquaries I've seen at the Met in New York."

"When do you think the theft occurred?"

"It was here this morning," Sandra said. "I helped change the altar cloth."

"And no one saw anything?"

"Don't you think we would have already told you if we had?" Josh asked.

Yang forced herself not to roll her eyes. "Do you have security cameras?"

"In the sanctuary?" Josh asked, incredulous. "Of course not. The eyes of God saw the culprit, of course, but those are the only eyes watching in here."

"Okay then," she said, taking care to address Sandra instead of her more flustered companion. "What can you tell me about the artifact itself?"

"Only that it appeared to be old," Sandra said, seemingly oblivious to her colleague's outbursts. Or perhaps she was just trying to move past his eccentricities to get some answers about the crime. "Centuries old, probably of Spanish origin judging by the detail and craftsmanship. It was just part of the cross, though—the beam that would have held one of Christ's arms. I don't know when or how it broke, but that piece was all the church got. The altar itself was built to hold it, so its being broken predates Flagler's gift at the very least."

Two historic locations created by Henry Flagler in town had already been vandalized within a matter of hours. Had the old Hotel Alcazar "contraption" that had been broken at the Lightner Museum held a piece of this cross as well? If so, and if the cross had at some point been broken at its intersection, perhaps there were two more pieces still out there.

This was far from over. The timing was particularly interesting. Using the new information to evolve her working theory, whoever had killed Bouvier and burned down his shop must have stolen a document or something describing where Flagler had hidden the pieces of this old Spanish cross. And now, armed with this knowledge, he or she was running through the industrialist's old haunts and gathering the artifacts from their hiding places.

It fit. She had been right. The arson at Bouvier's shop was meant to cover up more than just a murder. The culprit had stolen something valuable, something that was leading them to the pieces of a golden cross from the city's ancient past.

And yet, even though her theory had been all but confirmed and buttressed by the new information, she realized that she now had even more questions than before. Two in particular plagued her now.

Why had Flagler hidden the pieces of a centuries-old Spanish cross?

And why were their hiding places worth killing for?

Chapter 27

Jon was catching strong Venetian vibes as he approached the church. That was Flagler's purpose, of course. Memorial Presbyterian Church, his ecclesiastical crown jewel in Gilded Age St. Augustine, was designed after St. Mark's Basilica in Venice. Though Memorial was smaller and lacked the ancient mystique and grandmasters' artistry of its Italian inspiration, it remained a commanding presence, perhaps the most visited church in historic St. Augustine today.

"Wow," Liz cooed at his side. "It's incredible. I didn't expect to see something like this here."

"Apparently Flagler got his old-world architecture a bit mixed up," Michael said. "He was trying to make his revitalized St. Augustine into a mythologized version of the city's Spanish past. Instead, he must've seen St. Mark's in a picture book, thought it was pretty, and built one of his own."

Michael's cynicism was a bit thick, but he had a point. Flagler, for all his wealth and grand visions, never really left the country to see the world like so many of his counterparts did. Thankfully, he enlisted some of the finest architects and builders around for his creations. As with Grace United Methodist and the Alcazar Hotel, Memorial Presbyterian Church had been designed by Carrère and Hastings, who had plenty of experience with a variety of architectural styles, from Neoclassical and Beaux-Arts to Spanish Revival and Italianate. Their expertise, coupled with Flagler's vision and money, had made Memorial a lasting presence long after its architects and benefactor had passed on.

Faint echoes of worshipful organ refrains emanated from within, growing louder and bolder as the trio approached the edifice. Entering the church through the south transept, they quickly browsed through an exhibit about the church's construction and history. As they expected, Flagler's name was all over the displays, but there was nothing about his "seat under heaven" that Jon could see. But he wasn't expecting to get his answers from a museum-style model when the real thing was just feet away.

"The mausoleum," Michael said quietly. "Flagler's wife, daughter, and granddaughter are buried there. The church itself is dedicated to the memory of his daughter. Nowhere else has his mark as strongly on it."

"Why would he want people disturbing his family's grave?" Jon asked.

"Who said anything about disturbing it? The hunt's intended participants would just have to see the artifact to win, not steal it like we're doing."

"So we're adding grave desecration to our list of crimes today?"

Michael gave him a knowing look. "It wouldn't be the first time."

He had a point. But Jon had another idea.

"Go check it out if you want. There's something else I want to see."

Chapter 28

Caeden Monk had them right where he wanted them. Concealed in a shadowy corner, he watched as the older Rickner son—Michael, if memory served him correctly—crossed the sanctuary with the girl. She was a wild card, but he had faced off against unknown adversaries before, and had come away victorious every time. Not that it mattered. It was clear that the Rickner boys were running this show. And he knew them, at least well enough to beat them at the game he had started.

They were headed toward the crypt, just like Monk had anticipated. A logical place for the cross piece to be. His wife, daughter, and granddaughter had been laid to rest in the specially built mausoleum, its marble interior visibly open to visitors while barricaded by a steel gate. But somebody would have a key. Someone would *give* him a key once he was done with them. For the moment, though, he needed to acquire the first two pieces of the puzzle and to take out these other players who had royally screwed up his perfect plan.

Two birds. One very hard stone.

Michael and the girl had reached the entrance to the mausoleum, facing away from Monk's position. Monk left the safety of the shadows and crossed the north transept, walking briskly but mindful of his footfalls on the marble floor. The organ's deep bass notes and resounding chords helped to cover his approach. With a quick glance around the largely deserted sanctuary, Monk pulled his pistol from its hidden holster and jabbed it into the girl's back, using his body weight to push both her and Michael deeper into the mausoleum's small antechamber.

"Remember me?" Monk relished the shock and defeat that flashed across Michael's face when he turned.

He was quick to shush his quarry. "If you yell or make any sudden movements, your girlfriend here joins Flagler's dead family. And you won't be far behind."

"What do you want, Monk?" Michael asked, eyes darting back and forth between Monk's and the girl's.

"You know what I want. The pieces you've already stolen from me. And the final clue to the hunt."

Something glinted behind Michael's eyes as Monk spoke those final words. A mistake, perhaps—Monk had admitted that he didn't have the complete set of clues, despite being able to anticipate their arrival here. No matter. Soon enough, Michael would be out of the picture and Monk would once again be the only player in the game.

"And you'll let us go if I give you what you want?" Michael asked, his eyes flitting about the church, impotently looking for a way out.

Monk couldn't believe a Rickner would be this gullible, but perhaps the apple had fallen far from the tree for this one.

"Of course," he lied. "I only want what was stolen from me."

"He's lying, Michael," the girl said. "That's the only thing keeping us alive. You can't trust him."

Michael glanced over Monk's shoulder then gave her an apologetic look. "Sorry, Liz. We don't have a choice.

"The Catholic Cathedral just up the road," he said, redirecting his focus to Monk. "Flagler was instrumental in its rebuilding after a fire in 1887. He hid the final piece there. In the bell tower."

Monk knew the place. The congregation was as old as the city itself, established in 1565 and persisting through centuries of hardship. The first cathedral was burned to the ground when English privateer Sir Francis Drake attacked the city in 1586. But the pioneer spirit that later Americans would claim as their own was strong in St. Augustine, with the colonists completely rebuilding the cathedral mere months later. This one too burned down, in 1599 from natural causes, while a third cathedral would be destroyed in another English attack in 1702. For most of the rest of the eighteenth century, St. Augustine would be without a cathedral—royal funds designated for new construction were misappropriated, and two decades of British rule in Florida had changed the city's priorities. But less than a decade after St. Augustine returned to Spanish hands in 1784, a new cathedral began to rise. In 1797, it was completed and consecrated, making it the oldest church in Florida.

An old enemy showed up again in 1887, as fire devastated the cathedral. This time, however, the damage was far from complete, and instead of rebuilding from scratch, the congregation—armed with cash from Henry Flagler—hired St. Augustine resident James Renwick to restore the church. Most famous for his design of St. Patrick's Cathedral in New York, Renwick added a Spanish Colonial feel with soaring Renaissance Revival flair to the church, giving the restored cathedral the same mythical Spanish ambiance that Flagler had been so purposeful in constructing across his St. Augustine.

Another famous church that fit the timeline and had Flagler's fingerprints all over it. And yet, something smelled wrong about it. Something about the cocky look in Michael's eyes. He was holding back. Or lying entirely. That was the thing about living a life steeped in deception. You got pretty good at spotting a bad liar.

Liz groaned as Monk twisted the gun deeper against her back.

"You seem to think I'm an idiot," he said, twisting his lips into what he thought was a menacing sneer. "You forget that I was at this long before you were. You hadn't even heard of the Flagler hunt before today. So don't think you can fool me. I'm going to give you one last chance, and then I'll kill you and your friend, take the pieces of the cross for myself, and smash apart St. Augustine until I find what is rightfully mine."

Michael was stubbornly silent. Liz whimpered and shook.

"I will count to three."

The organ kept on playing, but Michael said nothing.

"One."

"Just give him what he wants, Michael," Liz pleaded.

"Two."

Liz started shaking harder. Michael pressed his lips together in defiance.

Fools, Monk thought as his trigger finger began to tense.

"Three."

Chapter 29

As soon as Michael and Liz had left the church's historical exhibit in the south transept, Jon made a beeline for the center of the sanctuary. There was a reason CNN had called the church one of the eight religious wonders in the United States. The hall was filled with rows of dark walnut pews, with white marble walls soaring up toward a magnificent mosaic dome depicting the splendor of the celestial kingdom. The English word *ceiling* and the Spanish word *cielo* had the same etymological root. *Cielo* meant "heaven," and of all the ceilings in St. Augustine, Memorial Presbyterian's was certainly the most heavenly.

Directly beneath that representation of heaven was a particular pew, designated by an extra railing around the periphery and a plaque identifying the man who regularly attended
this church and sat in this seat every Sunday morning he was
in town.

Henry Morrison Flagler.

After checking the sanctuary for attendants or other tourists looking in his direction, he dropped to his knees, disappearing
from view. He ran his fingers along the underside of Flagler's pew
until they touched what felt like a thin groove. He paused, rubbing
the groove thoughtfully, then smiling. With a single index finger, he
traced it until it made a ninety-degree turn, and then another, and
another, and another. A perfect rectangle.

He ducked his head below the bottom of the pew. There
it was. Just big enough, too. The edges were barely noticeable
unless you were looking for it, too narrow even to get a screw-
driver in to pry open the compartment. But then, the hunt's
nineteenth-century participants wouldn't be carrying around
screwdrivers. There had to be another way. A hidden way.

Jon tried to slide the panel to one side, but it wouldn't
move. So if it wouldn't slide, then perhaps...

He heard a click as he pushed the panel straight up, toward
the celestial ceiling above. As he let go, the panel slowly swung
out on hydraulic-fueled hinges, primitive versions of the ones
on cabinetry in modern high-end kitchens. And fastened to the
backside of the panel was an object glinting with gold.

The third piece of the cross.

Using his knife, Jon pried the piece free and closed
the panel. Unlike their previous destructive finds at Grace
United Methodist and the Lightner Museum, there wouldn't
be any trace of this discovery until they revealed the whole
thing at the conclusion of the hunt. With a grin on his face at
figuring out the clue before his older brother, Jon stood up
and looked toward the mausoleum—and froze.

He couldn't see his brother or Liz from there, but he could
see another man, with clothes Jon recognized from earlier in
the day, and flaming red hair he would never forget.

Monk. He was here. And he had Michael and Liz.

After slipping the cross piece into his cargo pocket, Jon
kept low, casually walking toward the rear of the church so
he could skirt the pews and cross the church behind Monk.
When he was reasonably sure no one was looking, he snagged

a heavy-looking candlestick from a table and concealed it against his leg. He was right. It was heavy. Heavy enough for his purposes, anyway.

He crept up behind Monk, his eyes at one time meeting Michael's. *Don't worry*, Jon tried to telepathically tell his brother. *I got this.*

A few more steps and Jon would be on their assailant. Over the sounds of organ playing, he heard Liz saying something, her tone pleading and distraught.

"Two," he heard Monk say.

Jon was right behind him now. He raised the candlestick aloft.

"Three."

He slammed the candlestick into the back of Monk's head, causing him to stagger and slump to the ground.

"Come on," Jon urged in a stage whisper, wanting to get out of the church before anyone noticed what had happened.

Liz was trembling. Michael grabbed her arm and helped escort her out of the mausoleum's antechamber. Jon replaced the candlestick on the table, slightly bent now, but only if you were looking for it. They were almost at the nearest exit when a woman gasped behind them. Someone had seen Monk's fallen form.

Against his better judgment, Jon looked back. It was worse than he'd feared. It wasn't just that someone had seen Monk collapsed on the floor. They were seeing him stagger to his feet, clearly dizzy but very much conscious.

And very, very angry.

Jon turned back toward the exit and breached the doors.

"What?" Michael asked.

"Run."

Chapter 30

For Audrey Yang, the pieces of the puzzle were already starting to come together. She couldn't see the whole picture yet, but shapes were beginning to emerge. And they all looked a lot like Henry Flagler.

She was just arriving at the Lightner Museum when she heard the dispatcher sending an officer and an EMT team to Memorial Presbyterian Church, where a man had been attacked at the entrance to the mausoleum of Flagler's wife. This whole thing was getting way out of hand. But she was about to get to the end of it.

Gavin Pereira met Yang at the entrance to the museum. Tall, black-haired, and about a decade past movie-star handsome, Pereira looked far less bookish than Yang had been expecting. The curator was on vacation, as it turned out. Pereira was the Lightner's spokesman, and so the duties of describing the crime fell to him.

After introductions were out of the way, Pereira led Yang into the museum and up to the second-floor displays, pointing out the piece that had been vandalized.

"From the Alcazar's hotel days?" Yang asked.

Pereira looked surprised. "Actually, yes. The hotel was renowned for its state-of-the-art health facilities, the Gilded Age version of a modern-day spa."

Yang moved closer to the apparatus. "So what was inside here?"

"Inside?" Pereira squinted at the broken area where Yang was looking. "Nothing. It was just pipes to hold it all together."

She pointed with the tip of her pen. "Did the Alcazar put gold in all of their pipes back in the day? I know Flagler was filthy rich and it was the Gilded Age, but that just seems wasteful."

She moved out of the way as he stepped closer to see what she was pointing at.

"What in the world?" Pereira said, pinching from the broken pipe a tiny gold shaving.

"So if something gold was hidden inside the pipe, that jagged edge could have accidentally cut this shaving off the larger whole when it was being removed," Yang mused. "The question is, why would something made of gold be hidden in nineteenth-century spa equipment?"

A flash of shock giving way to inspiration passed across Pereira's face. "Have you heard of Henry Flagler's Great St. Augustine Treasure Hunt?"

Now it was Yang's turn to look shocked. "Never. What is it?"

"*Was* it," Pereira corrected. "Although to be more accurate, it never even was."

The spokesman gave her an expectant look. This was going to be a longer story, it said, and if she didn't want to hear it, now was her opportunity to bail.

Not a chance.

"Go on," she said.

Pereira smiled, like an uncle about to share a favorite story with his beloved niece. "It was 1891, and Henry Flagler was looking for a new way to lure more rich visitors from up north. He had built the most magnificent hotels in Florida and invested heavily in the infrastructure of the city, offering electricity and all the modern amenities they would expect from the leading hotels of the day, along with the fresh air, sunshine, and warmth missing from the winters of New York and Boston. But Flagler wanted something to bring crowds down year-round. He needed a gimmick. And he found one in pirates.

"Robert Louis Stevenson's *Treasure Island* had come out just a few years before, and many in Flagler's target demographic had become enamored of the swashbuckling adventuring so removed from their staid city lives. So Flagler decided to tap into that vein by creating his own treasure hunt right here on the sunny shores of St. Augustine, which had seen firsthand the rise and fall of the golden age of piracy and in which he had invested millions to make it look more glamorously historical. Flagler's St. Augustine already looked the part of a pirate adventure, so he created a treasure hunt to entertain his guests and draw even more people down south."

"I've never heard of this before," Yang admitted.

"I'm not surprised. Most people haven't. Even most locals. I've spent the past decade or so piecing together the rumors about it. There's precious little evidence beyond some secondhand anecdotes, an advertisement proof intended to publicize the event in the big northern papers, and a handwritten note Flagler left for his son."

"His son?"

Pereira grinned. "Follow me." He led Yang deeper into the bowels of the museum, then through a side door and into the archives. After a few turns through a box-riddled warren, he pulled a file from a drawer and set it on a table.

"Here," he said, sliding from the file a yellowed piece of writing paper sealed in a protective ziplocked bag. Yang bent down to read.

> *My dearest Harry,*
>
> *I know that you were excited for the treasure hunt we had planned in St. Augustine, and I am equally sorry that we were forced to abandon the idea. There were unforeseen circumstances in the artifact we had recovered, circumstances that threatened to destroy everything we have built in the city. The pieces hidden at the hotels were closed up, since those locations are still under my purview. I have enclosed the record Mr. Edison made for me, so you can always hear my voice, promising the adventure we had planned together. The adventure we could never share with the world, but that we shall always cherish. All four pieces remain where they were hidden, so when you return to my St. Augustine, walk the path once more and remember the adventure that almost was.*
>
> *Your father,*
> *Henry Flagler*

"In his will," Pereira said when Yang looked up from reading, "Flagler bequeathed a wax cylinder and this note to his son in a secret bequest. The note came to us after Harry's death in 1952, but the cylinder has been lost to time. Harry was born just a month shy of Henry's fifty-first birthday, and he was his only child to survive his St. Augustine years, burying his oldest daughter at Flagler Memorial in 1889 along with his first wife and granddaughter. Shortly after Henry died in 1913, records show that Harry came down from New York to St. Augustine, stayed for a week, then left. Whether or not he 'walked the path' of the treasure hunt is unknown, but no treasure was ever reported to have been found."

"So what was the treasure?"

"No one knows. Perhaps something golden, if your theory about that sliver we found in the pipe back there holds. Perhaps even something from our city's ancient Spanish past, which surely would have delighted Flagler. Theories circulate that, if there was a treasure, it was likely something he had discovered while excavating the foundations for one of his many buildings in the city. We see it all the time in old cities. They're digging a new subway line in Rome and accidentally discover a secret underground church from Nero's day. King Richard the Third was found buried under a London parking lot. But as for what the treasure actually was, or where Flagler hid it, neither history nor rumor records those answers."

Treasure hunting fit with what she had seen thus far—vandalism of three sites associated with Flagler's St. Augustine, and the murder of an antiquarian and burning of his shop to cover a suspected theft. If she looked at Bouvier's records, she wouldn't be surprised if she were to find an early wax cylinder recording among his inventory. The missing one that once accompanied this note.

"He says 'all four pieces,'" Yang said. "So four unique treasures?"

"Perhaps. Or four pieces of the same treasure. If Flagler found something from the early Spanish era, centuries of building, destroying, and rebuilding on the land could definitely break a single artifact into multiple pieces."

"Like a cross," she said, remembering Josh and Sandra's description of an ornate piece of a centuries-old golden Spanish cross. That also would explain the golden sliver left inside the pipe. And how they could fit the cross in there in the first place. Four pieces of treasure, four bars of a broken cross.

"Sure, a cross could definitely be broken into four pieces."

Four pieces. Three Flagler sites vandalized already. Only one more to go.

"And you have no idea why he abandoned his plans to implement the treasure hunt?"

Pereira shook his head. "Unfortunately, no. Apparently he pulled the plug on the very eve of its announcement. Had to call in some favors to get the ads removed at the last minute, before they went to press. But other than this cryptic reference in his posthumous letter to his son, there is no record of the reason for his eleventh-hour termination of the project."

Which only brought more questions. Henry Flagler was one of the most powerful men in the country, and the city had reaped tremendous financial dividends from the stream of wealthy tourists he brought to St. Augustine. He was all but untouchable, with friends in the highest of places. So what on earth could destroy everything he had built?

Yang continued to mull the question as she thanked Pereira for his time and left the archives. The lost history of the hunt may have opened up new mysteries even as it solved old ones, but one word in Flagler's note stuck in her head. An unintentional clue to uncovering the truth. But her window of opportunity was quickly closing. Once they found the last piece, the treasure hunters would leave town, taking any chance she had of solving these crimes—and potentially a much older mystery—with them.

Fortunately, she was no longer playing from behind. She finally had an advantage.

Yang knew where the final piece was hidden.

Chapter 31

College students. They were everywhere, and they were setting Miriam Caan on edge.

She may have been a millennial herself—albeit just a few years this side of the Generation X cutoff—but her life was worlds removed from that of the coeds who roamed the palatial main campus of Flagler College. She had been places, seen things, *done* things that most of them never had and never would. There had been highs, yes, from the thrill of discovery accompanying a major find to the rush of wonder at cresting a hill to gaze upon the majesty of an ancient vista beyond. But none of that took away her jealousy of the naiveté these young students took for granted. She had once stood in their shoes, and then, right in the thick of what should have been the most important moment of her academic life, she had cast her lot with the devil. Never again would she experience the carefree joy of learning in an environment like this. But Esther could.

Everything that she did today would not only set her free from Monk's claws for good, but would also give her younger sister the opportunity for the kind of life Miriam had thrown away. Esther had already suffered enough for Miriam's mistakes. It was time to make things right.

The throngs of students were starting to thin out. Classes were done for the day, with the Florida sky ablaze with a stunning sunset. Overheard conversations portended an evening along the Matanzas, eating and drinking at one of the many pubs and restaurants along Avenida Menéndez or St. George Street, or crossing the Bridge of Lions to the beaches of Anastasia Island to watch the sun drown itself in the endless waves of the Atlantic. The relatively innocent camaraderie stirred another pang of regret in Miriam's chest, but she repressed it more easily this time. Fewer students meant fewer witnesses to what was about to go down.

Miriam stalked the second-floor balcony above the main courtyard, trying to imagine what the complex would have looked like thirteen decades ago, when Henry Flagler first opened his flagship hotel, the Hotel Ponce de Leon, to the world. Replace the students with a who's who of the day's rich and famous, ditch the air-conditioning and other twentieth-century modernizations, and replace the teachers and staff with white-gloved concierges and servants, and you were there. The structure had remained virtually unchanged for more than a century, despite its switch from hotel to World War II naval training base back to hotel and finally to college during its lifespan. And, it would seem, so too had Flagler's hiding place of the final piece of the cross remained undisturbed for all this time.

The cross was a valuable relic, no doubt—it was centuries old, had elaborate craftsmanship, and was hewn of gold likely mined from Spanish colonies in Mexico or Peru. The fact that it had been broken into four pieces would no doubt diminish its resale value, but the cross itself was not the goal. It was the message hidden in the completed cross, once all four pieces had been reassembled, that would change her fortunes. Ironic, she felt, that an atheistic Jew like herself would find salvation in the cross. It was equally ironic that a churchgoing man like Henry Flagler would have been destroyed by that cross's true meaning.

Without the final clue that had been destroyed when Monk dropped the cylinder hours earlier, she stood no chance of finding Flagler's hiding place. But soon enough, assuming her guess about the obvious conclusion to the nineteenth-century treasure hunt was correct, the Rickner boys and their newfound friend would be arriving at the former Hotel Ponce de Leon to lead her straight to the final piece. And with them, the other three pieces.

Miriam was close to the finish line but not close enough to fully leave her longtime partner, though in her heart she had already moved on. For now, at least, she had to keep Monk on her side. Any evidence of betrayal and he would surely kill her. She just had to make sure that when she made her move, she would be ready to disappear forever.

She squinted from her vantage point toward the massive wrought iron gates at the open entrance to the college. Speak of the devil. The trio of interloping adventurers had come after all. She sighed to herself. *Once more unto the breach.* She pulled out her phone and began to dial.

Chapter 32

It was just as beautiful as Jon remembered it. Flagler College, in all its terra-cotta beauty, was an exemplary fusion of Spanish Renaissance elegance channeled through Gilded Age opulence. A sprawling structure more akin to a sixteenth-century Spanish palace than an American hotel, the Hotel Ponce de Leon had been the crown jewel in Flagler's St. Augustine project. The terra-cotta roof was punctuated by a pair of spires that once housed water tanks to offer hotel guests quick access to fresh water. Utilizing the unique composition of locally sourced coquina, the building was the first poured-concrete structure in the United States and one of the first to have electricity, supplied by generators from Thomas Edison himself. It was considered the height of grandeur in the age of extravagance, and today, in an era of prepackaged mass-produced everything, its hand-crafted majesty was even more impressive.

A bronze statue of Henry Flagler stood proudly just outside the main entrance to his greatest creation. In between imposing brick columns, a series of wrought iron gates, forged in a long-dead blacksmith's fire, rose twenty feet above their heads, offering a sense of permanence and security to the present-day students as it had to its wealthy guests more than a century before.

To Jon, they also signified a cage. A prison. A trap. It was all but inevitable that Flagler would conclude his hunt at such a mesmerizing location, though the actual hiding place in this sprawling complex would be harder to ascertain. But Jon had no doubts that this landmark hotel wouldn't escape Monk's notice. Sooner or later, Monk would be coming. They just had to make sure they found the final piece before Monk found them.

"It's incredible," Liz said as the trio passed through the gates and into the central courtyard.

"Flagler knew his clientele would require the best if he expected them to make the long journey south every year," Michael said. "He delivered, and then some."

The courtyard was ringed by a four-story colonnade, beyond which lay guest suites, lounges, and other amenities designed to cater to the turn of the century's most demanding tourists. At the center of the artfully designed cloister was a tiered fountain, replete with terra-cotta frogs and turtles. A pillar shot up from its core, capped by a ring of lion heads from which water spouted.

"A sundial," Jon said, running across the courtyard at the realization.

"What are you talking about?" Michael said, chasing after him. "And don't run. We don't need to draw any extra attention, if you've forgotten."

"The final clue. 'Look deep into the face of time,' it said. Check out the markings on the ground." Jon pointed to a series of lines and roman numerals inscribed in a golden arc across the northern side of the fountain, then checked his watch. "See, it almost matches with the current time."

"Almost?" Liz asked.

"It's later in the year, so the sun is setting earlier, throwing off the original calibration, but it would have been close enough for Flagler's guests to see what time it was without having to go back inside. The guests were on vacation, so this was just one more thing Flagler would have included to make things easier for them. No use relaxing and taking in the sun if you're shackled to your pocket watch the whole time."

"Good eye, Jon," Michael said, slapping him on the back. Jon swelled with pride at his brother's praise but tried to stay focused.

"So which face is the clue referring to?" Liz asked.

A good question. There were a number of women and half-human mythological creatures carved into the fountain's menagerie, but none of them stood out as having *the* face of time. No hourglasses, no sundials, not even a memento mori symbol accompanied any of them to betray their particular connection to time. No crosses, no secret *F* for *Flagler* or *T* for *treasure*, no obvious buttons or switches or sliding compartments in which to hide the final piece. But it had to be here somewhere. Didn't it?

"Maybe I jumped the gun," Jon said, starting to regret the pride he'd felt at his brother's praise, which suddenly seemed premature and undeserved. "This is a big place. Maybe it's somewhere else."

"This is a big place," Liz said. "You don't think he would have hidden it in one of the guest suites or dorm rooms or somewhere we can't get to, do you?"

"I doubt it," Michael said. "He would have wanted it to be somewhere publicly accessible to all the hunt's participants, not locked away for only a single guest."

"Unless it was like a raffle?" Liz offered.

"Then why have them run through all the hoops of the rest of the hunt, only to be stopped at the end from completing it because they booked the wrong room?"

"Not only that," Jon said, "but what about the privacy of that winning guest? Everyone who learns where that last clue is would be banging on their door day and night. Not the kind of experience that engenders repeat business."

Michael was rubbing his temple with a thumb, a habit Jon knew was associated with his brother being in deep thought. Usually it portended something good, a revelation of sorts.

"What are you thinking?" Jon asked.

"About the stars," Michael said, looking at the first twinkling luminary appearing in the darkening eastern sky.

"Uh-huh." Jon was afraid that he had been wrong. He had been expecting a breakthrough from his brother. Instead, he got cosmic philosophy.

"We don't have time for stargazing, Michael," Liz said. "If you haven't forgotten, we're kind of in a hurry here, what with the psychopath Monk guy and the police and all. What about the clue?"

Michael stopped rubbing his temple and grinned. Tearing his gaze from the heavens, he beamed at Liz and Jon. "The clue? Flagler hid it in the stars." He turned and started up the stairs to the old hotel's main entrance. "Come on. I think I know where the final piece is."

Chapter 33

The Rickner boys were going to die. The girl, too, but the Rickner brothers had it coming full force. Once Caeden Monk had his prize in hand, he would happily end their lives. And he was getting close. Very, very close.

Miriam had already spotted them at Flagler College—the old Hotel Ponce de Leon. Of course Flagler would have set the hunt's climax at his architectural magnum opus. And ten points to Gryffindor for Miriam's foresight to be waiting for them there. But something didn't sit right. He was so close. But he wasn't quite ready to break out the champagne. Too much could still go wrong. Too much already had.

Monk staggered down Valencia Street, endeavoring to normalize his gait as much as possible. His head still throbbed from Jon's attack, and every few seconds he had to blink to clear his head of the dizzying double vision that threatened to destroy his mission in these final moments. He'd refused the church staffers' insistent offers of medical attention, popping a few Tylenol gelcaps and returning to the hunt. After each encounter with the Rickner brothers, his grievances became more personal and more acrimonious. They had stolen his cylinder, destroyed the recording of the final clue, humiliated him, and assaulted him. His legacy lay at the end of this quest, and they would not succeed in stealing that from him. Instead, he would take back from them everything they had taken from him, with interest. They had messed with the wrong man. He had tried to play nice, but that ship had long since sailed. They deserved everything that was coming to them.

What they didn't realize is that they were walking straight into a trap. In fact, Monk would wager they'd already passed the point of no return. With Miriam already ahead of them and Monk closing in from behind, they would soon find themselves overwhelmed with no way out. And that was just the way Monk wanted it.

His phone buzzed again. Another text from Miriam. Its content made Monk smile. He didn't bother texting back. This would all be over in a matter of minutes.

He turned a corner and saw the backside of Flagler College through the trees. His head was getting better now. He was preparing to finish what he had started, once and for all. His anger purged the pain and channeled it into his lethal plan of action.

In the distance, through the lead glass windows of the great hall, he could see painted skies offering starry stories of legends past. Hercules and Cortez had already had their days. It was time for Caeden Monk to write the last chapter of his legend.

And it started with revenge.

Chapter 34

Detective Yang's phone rang just as she left the Lightner Museum. Her first instinct upon seeing the caller ID was to ignore it, let it go to voicemail. But she knew she couldn't do that. Against her better judgment, she answered.

"What is it, Weiss?"

"Yang? Sarge has been asking about you. He says you're not answering his calls. Where are you?"

"Following up on a lead. It's all connected, starting with this morning's arson." She gave him the Cliff's Notes version of the string of vandalism incidents at sites built by Henry Flagler and what she had learned about his abandoned treasure hunt from Gavin Pereira.

Weiss let out an exasperated sigh. Despite the lack of syllables, she recognized the meaning. Her mother had long ago given her a graduate-level course on disappointed sighs.

"Look, kid," he said. "I know you're smart and I know you want to make a name for yourself. But come on. First you're Columbo, and now you're Indiana Jones, chasing buried treasure and cryptic legends."

"I saw a piece of the gold myself," she argued.

"Great. Regardless, we've got actual evidence to sift through from an actual murder scene. *This* is your chance to prove yourself, Yang. A very legitimate case with a pair of very serious crimes. But you're throwing it all away for a Hollywood dream. This is real. A real opportunity. But if you don't stop running off on your own, you're going to lose it all."

"Thanks, Dad," she said, instantly regretting it. Weiss may have seemed obstinate to her, but then what did he have to go on? He hadn't seen everything that she had today, hadn't followed the clues and talked to the experts at Grace United Methodist or at the Lightner Museum. Furthermore, it was no secret that she was ambitious, perhaps too much for her own good at this stage in her career. She had yet to prove herself as a detective, and her first act when being handed a big case was to abandon protocol and her partner, going off on her own.

"I'm sorry," she said, her conciliatory tone genuine. "I didn't mean that."

"Look, I haven't told Sarge what's going on with you yet, but this can still be fixed." Weiss sounded less flustered than before, trying to bring her back into the fold as any good mentor would. "Come back to HQ and we'll make this right, together."

See, you need a man to fix your mistakes. Right on time. Her mother's voice never failed to show up and heap her posthumous disappointment on top of Yang's own problems. *Even your partner knows you're not cut out for this. Stop playing at being a detective and go be the nice girl I raised. You've wasted enough time with this silly dream. Give me a son-in-law and some grandchildren already.*

She passed through the inner courtyard of the old Alcazar Hotel, into a block-wide plaza of concrete paths, statues and plaques celebrating long-dead luminaries, and a veritable maze of shrubberies. But beyond all that, across the street, the majestic red spires of Flagler College rose to pierce the darkening sky. No vandalism had yet been reported there. And her gut told her that if there was just one more piece of the cross hidden in St. Augustine, Henry Flagler would have concealed it at his flagship hotel, the Hotel Ponce de Leon.

"Yang, you still there?" Weiss said, still waiting for a response.

Trust yourself, came a different voice from within. Her father's. He had gone against the grain and changed up his approach when unique circumstances called for it. Yang felt fairly certain that a forgotten treasure hunt, a string of vandalisms, murder, arson, and the resurfacing of a lost legend all constituted a fairly unique set of circumstances. This could still go very wrong in a number of ways, from demotion or termination from her job to criminal prosecution or even getting killed by a clearly driven treasure hunter who had already shown he had no compunction about murder.

"I'm sorry, Weiss. I can't come in just yet."

"Don't do this, Yang. Where are you?"

Yang smiled to herself. "Meet me at Flagler College ASAP. I've got a feeling the proof you want will be waiting for us."

Chapter 35

No one ever noticed ceilings anymore. The world of hand-sculpted crown moldings and Michelangelo-painted masterpieces had given way to popcorn ceilings and generic, factory-made panels, a byproduct of the utilitarian architecture schools that gained popularity in the postwar era. The ubiquitous blandness of ceilings had become a given for modern life, so much so that when hard work and true artistry had been put into creating a beautiful ceiling, no one looked, visitors believing there would be nothing up there worth seeing.

The Hotel Ponce de Leon was a notable exception. The foyer through which Jon, Michael, and Liz had entered the building a few minutes ago was a masterpiece in and of itself, with skilled hands having shaped dark walnut and oak into works of art. Columns bore the busts of great explorers and mythical figures, while the soaring dome illustrated the site's unique history in the same masterful fashion that a similar entryway would have in the great houses, museums, and universities of Europe.

But that was nothing compared to the dining hall. A vast, open space full of natural light from an array of windows at either end, the great hall of the hotel had originally been used for banquets and balls, majestic celebrations and gatherings of all kinds. Today, it served as the dining hall for the students and faculty of Flagler College, with the original hotel kitchen updated with modern appliances. Some of the hotel's chairs still graced the hall, though most had by necessity been replaced. A fountain drink machine offered beverages to students near an entrance to the kitchen area, but otherwise, the room looked much the same as it did more than a century ago.

Over the years, Jon had visited some of the great historic universities of the world, from Oxford and Harvard to Bologna and Salamanca. The sense of history in those places was thick, as centuries of students—many of whom went on to change the world in massive ways—had left a tremendous legacy across those ancient campuses. But this was special in a whole different way. While those esteemed institutions had been constructed for the education of future kings, lords, and other history makers, this building had been created for the enjoyment of men and women who were already making history. Influential members of the nation's elite blue blood families, revolutionary authors like Hemingway and Frost, even larger-than-life personalities like Teddy Roosevelt, Babe Ruth, and Mark Twain, all breeds of the rich and famous came to St. Augustine to escape into Flagler's constructed fantasyland of history and legend. And now, where once the world's wealthiest and most influential celebrities

Jeremy Burns

sought refuge from the bitter cold of New England winters, college students just like Jon and Michael slept in the old guest suites, dined in the old great hall, and played across the old lawn. It was truly something.

Also impressive was the artistry of the ceiling here in the dining hall, a fanciful mural of starry skies that could certainly hold a secret or two.

"Constellations," Michael explained. "For millennia our ancestors used them to chart the seasons. And they person-ified them with the identities of their gods and goddesses, their heroes and monsters. The artifact must be somewhere in one of their faces."

"But which one?" Liz asked.

The ceiling's false sky was full not only of constellations, but of the flagships of Spanish explorers, key scenes from St. Augustine history, and mythological personifications of Wisdom and other Greco-Roman goddesses that had been adopted into the Christian pantheon of noble virtues.

"What about this one?" Liz asked. She pointed skyward to Providence—the beneficent giving aspect of God—de-picted as a comely woman pouring blessings upon a hungry colonial populace from a massive cornucopia. "Like how the blessings of God are timeless and unending?"

Jon examined the celestial face then shook his head. Though painted with the same masterful hand as the rest of the ceiling, the face of Providence looked essentially identi-cal to the other virtues personified across the celestial ceil-ing. That would make sense from an artistic standpoint, as not only were they likely painted by the same individual but they were designed to be different aspects of the same God. For their purposes, though, they needed something that would stand out to Flagler's guests. Nothing in Providence's face did so.

"Oh my gosh," Michael said. "*Memento mori...* Of course."

Jon ran over and looked at what Michael had found. A skull with wings sprouting from either side had been tucked away into one corner of the ballroom. It was one of sever-al symbols collectively referred to as *memento mori*, Latin for "remember that you must die." Hourglasses, skulls, and scythes, often with wings, were among the common compo-nents in the symbology that had been reminding churchgo-ers and cemetery mourners for centuries about the fleeting nature of their time on earth. Though it was clearly *one* face of time, Jon quickly noticed another winged skull in the next corner. Just like the face of Providence personified, the memento mori skull was not unique enough to hide the final piece.

Then, amid the elaborate starscape of mythical beings and legendary heroes, Jon noticed an entirely different sort of figure. Standing atop the old orchestra balcony from which dinner guests and ball attendees would be serenaded by string quartets stood a black-haired woman. From her elevated vantage point, she seemed to be watching their every move. Then, upon realizing that Jon had noticed her, she lifted a rifle from the bag next to her. Aiming it squarely at him.

Chapter 36

Her perch hadn't been as invisible as she was hoping, but that mattered little now. Miriam Caan was prepared for this eventuality. The one who was closest—the younger Rickner brother—would be her conduit.

She tossed him a prepaid cell phone, which she immediately began to call using her own disposable unit, linked to her Bluetooth earpiece so she could keep both hands on the rifle. Clearly wary of this new development, he answered on the second ring.

"You know what I want," she said. "And you're going to give it to me. It's just a matter of whether you and your friends get shot in the process."

"I don't know what you're—"

"Really? Playing dumb seemed like a good move to you?" She sighed. "Jon, is it?"

"You're working with Monk?"

"I am." *For now.* "Look, I'm going to make this very simple. Give me the pieces of the cross you've collected, and tell me what the final clue is. Then I'll let you go. Lie to me or make a move I don't like…"

133

Jeremy Burns

"Why are you doing this?" he asked, looking up at her while edging across the carpet.

"Isn't it obvious?"

"The cross is valuable, I'm sure, but it can't be worth killing over."

Monk had been right. They were clueless about the real prize.

"You might be surprised," she said.

"The secret treasury?"

They knew? How? Did they already know what it meant or where it was?

"What do you know about that?" She tightened her grip on the rifle, her finger moving ever closer to the trigger.

"Enough to be sure you'll never get your hands on it."

He was bluffing. He had to be. The full cross was needed to reveal the complete message, and they only had three of the pieces.

"Cute. But I'm the one with the gun."

"You kill us, that last clue will be lost forever. Along with your precious treasury."

He was definitely bluffing. The word treasury—in Latin or Spanish or whatever language the message had been written in—must have been on one of the parts they had. But it wouldn't be enough for him to find it. And if that was all he understood of the hunt's final phase, he still had no idea what was at stake, or how it had gotten to this point in the first place.

"Well, I know it's here at the Ponce, and with the three of you out of the way, I'll have enough time to find it with or without the last clue. I'd rather do it more quickly, though. And with less blood to clean up."

He said nothing, appearing to consider her proposal. Her first instinct was that he was stalling. Hoping that someone else would come into the room and save them, perhaps, or looking for a way to extricate himself from the situation somehow.

Meanwhile, she needed to hurry this along. She had been forced to contact Monk. It would all be over for her if he found out she had kept him out of the loop and attempted to steal the cross for herself. But if she could obtain the cross before he arrived, she could use it to secure the treasure for herself and be long gone before he knew what happened. All it took was

134

some subterfuge, a skill Monk himself had taught her over the past several years. That, and some speedy cooperation from Jon.

She smiled at him over her rifle sight. "Let's start with something simple. I'll give you to the count of three to tell me the final clue. If I get to three and you haven't told me, you will be an only child. Then we'll try again, and if I get to three that time, your new girlfriend will quite literally lose her mind, all over the carpet. And, if you're stupid enough to let things get that far and I reach three a third time, you can join your friends in finding out if there's an afterlife."

"Oh my gosh," came the cry from across the room. Miriam looked up to see that Jon's compatriots had noticed her. Michael started running toward his brother, while the girl looked for cover.

Time for Miriam to start the countdown. "One."

"What guarantee do I have that you'll let us go once you have what you want?" Jon asked.

"The only guarantee you have is that if you *don't* give me what I want, all three of you will die in this room. Two."

"What's going on?" she heard Michael say below. It was too late for Jon to bring him up to speed. Jon could give her what she wanted. But he needed the proper motivation. Centering Michael's skull in her sights, she started to pull the trigger.

A crash sounded from her left as someone slammed through one of the hall's entrance doors below. In an instant, she realized that she was too late.

Monk had arrived.

Chapter 37

Afraid to take his eyes off the sniper on the balcony, Jon glanced toward the intrusion and saw his worst nightmare. Caeden Monk was here now, double-teaming them and barring yet another potential avenue for escape. Yet when Jon looked back up at the woman, he could have sworn he saw a flash of disappointment as she recognized who had come barging into the room.

Interesting.

"We just keep running into each other, don't we?" Monk broke off the back from a chair and used the twin supports to bar the door through which he'd entered. Then he turned to Jon and Michael and sneered. "Frankly, I'm getting sick of it. Let's make this our last meeting, shall we?"

Nothing would make me happier, Jon thought. He was pretty sure he and Monk disagreed on exactly how that ideal scenario would play out.

"Plain and simple, just like my esteemed colleague I'm sure informed you. You give me what I want, you walk away. You fail to do so, I take what I want anyway while leaving a mess for the college and the police to clean up."

Michael stepped forward, trying to box out his brother, protect him from Monk's line of fire, forgetting that the woman on the balcony had her own weapon aimed in their direction. "It's easier for everyone the first way, huh?"

Monk must have detected the subtly snide tone in Michael's delivery. "Let's not try to get cute. I know you've done a lot of exciting crap across the world due to your parents' travels. Lots of narrow escapes from tight spots that make you feel invincible. This is not one of those times, boys. Your little adventure ends here, one way or another."

Jon looked for Liz and saw her still cowering behind a table halfway across the dining hall. Smart girl. Hopefully Monk wouldn't notice her, though Jon wasn't exactly expecting to rescue her the way he had back at the Memorial Presbyterian mausoleum. One, she seemed a bit more timid when it came to violence and these sorts of exploits in general. And two, Monk wasn't alone this time. Any attempts at sneak attacks would be stopped from the balcony long before they stood any chance of success.

"You seem to know so much about this Flagler hunt, and we have the pieces of the cross and final clue," Michael said. "Maybe we can be partners in this. Split it fifty-fifty?"

"Says the man with no gun and no leverage. The only thing I'll share with you is the chance to still be breathing when this is over." Monk stepped closer and leveled his pistol at Michael. "The final clue, please."

"If I'm dead, you get nothing."

"If you're dead, I no longer have any competition in completing the cross. I take the first three pieces from your backpack, let things die down a bit, then tear apart the old hotel here until I find what I need. Meanwhile, you'll be down with the Huguenots, rotting in the cemetery. Obviously, plan A is far more expedient for us both, but my patience is wearing thin."

Jon crossed behind Michael and gripped the back of a chair. He pretended to casually let his eyes drift upward, toward the ceiling over Monk's head.

"Please, don't hurt us," Jon said, putting a little quaver into his voice. "I'll give you the clue if you promise to let us go."

"Jon..." Michael warned under his breath.

Monk's eyes lit up at the prospective breakthrough, then darkened again as he adopted his posture of menace. "Don't make me repeat myself. The clue. Now."

Jon took a deep breath, as though he were making a heavyhearted decision. "The final piece is hidden 'beneath the emblem of the explorer most true.'" He looked again at the ceiling over Monk's head, where the names of Juan Ponce de Leon, Christopher Columbus, Hernando de Soto, and Pedro Menéndez de Avilés and their flagships had been hand-painted over a century ago.

Monk couldn't help himself. Being so close to the prize he had sought for so long, he looked. Jon flung the chair at his head.

"Liz! Come on!" He nudged his brother as they both moved to rush Monk. This was their only shot at escape.

Monk looked back just in time to lift an arm and halfway deflect the chair. The impact only knocked him back a little.

Just a few more steps.

The bang made Jon stop cold. Monk had shot while stumbling, but it was enough. Michael's scream devolved into a pained growl as he suppressed the agony of absorbing a bullet. Blood spurted from his upper leg. Michael grabbed hold of a nearby chair to support himself.

"Enough!" Monk yelled at Jon, his reddening face contorted with fury. "The next shot will be lethal. Tell me what the real clue is or your brother dies."

He didn't have a choice. But then, he didn't for a second believe that Monk would let them live once he had what he wanted. There was no way out.

Liz was just a few yards behind them now, having left the relative safety of her hiding spot. Shaking in terror, she positioned herself in front of the sniper's balcony, angled away from both the black-haired woman up there and Monk down here. But it wouldn't be enough once the bullets began flying. Not for any of them.

Jon looked from the tortured face of his brother to the choleric rage of Monk's, racking his brain for something, anything, to do to get them out safely.

"Fine," Monk said, seething. "We do it the hard way. Say goodbye to your brother."

"No!" Jon yelled. But the sound of his voice was drowned out by another as the door behind him crashed open.

Chapter 38

With his nerves frayed to the breaking point, Monk's hand was quivering ever so slightly as he aimed a lethal shot at Michael Rickner. It was all starting to come to pieces. And then, as the door at the far end of the room opened, the door he hadn't even realized existed, he realized how badly this whole enterprise had already gone.

"Freeze!" yelled the cop, a young Asian woman who looked like she meant business. "Drop your weapon! Now!" She must have been working security for the college, drawn into the dining hall by his gunfire. And now she was aiming her own weapon at him.

He had come too far to give up now. The cop wouldn't have noticed Miriam up in the balcony yet. Which meant he had the advantage.

"All right, officer. I'm putting my weapon on the table here." Monk moved toward a nearby table and feigned laying down his weapon. At the last second, he flipped the weapon back into firing position and unloaded three shots at the cop. Across the room, she yelled out in pain as at least one of the bullets hit the mark.

Four more bullets were sent in his direction as the cop fired while taking cover. Monk felt the searing slice of supersonic hot metal as a bullet tore into his left arm. He cursed, dropping to the floor to take cover from the cop. He had to finish this quickly. She had body armor, a radio, and backup. All he had in the way of backup was Miriam, but she was busy making sure the Rickner brothers and Liz stayed put. He tried to push the pain down, isolate it, and deal with it later. He was a good shot, but there were easily a hundred feet between him and the cop. His bleeding arm—not his shooting arm, thankfully—would be a distraction, but he had to do what he had to do. The cop would go down. And then so would Liz and the Rickner brothers.

"Give it up!" the cop yelled. "We know all about the Flagler hunt. You're too late."

Too late? What did that mean? Someone had already discovered the treasury? But he would have heard about such a newsworthy event—unless someone like him had already found it in secret, squirreling it away to private collectors through the black market, obscuring its true provenance to protect the secret of the hunt. Or had Flagler or someone else destroyed the treasury, fearful of what it could mean for his legacy? But as of a few hours ago, the pieces of the cross concealing the treasury's location were still in their original hiding places. The recording on the cylinder, damaged though it was, had proven that.

"What are you talking about?" he shouted back, hoping she'd fill in the gaps with whatever she knew. She grunted again, perhaps repositioning herself while fighting through the pain of her wounds, but she gave no other response.

No, the most likely scenario was that the cop was bluffing. How she knew about the hunt and that he was pursing Flagler's long-forgotten secret was a mystery. But considering the trail of historical destruction and other crime scenes he and the Rickner brothers had left in their wake today, she could have put the pieces together. He still had the advantage, though. He knew far more than anyone else could. Anyone, that is, except for Jon, Michael, and Liz—the only ones alive who had heard the last clue before it had been destroyed. As soon as he was done with this cop, he would deal with them and have his long-deserved prize.

He crept to the corner of his table. His gun at the ready, he peeked his head out to see if the cop had exposed herself for a shot, quickly ducking back down after. He didn't see her. Which gave him an opportunity to sneak closer, flanking her.

On hands and knees, blood pounding in his ears as adrenaline and the thrill of the hunt fused into a grand primordial energy boost, he crawled across the lush carpet from one table to the next before finally reaching a load-bearing pillar. With his back pressed against it, he slowly stood. He had never killed a cop before. Not an American one, at least. First time for everything.

He glanced across the room toward the balcony, hoping that from Miriam's hidden vantage point she could help him ascertain when the cop was exposed, allowing this fiasco to finally come to a swift end. Miriam was pointing toward the cop's position, giving him a thumbs-up. Perfect.

Then he noticed the door through which he had originally entered the dining hall. The chair back he had used to bar the door was lying on the floor.

Jon, Michael, and Liz were gone.

Chapter 39

Once the cop had burst into the room, the sniper on the balcony had been distracted by the firefight between Monk and the officer below. It was the only opportunity they were likely to get, so Jon took it. Dragging his brother alongside, with Liz opening the door for them, the trio made their escape from the dining hall while Monk attempted to get the drop on the police officer. Jon hoped she won that fight, but in the meantime getting his brother to safety and—if it was still possible—solving Flagler's persistent riddle took top priority.

Half running, half stumbling, he helped Michael down the stairs from the dining hall entrance. Michael tripped on the second-to-last step, falling to the floor with a repressed yelp as he landed on his wounded leg.

"Michael!" Jon dropped to his brother's side.

"I'm fine. Just stepped wrong." Michael grunted as he tried to get to his feet. "Help me up."

Jon scrambled to his feet and pulled his brother upright.

Liz had run several steps ahead before stopping. She turned back, her face stricken. "We've got a problem."

"What?" Jon asked.

"Cops entering the lobby. Headed this way."

The cops would eventually be an ally, but without the completed cross and the message Flagler had tried to suppress, there would be no way to prove the reasoning behind their thievery. Jon, Michael, and Liz would go to prison for a long, long time, leaving the devious Monk to make off with a historical treasure.

"Then let's avoid the lobby," Jon said. "Come on, this way."

The trio darted to the right into a side hallway. As soon as Jon turned the corner, he encountered a pair of female students, who stared in shock before doubling back. He hoped they returned to their dorm rooms, or headed to the beach, or just went out for the evening. Anywhere but to the cops descending on the college and surely on the lookout for the three of them.

They made a quick left at a T-intersection and found themselves in another hall, still heading away from the altercation in the dining hall. He and Michael had only been here once or twice, years ago. He wished he had time to map out the building, to figure out where the exits were and what routes they could take to get there. But they were flying blind, with adversaries on both sides of the law after them and unknown numbers of witnesses to betray them to the authorities.

"...looked like a gunshot wound, maybe." The voice—scared, female—came from ahead of them, nearing another T-intersection at the far end of the hall.

"In here," Liz said, throwing open a door to their right and diving inside. Jon dragged his brother through the door, with Liz shutting and locking it behind him. It was only once they were inside that his brain processed the plaque outside the room: *The Flagler Room.* The voices in the hall outside grew louder, as a cop and his witness came closer, zeroing in on their position.

Inside the Flagler Room, the three hunted vigilantes held their breath, praying they would go away. The voices stopped. And then, the door handle began to move.

Chapter 40

Audrey Yang's lungs were screaming. She had been shot twice, though thankfully both rounds had hit her vest. Kevlar vests were invented to prevent bullet penetration, but her body had still been hit by two supersonic projectiles, the impact of which had likely cracked a rib. But she wasn't going down without a fight.

Yet she was outnumbered and outgunned. She had seen the woman on the balcony as she ran for cover but hadn't checked since hunkering down to assess from her wounds and figure out her next move.

Shouting about the hunt had been impulsive but one that clearly struck a nerve. Her assailant yelled back, but she let him stew, hoping he'd make a mistake. She wasn't foolish enough to let him sonar his way to her position by getting into a Marco Polo–style shouting match. Still, she had to do something. The gunman had been silent for too long now. If she were in his shoes, she would be trying to sneak around, flanking her position to get the drop on her.

Well, two could play at that game. She repressed a grunt and pushed herself to her knees, her chest burning from the movement. Checking how much cover she had and choosing her next hiding spot, she prepared to move.

Behind her, the door through which she'd made her entrance moments ago opened. She turned to see her partner, Kyle Weiss, step into the room.

"Weiss!" she shouted. "Get down!"

His eyes widened, sweeping the room as he dove behind a nearby table. A good partner indeed, Yang realized, as doubling back through the door would have been much safer for him.

Instead, Weiss had jumped into the fire along with her, ready to confront whatever adversary she was facing.

"What's going on?" he asked in a stage whisper.

"Two confirmed shooters, one on the balcony, one across the room, possibly using cover to flank my position. I think the three underneath the balcony are the ones from Bouvier's shop. The ones who tried to put out the fire and save the victim."

Weiss looked at her like she had hit her head. Carefully, he peeked out from behind the table to survey the room.

"Who are you talking about?" he asked.

Yang gave him a similarly befuddled expression. Taking some small measure of comfort from the fact that her partner's entrance hadn't drawn fire, she popped out to quickly survey the room.

The trio under the balcony was gone. So too was the woman standing atop it. The fact that neither she nor her partner had been fired upon when exposing themselves led her to one horrible, obvious conclusion.

She had been hiding in an empty room.

Her assailant had already escaped.

Chapter 41

Miriam Caan wasn't sure if she was grateful for the cop's arrival or not, but it had certainly complicated her plans. She was hoping the cop and Monk would kill each other, allowing her to sneak away unfettered. But Monk escaped with only a flesh wound and the cop spotted her position on the balcony. Once Monk noticed their quarry had escaped, there was no reason to stick around, so he headed for his exit while Miriam disappeared through the curtain at the rear of the balcony.

Now she found herself hopelessly lost in a labyrinth of third-story service corridors. They weren't nearly as well lit as the rest of the former hotel—no Tiffany windows or elaborate sconces for Edison electric bulbs. These were the hallways exclusively used by the hotel's servants, the "dark angels" as one prominent guest had observed in 1889. But since they all but lived in the hotel year-round, the servants didn't need clear markings to navigate these passages. They knew them like the back of their hands.

Miriam didn't. She made a wrong turn somewhere, and she wasn't sure how far back to trace her steps. She hadn't even run across a stairwell yet, something to take her downstairs toward the more familiar guest areas. And now, somewhere below, Monk would be closing in on the treasure and her path to freedom would be closed forever.

Monk hadn't been on point at all today. Bouvier's deception had thrown him for a loop, and the Rickner brothers had kept him a step behind ever since. Of course, Miriam liked to think she had played some small part in his failures. She only wanted him to succeed to the point where victory was within her grasp alone. And then she could make her move. That point was rapidly nearing. But she was not there yet. As much as she hated to admit it, she still needed him.

She turned another corner, only to be faced with yet another featureless corridor. Had she seen this one already? She felt like she was going in circles. Without the distinctive features the rest of the building had, orienting herself was incredibly difficult.

She ignored the next junction, continuing on until she reached another narrow hallway, stretching into oblivion. There, on the wall, was something she had seen a few times before. A narrow sliver of wood set into the wall panel. Could it be?

Trying to think outside the box, setting herself in the mindset of a servant from one hundred and thirty years ago, she touched the sliver. It was the right height. It was one thing to not know where you were going in these passages, but she hadn't seen a door handle or anything in ages. This might have been why. The servants would have only used these corridors for traveling unseen through the bowels of the hotel. Their jobs would have been conducted outside these hidden hallways, turning down guest rooms, laundering bedding, cooking, cleaning, and otherwise satisfying the needs of the hotel's esteemed guests. All sorts of prospective destinations would have to be easily accessible from these passages while still keeping up the illusion of being invisible to the average guest's naked eye.

She pressed on the thin wooden piece set into the wall until she heard a click. The panel swung inward. A hidden door.

Freedom.

With her rifle secreted away in her bag, she casually stepped into the hallway, taking tremendous joy in the fact that it was richly decorated and well lit. She was back in the hotel proper now. Back in the hunt for the Rickner brothers, for Monk, and for the treasure.

She just hoped she wasn't too late.

Chapter 42

Jon held his breath, waiting for the police to burst through the door and arrest him for all manner of crimes, real and imagined. The door handle turned. And then it stopped. The lock had engaged.

"Is this door supposed to be locked?" said the voice Jon guessed belonged to a cop.

"I don't know..." said another voice, possibly the coed who had spotted them in the hall earlier.

The cop's radio interrupted. "Shots fired, officer down in the dining hall, repeat, officer down in dining hall."

Jon felt a guilty sense of relief as footsteps pounded away from the door. He hoped that officer was all right. Whether she knew it or not, she had saved them from Monk's wrath and now from the investigating officer outside. Jon had to make sure they didn't waste this opportunity.

"Now what?" Liz whispered.

Jon turned from the door to take in the room. It was originally created as the ladies' parlor, a waiting area where female guests would gather and socialize while their male counterparts conducted hotel business in the main lobby. Portraits of high-class ladies dressed in the turn of the century's finest as well as pastoral scenes of idealized natural

Jeremy Burns

beauty adorned the walls. The ceiling overhead was painted a distinctive robin-egg blue that the upper-crust ladies who once gathered in this room would have immediately recognized as Tiffany Blue. The legendary artist Louis Comfort Tiffany had been the interior designer for the Ponce de Leon, and his famed Tiffany glass adorned the windows and lamps throughout the room.

And set into the marble mantelpiece in the center of the room, a beautiful white onyx clock, its gilded hands stuck at 3:26.

"Of course," Jon said. "It's so obvious."

"What?" Michael said, hobbling over. Liz joined them seconds later.

"'The face of time.'" Jon pointed to the clock, perpetually frozen in time. "A *clock* face."

"I remember this one from the last time we were here," Michael said. "It was years ago, but this one stuck with me. This was one of the first electric clocks in the country to be displayed in a public place, provided by none other than Thomas Edison himself."

"If it's such a big deal, why is it stopped?" Liz asked.

Michael smiled, slipping into the teacher mode he had so long enjoyed with Jon. "Because no one can get to the inner workings of the clock. The whole thing is encased in marble, and the clock face is the single largest piece of white onyx in the Western Hemisphere. Ever since the clock stopped back in 1968, no one has been able to figure out how to get inside to repair it. So it's been stuck at 3:26 for half a century, a beautiful relic of a forgotten past."

"And apparently housing another relic from an even older, more forgotten past," Jon said. "The last piece of the cross."

Liz shook her head. "But all sealed up and opaque like this, Flagler's guests, the original treasure hunters, never would have been able to see the cross piece to know they'd solved the final riddle."

"Maybe it was like the pipe in the influencer machine at the Lightner. Encased in something clear—a glass clock face, perhaps—and then the setup was changed when Flagler decided to pull the plug on the hunt."

"But how do we get inside?" Liz asked. "If fifty years of engineers and historians haven't figured out how to get in there to repair it, how could we expect to puzzle our way in."

146

"Puzzling our way into things is kind of our favorite pastime," Michael said with a grin. "After all, we've gotten this far in the hunt, over a century after Flagler buried his plans and covered his tracks. If anyone can find a way into this clock, we can."

Jon and Michael got to work, studying the clock face, the marble surrounding it, even the walls adjacent to the mantle. For Jon's part, he couldn't find anything—no hidden levers, no recessed switches, no potential secret mechanism of any kind. If Flagler had sealed the final piece of the cross inside the clock, he had done a very good job of keeping it hidden. Unless, once again, he had gotten this last clue wrong.

"Are you having any luck, Mi—" He stopped midsentence, seized by the sight of Liz swinging a fireplace poker at the mantle. With a sickening crunch, the beautiful antique clock face cracked, fissures spilling out from the poker's impact point.

"What are you doing?" Jon tried to keep his voice down, but the shock of Liz's assault on the clock made it difficult.

She swung again, cracking the exquisite gemstone completely through in one place. The noise was louder now, too loud. But they had passed the point of no return. One more swing broke a sizable jagged hole in the center of the clock, the mangled golden hands bent and broken with no time demarcation to point to. But despite the horrific damage to a historic treasure, Liz, staring into the hole she'd just created, began to smile.

"Hello, beautiful."

Chapter 43

Caeden Monk swept the corridor with his eyes as he stalked through the old hotel. He was both hunter and hunted now, seeking the escaped trio while avoiding the growing police force swarming the premises.

It never should have come to this. Of course, if Emerson Kirkheimer had lied to him on that Vermont mountaintop the day before, he would be even further from his prize. But ever since he'd arrived in St. Augustine, everything had gone wrong. The boys who were supposed to lure away Bouvier had only drawn out the Rickner brothers. The fact that the Rickner brothers were in town at all, much less throwing their own particular monkey wrench into the gears of his plan, was a disaster all on its own. Monk had fallen for Bouvier's deathbed deception, grabbing the wrong wax cylinder recording and nearly burning the real one in the process. Then, after listening to the recording, Jon Rickner had damaged the cylinder, destroying the final clue in the process.

Every step of the way, they had been half a step ahead, managing to squeeze out of confrontations outside Ripley's, in Memorial Church, and now in the dining hall. Next time, he would shoot first and worry about the questions later. And there would be a next time. Monk would never stop until he had his prize and the three troublemakers were dead.

Of course, too much had gone wrong inside the dining hall that wasn't exactly his fault, though he could certainly assess the situation better in hindsight. But who could have anticipated that a cop would come bursting in? That wasn't an accident. She hadn't just been drawn by the gunfire. She knew what he was after. And she claimed it was already too late.

And she had shot him. It wasn't lethal by any stretch of the imagination, but it was bleeding a fair amount and hurt like the devil. He had torn a small Flagler College banner from a post in the hallway outside the dining hall and fashioned it into a tourniquet. His new accessory wouldn't stop him from standing out, but it would stymie the blood loss, not only helping him keep his strength up for this final pursuit but also ensuring he didn't leave a crimson trail for the police to follow.

Even Miriam, his most faithful associate, had failed him by allowing the Rickner party to escape while he tried to deal with the cop. He would extract her penance after this was all over. He could not allow mistakes like that to go unpunished.

Another cop. No, two of them, dashing straight toward him. He didn't bother glancing around. There was no escape. He would have to fight his way through.

Unless... The cops would be issuing orders if he were the subject of their interest. "Get on your knees" and such. They weren't saying a word. In fact, they seemed to be focused on a point just behind him.

Monk pretended to study a bulletin board next to him, pivoting so the tourniquet wasn't as obvious to the approaching officers.

They ran right past him. Headed, no doubt, to the actual scene of the crime. The dining hall.

Monk breathed a sigh of relief as he realized how close he had just been to losing everything he had worked for. After all that had gone wrong for him today, it was about time karma started working in his favor again.

He stayed against the side of the corridor for a moment, pretending to read the bulletin board before continuing on. He may have survived that encounter, but eventually the cops would figure out what he looked like. Further, his quarry was still loose in the building, armed with the first three pieces of the cross and knowledge of the final clue. Eventually, they would find the final piece and, if the Rickner brothers were as smart as their father, they would figure out why Flagler had deep-sixed the hunt—the secret behind the secret, as it were. Monk's ultimate goal. And his window for finding it before the Rickners was closing fast. He was caught between the carrot and the stick, and they were both moving too fast, with him flying all but blind.

A crash sounded from nearby, away from the dining hall. The only other reason Monk could think of for a sound such as that would be another act of vandalism by the Rickner party.

Another crash, then another. Each noise diminished somewhat by distance, but it was enough for him. He started off toward the sounds of destruction.

They had found the hiding spot. It was the only answer. But in doing so, they had also ensured that Monk would find them.

Chapter 44

Inside the freshly broken hole, caught between the gears of the Edison Electric clock, a twinkle of gold gleamed at Jon.

"Occam's razor strikes again," Michael said as the three of them stared at their prize. Liz beamed. It wasn't the approach Jon would have taken, but it had worked. And more than that, he had been right. The final piece of the cross Flagler had hidden was behind the clock face.

Jon thrust his hand into the jagged aperture, feeling around for the texture he had become quite familiar with over the past few hours. Finding it, he wrapped his fingers around the artifact and gently pried it loose from the gears. Almost immediately, the clock began ticking.

"Fixed your clock," Jon said to the ether as he pulled the cross piece from its mechanical coffin for the first time in well over a century.

"More Latin." Michael took the other pieces from his backpack and set them on the table. Once Jon had added the fourth piece, they arranged them into the finished cross, battered by time but still beautiful.

Jon leaned over the cross and started to read the Latin inscription aloud, pausing once or twice when the breaks between the pieces partially obscured a letter. When he finished, he looked at his brother.

"Do you realize what this means?"

Michael, wide-eyed with his trademark goofy grin, nodded. "If it means what I think it means, this is huge."

"Huger than huge," Jon said, his own ecstatic expression mirroring that of his brother. "No wonder Flagler canned this whole thing."

"Guys, sorry but I'm a twenty-first century girl. No speaka the Latin. Clue me in?"

"Oh, sorry, Liz," Jon said. "Basically what it says is—"

A bang on the door interrupted him. Not just a knock. Much more forceful. Followed by another.

"Time to go," Michael said, scooping all four cross pieces into his backpack.

Jon looked across the room, scanning the wall for other exits. He ran to one door and opened it, only to find himself staring into a closet stuffed with folding furniture. He ran down to the next door. More furniture.

"Anything?" Michael asked, shouldering his pack.

"Not unless one of these closets leads to Narnia."

With a final percussive bang, the entrance door flew open, splinters flying from the locked jamb. A quake of fear shot through Jon's body as he looked toward their only way out.

The doorway that was now filled with the furious form of Caeden Monk.

Chapter 45

Jon's body was moving before he'd even had time to consciously process the gun that Monk was aiming in his direction. The same primordial instinct that caused the rabbit to flee at the sight of a wolf moved Jon's head just far enough out of the bullet's path to send the deadly projectile into the wall behind him instead. But Monk wasn't wielding a Derringer. He had plenty more bullets where that came from.

But there was one way out they hadn't considered. Self-defenestration.

Jon ran to his brother's side and tucked his shoulder under Michael's arm. "Come on, both of you. The windows are our only way out."

Liz was yelling, terrified by the gunfire. "Are you serious?"

Monk was moving toward them now, angling into the room so he could get a solid line of sight on his targets.

"We go now or we die!" Jon yelled back, already moving in a three-legged race with his brother.

A transformation came over Liz as she seemed to realize the severity of their situation. Jumping out a window was hardly ideal, but it certainly beat the alternative. She ran ahead, grabbing a chair on her way and smashing it into a window. Between the clock and the window, Jon thought she must have missed her calling as a Home Run Derby slugger.

By the time he and Jon were within a few feet of the window, she had already knocked out the plate glass. The sizable shards that had fallen on the ground below would cut deep if they landed on them.

"Go!" Jon yelled. Liz took the hint and leapt. Inches from her heels, a flower-patterned turn-of-the-century armchair spit cotton fluff as a pair of bullets punctuated its exterior.

Jon turned to see Monk, closing the distance between them as he changed magazines.

"Together." Jon locked eyes with his brother. "We jump together."

Michael nodded. Jon gritted his teeth and, his arm wrapped tight around his brother's torso, jumped through the window and into the twilit dark.

A dozen feet below, a bed of landscaping woodchips cushioned their fall. Jon scrambled to his feet, helped his brother up, and resumed their race to safety. Just a few dozen more feet and they'd be around the corner and away from here.

"Hang in there, buddy," Jon said in between panting breaths. "We're almost home free."

Michael screamed and collapsed. Jon hadn't heard any more shots fired. Plus they were no longer in direct line of sight with the windows. Had Monk shot him again?

Jon crouched next to his brother and almost immediately saw the culprit—a gopher hole. Michael had stepped in it and twisted the ankle of his one good leg, then fallen on his gunshot wound. Jon tried to help him to his feet, but to no avail.

"Over here!"

Jon looked up to see who was yelling. The blue uniforms of the officers brought no comfort. Not now. Not when they were so close.

Michael grabbed his brother's hand and fixed him with a pained but purposeful look. "Go. Get out of here. Take the cross and finish this."

"I can't leave you, Michael."

"You have to. You don't have a choice. It's up to you now. Make this right. Don't let him win."

Jon squeezed his brother's hand and nodded, grabbing the backpack from where it had fallen beside Michael. He winced. This went against everything he believed about brotherhood. You never left your brother behind. And yet, that was the only path to salvation now for either of them.

They were still in the shadows, but the sweeping flashlight beams would soon betray their position. Keeping low,

Jon rose and ran to the shelter of the bushes lining the street at the edge of the property. So close. And yet so far.

Once concealed, he turned back just in time to see two police officers descend on Michael, their guns trained on their new prisoner.

Jon felt a tap on his shoulder. He turned to see Liz, concern etched across her shadowed face. She didn't say a word. She didn't have to. Michael was out of the hunt now. And the only way to prevent a litany of charges from being filed against him—and to prevent Monk from executing a crime of historic proportions—would be to discover and bring to light the unthinkable truth behind why Flagler buried his own treasure hunt.

Slinking out of the bushes and onto the darkened street, Jon and Liz disappeared into the night. One way or another, history was about to be made.

PART THREE

MENÉNDEZ

Chapter 46

Miriam Caan heard the screaming before she even opened the door. She had heard that scream before, and it never presaged good things for anyone who had caused it.

"They escaped?" she said upon entering the room. Her voice was low, intended as a calming agent. It didn't work.

Monk spewed off an expletive-riddled rant that, in his flustered state, made him sound a bit like Yosemite Sam. Vintage furniture went flying as he kicked over tables, ripped paintings from the wall, and battered chairs with his empty pistol.

She walked over and placed a hand on his shoulder, a soothing motion that she had used on him many times before when he got this way. Touching him sent an unnerving sensation up her arm and down her spine, a strange combination of remorse, desire, and nausea. He had been her first and only. But soon enough, that would be behind her, with a whole new life of luxury and freedom to salve everything he had put her through. Everything she had put herself through.

He turned at her touch. Frustration and fury were still thick in his eyes, but his face seemed to soften in that almost imperceptible way that only longtime lovers could detect. Miriam detected it. And she hated herself for it.

"They got it," he said, jabbing a finger at the broken clock face. "The last piece. And now they're gone."

"Do you think they know?"

"If they don't already, they definitely will now."

"They got the older brother."

Monk brightened at that, then let his face sag. "I'm not sure if that's a good thing or a bad thing. If he already knows the truth, if he tells the cops..."

"Would you believe it if you were the one interviewing him?"

"No. But that one cop did." He pointed to the bloody tourniquet on his left arm. "You remember, the one who you let shoot me."

157

"Monk, I'm sorry. There was no way either of us could have known."

Immediately she realized her mistake. For most people, her attempt to absolve herself and her accuser of responsibility would be useful, tying their fates together and granting both immunity from their errors. But for Monk, any perceived accusation of his own failures was a trigger point.

His face darkened. "So you're saying this was my fault?"

"No, of course not."

"Now you're saying I've got a hearing problem?"

"Come on, we've got to get out of here. The cops will be here soon."

He backhanded her with such force that it knocked her into an armchair, one of the few Monk hadn't destroyed in his fury moments earlier. The chair tumbled over, and she fell to the floor.

"Please," she said, trembling. He liked it when she cowered, got off on the absolute power he felt he had over her. If he only knew.

"This whole thing has been a disaster, ever since we got into town." He aimed his gun at her. "I blame you."

"We are still so close. We can still make this right."

"How?" His hand was shaking, but at this close range, he would be hard-pressed to miss his target.

Miriam smiled with a confidence she only half felt. Pretending to ignore the gun aimed at her skull, she climbed to her feet and started heading toward the door.

"Come on," she said over her shoulder. "I'll tell you on the way."

Chapter 47

Jon tried to keep to the backstreets. He didn't know if there was a BOLO alert out for him or Liz, but he didn't want to find out the hard way.

They were heading north, cutting across the city to avoid the dual major north–south tourist thoroughfares of

Avenida Menéndez along the coast and St. George Street farther inland. Better to bypass the downtown heart of the historic district as much as possible now. He had a destination in mind. Part of the completed cross's message was cryptic. The other part was unmistakably profound.

Sevilla Street dead-ended into Orange Street, and beyond the intersection, Francis Field. Used for local festivals and food-truck gatherings, the field was currently empty. Jon angled across the field toward the parking garage at the eastern end. Checking behind him once more, he led the way around the corner, the garage at his right, the famed Huguenot Cemetery to the left.

The cemetery's name was a misnomer, with most historians agreeing that none of its bodies likely belonged to the sixteenth-century French Protestant sect. Instead, it was the first American cemetery in the city, which needed a Protestant cemetery after the U.S. took control of the city in 1821. The Spanish-founded Tolomato Cemetery to the southwest continued to serve for Catholic burials, but the Huguenot Cemetery came at an ideal time. Within a few short years of its founding, a massive yellow fever epidemic hit St. Augustine, decimating its population and filling the new plots with fresh bodies.

Huguenot, like Tolomato before it, was considered one of the most haunted cemeteries in the country. Tonight, though, Jon had his own ghosts to contend with.

"Okay, hang on a sec, here," Liz said, stopping by the wrought iron fence that ringed the cemetery. "Where are we going? What did the Latin inscription say?"

Jon looked at his phone, checking the image he had snapped of the completed cross before Monk had ruined their revelation. "Roughly translated, it means 'to honor the Lord God Most Holy and to redeem this land for His purposes, Pedro Menéndez and Father Francisco López hereby sanctify this secret treasury for the promulgation of the Holy Faith throughout Florida. The treasury will be housed by the defenders of God, where the sacred trespass began.'" That wasn't all it said, of course, but it was all she needed for now. The rest would come when the time was right.

"The secret treasury? So where are the defenders of God?"

"Nowadays, I guess they would be downtown, at the Catholic Cathedral. But the original defenders would have been where Catholic Florida actually started. The 'sacred trespass' where Catholic Spain staked its claim to the souls of this land. The site of the very first mass in St. Augustine, conducted by Father Francisco López right after Admiral Menéndez and his ships landed in 1565."

He led them out of the tree cover surrounding the cemetery and pointed to the northeast. There, illuminated from below and stabbing 208 feet into the night sky, was a massive steel cross, one of the largest upright crosses on the planet.

"The Mission Nombre de Dios. That's where this mystery began. And that's where we're going to end it."

Chapter 48

Seated in a chair in the middle of the crime scene that the Flagler College dining hall had become, Audrey Yang brushed off the medical technician who hovered at her elbow.

"I'm fine." Physically, at least. Her ego had certainly been bruised, and now she was being kept here by red tape and bureaucracy. She had already given her preliminary statement to the Internal Affairs investigator, who got here a little too quickly for her taste. She could jump through their hoops later. But right now, this was a massive waste of her time.

"You were right, Yang," Weiss said. "I guess I should have listened."

She wanted to hit back with "Yeah, you should have," but she didn't care anymore. She had been right. And now she just wanted to see this through.

"He shot me, Weiss. He shot me, and he got away. I want back in."

"IA's still working on clearing you. As soon as they finish up..."

She glared at her partner. "How did they get here so fast?" She already knew the answer, but she needed to hear it from the horse's mouth.

"Sarge asked them to tag along."

"Because you told Sarge I had gone rogue."

"I was worried about you, Yang." He pointed to the bruising that had crawled its way through the neckhole of her undershirt. "With good reason, apparently."

"I was right and you ignored me. And when I reached out for official backup, you bring someone to investigate *me*."

"I'm sorry, Yang. It's not like you think, I promise."

"Get those IA jokers off my back and let me finish this, Weiss. You owe me."

Weiss sighed. "We've got half the cops in the city looking for the guy who shot you. No offense, but in a manhunt situation like this, how much of a difference do you think you could really make?"

An hour ago, she would have made all the difference in the world. Hotel Ponce de Leon was the final hiding spot in Flagler's treasure hunt. But now, after the last piece of the cross had been stolen from a clock in the old ladies' parlor downstairs, she had nothing to go on. The hunt was over. The bad guys had won. But they wouldn't get away with it. Not on her watch. Still, she had no clear next step for her investigation, no clue as to where her quarry would go next. But she had to do something.

"I can't just sit here screwing around with IA—the IA *you* brought here—while they're out there terrorizing my town."

"Who said anything about terrorizing?" Weiss said. "They're on the run. And we'll get them."

Yang started to protest, but her partner cut her off.

"I did pull some strings, however. You might be stuck here for the moment, but there's something you can do in the meantime."

"More paperwork?" Yang infused her response with as much sardonic faux-enthusiasm as possible.

Weiss, for his part, didn't bite. "Even better. We caught one of the guys you saw under the balcony. Thought you might want to ask him a few questions."

Yang smiled. She was back in the game. "Bring him to me."

Chapter 49

The Mission Nombre de Dios was closed to visitors for the evening. But Jon and Liz were not visiting.

The complex was a vast tract of land, especially considering its proximity to the historical center just a block to the south and the growing suburbs to the north and west. To the east lay the Atlantic, where Menéndez had followed in the nautical footsteps of Columbus, Cortez, Ponce de Leon, and de Soto. The difference? Menéndez had stayed, dedicating life and limb to gaining the allegiances of the native peoples and spreading the Catholic faith. He had built something lasting. And hopefully, something that had remained hidden for more than four and a half centuries. A secret treasury, founded for God, forgotten by history.

As well as being a working mission, Nombre de Dios had become a Catholic shrine in recent years, complete with grassy knolls, prayer gardens, and a sanctuary. A statue of Father Francisco López de Mendoza Grajales, arms outstretched and face turned heavenward, was the centerpiece of a reflective pavilion. In 1565 Menéndez landed in this spot, where Father López gave what many historians believed to be the first Catholic mass said in what would become the United States. All this was pertinent to the mystery Jon and Liz sought to solve. But nothing leapt out at him as fitting the clue hidden in the assembled cross.

"How could López and Menéndez fund a treasury that isn't in the historical record?" Liz asked as they explored the property.

"I don't know. All the precious minerals and gemstones mined from Spanish holdings in Central and South America were property of the crown. The king would have demanded detailed records and logs—how much of what was mined, which port it left from, which ship it was loaded onto, where that ship moored throughout its journey..."

"What?" she asked after he had drifted off midsentence.

"The *San Miguel*."

"The what?"

"The *San Miguel* was a Spanish treasure galleon that sank en route to Spain in 1568. Supposedly lost in a hurricane sweeping across the Atlantic. No one's ever found it, but the timeline fits."

"Okay, you've lost me. What are you talking about?"

Jon gave her a sympathetic grin. "Sorry, my brain was getting ahead of my mouth there. St. Augustine was founded for three basic purposes. First, to establish a permanent foothold on the American mainland. Second, to help spread the Catholic faith to the native population. And third, to help defend the Spanish treasure fleet from pirates and privateers. The ships, laden with treasure from Mexico and Peru, would make their final main stop at Havana before departing on the long trek across the Atlantic to Seville or Cadiz. St. Augustine was positioned right at that eastward curve to the Gulf Stream that the ships rode back to Spain, offering a last-minute friendly port of call if ships needed it. It wasn't as often as you might think, as the presence of St. Augustine and other outpost ports along the Florida coast helped to deter would-be pirates somewhat, but treasure galleons did moor out in Matanzas Bay plenty throughout the fleet's history."

Liz's eyes lit up as the pieces clicked into place. "So Menéndez could have off-loaded the treasure from one of the ships here, then sank it in the middle of the ocean, writing the whole thing off as a loss."

"Exactly. King Philip would never be the wiser, because storms sank many a ship back in those days. It was simply one of the risks associated with these bold transatlantic ventures, the cost of doing business."

"But why would Menéndez take that risk? Establishing a secret treasury here, behind the king's back? They'd hang him for that."

Jon looked out at the dark waters of the bay, empty save for a single pleasure yacht cruising in the distance.

"Do you know why the bay out there and the river that feeds it is called 'Matanzas'?"

"Should I?"

"It's Spanish for *massacre*. Named because of Menéndez's controversial mass execution of French soldiers in 1565. He did it twice, once just a few days after arriving in Florida, once about a month later. He accepted the French surrender, then killed all who were not immediately useful to him for his new city. Ten at a time, he would make his captives kneel at the water's edge, then ordered his men to slit their throats. French blood turned the river and bay red for days afterward."

"An act of piety in the face of what he felt was blasphemy? Or overkill?"

"That's surely the question Menéndez would have been asking himself. Father López's name makes this even more interesting. Perhaps the friar decided to capitalize on the enormity of the massacre by telling Menéndez that his eternal soul was in jeopardy if he did not pay the proper penance. As captain-general of the treasure fleet, Menéndez would have been uniquely positioned to siphon enough loot from the king's future coffers to fund a sizable secret treasury, ensuring the Church could continue its work in *La Florida* for generations to come. History records the great lengths he went to in order to gain the trust of the native tribes, promulgating the gospel deep into the swamplands of Florida while helping set up missions throughout the territory. Using other methods to help the Church's foothold in Florida wouldn't have been outside the realm of possibility."

"So where would they have hidden it?" Liz asked. "Because I'm not seeing anything here that looks like it was built to defend the faith."

Then it clicked. For sixteenth-century Catholic Spain, church and state were irrevocably intertwined. Menéndez may have answered to the king, but the king answered to God. Thus, in his mind and in Father López's, the very soldiers who defended the city of St. Augustine would have been defenders of the faith, a bulwark against the Protestant heresies of the French and English, a vanguard into the fertile hearts of the pagan natives.

"I'm so sorry," he said. "I don't think it's here at all."

"What, the treasure's gone?" She looked panicked.

"No, not that." He gestured around him. "I mean it's not here. This isn't where the defenders of the faith would have been."

"Then where?"

"The oldest building in St. Augustine," he said with a grin. "The Castillo de San Marcos."

Chapter 50

B ound in handcuffs with a bandage covering the su-
tured wounds on his leg, Michael was led back into
the dining hall of Flagler College. He recognized the
police officer from before, the one who had shot at Monk
and enabled him, Jon, and Liz to escape. Michael's own escape, of course, had ended prematurely, but he hoped Jon
and Liz had managed to get away. Jon knew enough to finish the unintended denouement to the century-old treasure
hunt, the reason Flagler buried the idea in the first place. He
just hoped he would find it in time to validate his story to
the police. And, most importantly, that he found it before
Monk did.

The officer who had confronted Monk earlier was seated at one of the hall's tables. "Take those off him," she said to
the cops flanking Michael. "I don't think he's going to try to
make a break for it on that leg." She turned to Michael. "Are
you, Mr. Rickner?"

"No, ma'am."

The cops complied, removing the cuffs before pushing
him down into a chair opposite the female officer.

"I'm Detective Yang, Mr. Rickner."

"Call me Michael."

"Well then, Michael," she began, her tone friendly
enough that Michael half suspected a trap. "Tell me about
what you've been doing today. And please, no lies. I know
more than you think."

He didn't doubt it. She had not only crashed Monk's
party just in time, but she also knew at least something about
the Flagler hunt. It was time to come clean about everything
that had happened thus far—everything, that was, except for
the Menéndez clue hidden on the cross itself.

So he told her. About their meeting with Mr. Bouvier
that morning, the young thieves posing as a distraction, the
antique shop inferno, meeting Liz, Mr. Bouvier's final words,
the falling ceiling beam that had killed the antiquarian, the
Edison recording, the confrontation with Monk, the clues
of the Flagler hunt and the decision—right or wrong—to
take the pieces of the cross with them to prevent Monk from
getting his hands on them. Yang nodded at key parts of the

story, his recollection seemingly confirming some of what she had already known.

"You've destroyed a number of priceless historical treasures," she said when he finished. "As the son of an eminent historian, I would have thought that they would mean something to you."

He remained silent. He didn't want to throw Liz under the bus just yet. After all, if she hadn't broken the onyx clock, the most valuable of the damaged hiding places, Monk would now have the final piece, and they would have no idea that the biggest prize was still out there.

"Well, you've shared with me," she said. "Here's something you might not have known. We found out who the sniper on the balcony was—Miriam Caan, one-time archeology student under the former professor. She left the program at Cornell shortly after Monk was forced out. Been seen with him in a number of countries over the past few years, with numerous warrants out for her arrest. No American warrants, though, for either of them. That is, until a few minutes ago."

"So you realize that they're the bad guys in all of this, not me. Not Jon and not Liz either."

"I've been operating under the theory that there was more to the murder of Mr. Bouvier and the torching of his shop than met the eye. That there were at least two different parties working separately, one meaning to harm Bouvier and his shop, one trying to save both. It appears my stance was vindicated. But that doesn't absolve you of wrongdoing."

Just as Michael had feared. Without Monk or Caan, the cops would go for the bird in the hand. After all, Michael had been a party to four separate acts of vandalism, damaging or destroying elements of historic sites, each of which would carry a hefty sentence behind bars.

Another officer called to Yang from across the room.

"Sit tight, Michael," she said, getting up to leave. "And don't do anything stupid while I'm gone."

He would have loved to have tried something she would consider stupid, like escaping. Outlandish and supposedly stupid maneuvers had gotten Jon and him out of more than a few pickles over the years. But not this time. The room was full of cops and crime-scene techs, each exit guarded by at least one officer. They'd draw down on him the moment he left his chair. No, there was no way to escape from this predicament by force or stealth. Only his mental acuity and carefully chosen words could save him now.

He tried to puzzle out how to get the police to let him go, but he found only dead ends. Crazy how he could solve a centuries-old riddle without breaking a sweat yet couldn't even see a light at the end of this maze.

Yang was walking back over now. More like speed-walking, really. What had they called her away for? Had they found Jon and Liz? Had Monk caught up to them and killed them? Or had the cops finally captured Monk and this Miriam Caan? His mind raced with the possibilities—good, bad, and ugly.

"What's going on?" he asked, anxiety obvious in his voice.

"Well, your story checks out as far as we can tell, except for one thing."

"What?" he asked. He had told her everything. Everything except for the secret Latin message engraved in the cross, something there was no way they could know about unless they had a hidden camera in the Flagler Room. Which, now that he thought about it, they very well could have. If the school had surveillance footage of that room, the cops could know exactly what had been discovered in that room. Though that was the worst omission he could think of that she might have uncovered, what Yang said struck fear into him on a whole new level.

She leaned across the table, locking eyes with him and sizing him up before finally answering. "There's something you should know about your new friend, Liz."

Chapter 51

The oldest masonry fortification in the continental United States, the Castillo de San Marcos was perhaps the most famous site in St. Augustine. Colloquially called "the Fort" by modern-day locals, the seventeenth-century stone fortress had been built almost entirely of coquina. Despite the relative softness of the material, the Castillo had survived the rise and fall of nations, watching over St. Augustine as the city fell to British hands, then back to the Spanish before finally becoming part of the fledgling United States of America.

And, if Jon's theory was correct, it had also watched over a secret fortune, forgotten by its caretakers and lost to history. Until now.

He understood why Flagler would have abandoned the treasure hunt once he realized what the Menéndez clue said on the cross itself. Flagler had spent a fortune investing in St. Augustine real estate and infrastructure. From his hotels, churches, and restaurants to his train stations, power plants, and luxury attractions, the magnate had utterly transformed the ancient city. The very grass Jon and Liz were walking across as they made their stealthy approach toward the Castillo's outer walls was once used as a three-hole golf course for guests of Flagler's hotels, the first-ever course in a state soon to be renowned for them.

But Flagler's fantasy had accidentally veered a little too close to the truth. It was one thing to conduct a controlled treasure hunt to entertain his well-heeled guests. That wasn't far removed from a city-wide parlor game, a clear fantasy tapping into nostalgic visions of *Treasure Island*-esque swash-buckling. But if word had gotten out that there was an ac-tual stash of pirate-era treasure buried somewhere in the city, Flagler's dreams would have been turned to ruin. Every man, woman, and child who could wield a shovel would be digging up the city—his city—in pursuit of long-lost buried treasure.

So he'd been forced to kill his fantasy treasure hunt, all to hide the presence of a real hoard hidden within the very foundations of the nation's oldest city. A city that, in many ways, had become Flagler's own.

Now they would see if Flagler's fears had been well-founded. Was the treasure still hidden beneath the Cas-tillo? Had it ever been there at all?

At the top of the slope leading to the fortress, Jon paused. A dry moat had been dug around the structure, and though it was devoid of water, it would make the as-cent over the walls that much more difficult.

He dropped down into the moat, using the embankment as cover as he crept around the fort. To the right was the main gate, through which tourists, researchers, and National Park Service rangers would enter the fort during the day. Now, in the dark of night, the last tourists had been gone for hours. The historical actors once clothed in period Spanish military uniforms had long since clocked out and returned to twenty-first-century apparel. And, most important for Jon's purposes, the portcullis had been lowered and the drawbridge raised. Just outside the entrance, a National Park Service hut stood sentinel, a single light within betraying the presence of a ranger on the night shift. Several years before, a vandal had tagged the centuries-old walls of the fort with graffiti, severely damaging the historical integrity of the porous coquina walls. With news of the vandalisms committed across the city today, the ranger would surely be on high alert.

Jon backed away from the guarded main entrance, moving counterclockwise around the fort, looking for some other way in. Liz followed close behind. The bad news was that the fort had been built to prevent invaders from getting in. And it had been successful in that regard, as the Castillo de San Marcos had never been taken by force. The good news was, unlike during its tenure as an active military fort, no one was up on the battlements shooting at him. Not yet, at least.

As he rounded the corner at the far end of the fort, a forge came into view. Long since dormant, the forge had once been used to smelt cannonballs and other armaments for the fort. This side of the fort was facing the Matanzas, the bay breeze tinged with the scent of saltwater. Across the bay, the lights of Anastasia Island twinkled as residents and tourists began their post-dinner evening plans. In the fort's earliest days, the locals staring out at the view would have been plagued with constant worries of pirates, enemy naval forces, hostile tribesmen, and the relentless torrents of Caribbean storms, not to mention starvation and innumerable deadly diseases. Flagler had helped to change all that, laying the foundation for transforming an insanely hot, mosquito-infested swampland into the world-renowned tourist destination that modern-day Florida had become.

Jon turned from the water, an idea taking root. The surface of the coquina wall was pocked with centuries-old impacts of cannons fired from enemy ships attacking from the bay. The soft resilience of the wall's materials had absorbed the blows, not fracturing along an impact fault line like regular stone walls did in castles and fortresses elsewhere in the world. But while those attacks hadn't destroyed the fort, it hadn't left it unblemished.

Jon began to climb, using the shallow pits punched into the outer wall as hand- and footholds. Ironic that it would be the failures of the heavily armed ships of the strongest navies in the world that would allow him, an unarmed civilian, to gain illegal entrance to the Castillo.

He was just past the halfway point up the wall when he noticed a flashlight beam in the distance. Glancing to his left, he saw that the park ranger had left his station and was beginning his rounds. Jon was past the point of no return, while Liz had just begun to climb, her feet only inches off the ground.

"Get down," he whispered as quietly as he could. Liz looked up and caught his gaze, which he redirected with a sharp look of his own toward the approaching ranger. Seeing the sentry, she slipped off the wall and took refuge behind the forge.

Satisfied that Liz wouldn't be climbing into the immediate line of fire, Jon scrambled up the rest of the wall. He reached the top and pulled himself over. The instant his feet disappeared over the edge, a flashlight beam played across where he had just been. Had the ranger seen him? Jon prayed for the guy to go away. The fort, like most historic buildings and sites throughout the city, was said to be haunted. Perhaps the ranger would just chalk it up to seeing things and move along on his route. Still, Jon remained in hiding, tempering his breathing as he waited for the danger to pass.

But the footsteps didn't continue on. From his hiding spot up high, Jon heard the man's tentative footsteps on the stone wall ringing the outside of the moat. The flashlight beam continued to dance below, occasionally breaching the top of the battlement where Jon's head would be if he had dared to peek over. He dared not. He hoped Liz was smart enough to stay quiet and hidden, especially if the ranger started circling the forge, forcing her to change her position. If not, it was all over. For both of them.

Finally, with a grunt that said *must have been seeing things*, the ranger moved on, continuing his patrol around the Castillo.

Thank God.

Once the sentry was around the corner, Jon peeped over the wall down at Liz. A sharp one, she was already starting to climb, wasting no time. A minute later, once she was in range, Jon reached down and grabbed her wrist, helping to pull her to safety.

They were in.

Chapter 52

The moonlight was a little too bright for Monk's liking as he advanced toward the Castillo de San Marcos. He preferred the darkness. It had shielded his approach from unsuspecting victims or vigilant authorities on many occasions. Tonight, though, he didn't have the luxury of choice. Jon Rickner was in the process of stealing his prize. Moonlight or not, Monk had to finish this now.

He passed by the Old City Gates, looking so much different than they had less than a dozen hours earlier. It wasn't just the deep shadowy crags cast by the stark moonlight in the otherwise black night. His perspective had changed. He had been so buoyant and sure of himself and his plan when passing through the gates that morning. Then everything had gone sideways. The cops were on his tail, the Rickner brothers had managed to acquire all four pieces of the cross, and while he should be sailing into the Caribbean with untold millions in lost treasure, he was still playing catch-up.

All that was about to change.

Michael Rickner was in police custody, out of the picture for the duration. Meanwhile, Jon and Liz were pursuing the treasure. But they were trapped. If they were already in the Castillo, there was no way they were getting out of there with the treasure. Monk would make sure of that.

Miriam Caan walked at his side. No words passed between them. None needed to be said. She had said plenty in the few minutes after leaving Flagler College. Now all that remained was to finish what he had started.

They crossed Avenida Menéndez and started up the slope surrounding the fort. A ghost tour, led by a young man in colonial clothing and leading the way with a lantern, passed nearby. But its participants were more interested in specters from the past than with any non-supernatural beings walking toward the Castillo. Monk himself was interested in both—the secret treasury of the long-dead Admiral Menéndez and the soon-to-be-dead Jon Rickner.

Halfway up the slope, Miriam broke off. She would remain outside playing lookout, ensuring his reclamation of everything he had worked for would not be interrupted.

A moment later, Monk dropped to the ground. A guard, perhaps a park ranger, was walking around the corner of the Castillo. Of course, this was public ground. It was only the Castillo itself that was off limits at night. Still, he didn't want to raise any red flags. He waited until the guard was around the corner again before continuing his ascent.

When he reached the edge of the moat, he readied the grappling hook he had retrieved from his Explorer. Building momentum by swinging the hook in a circle at his side, he tossed it over the wall, gripping the rope's end in his other hand. When it was over, he yanked back on the rope, trying to prevent too much distance between the hook and its eventual purchase on the far side of the wall. The longer he had to pull on the rope, the longer he was standing there exposed, waiting for the guard's next round to catch him in the act.

Unfortunately, he had yanked back too soon. The hook hit the edge of the battlements with a *tink* before sailing back toward him. Hand over hand, Monk gathered up the play in the rope, hoping to prevent the hook from hitting the ground with a *thunk*. The hook was coming back too fast, the rope doubling back and not offering enough easy grabs for Monk to pull in the slack. So he went straight to the source. Dropping the rope entirely, he leapt for the hook, snagging the rope just inches below its attached eyebolt and arresting its fall.

Monk took a deep breath, calming his nerves and listening for any change in the cadence of the guard's footsteps. He heard none. Readjusting the rope, he prepared for another attempt, swinging the hook again. He couldn't afford another misthrow. With a clench of his jaw, he tossed the hook. Feeling the rope play out through his hands, he waited a split second longer than he felt he should, erring the other way this time. Then he yanked back, prepared to catch the hook again if this attempt should also fail.

He felt the resistance as the barbs of the hook bit into the malleable coquina wall. Grinning in the moonlight, he gathered in the slack, looping it around his waist. Now at the base of the wall, he tugged twice on the rope. It held. With one foot on the ground, he tested the rope with most of his weight. The purchase was solid. He was good to go.

Monk gripped the rope and put his right foot on the wall. And he began to climb.

Chapter 53

She really is beautiful, Jon thought as pale beams of moonlight illuminated Liz's face. He thought back to the Indiana Jones movies he had always loved growing up. He had never cared for *Temple of Doom*'s Willie Scott, but *Raiders of the Lost Ark*'s Marion Ravenwood had been an enduring character, one Indiana seemed to have good chemistry with. Spielberg had even brought her back for the poorly received sequel in 2008. The aliens angle may have been stupid and hackneyed, but at least Indiana and Marion's chemistry remained. Who knew, perhaps after finding their own lost treasure tonight, something might happen between him and Liz.

"Why are you looking at me like that?" Liz whispered as they finished climbing down the stairs to the central courtyard.

"What?" Jon hadn't been prepared for being caught staring. "Nothing. I'm just... You're really pretty."

Liz looked away, Jon catching sight of a bashful half grin as she turned. But when she turned back, there was a sadness in her eyes. Hard to see if you weren't looking, but Jon was.

"Thanks."

That's it? Jon thought. *That's all I get?* A dead end if he'd ever seen one. And yet, considering all that was going on right now, with her uncle's murder, her father's recent death, being pursued by the police and a pair of mad treasure hunters, and the presence of a long-lost treasury hidden somewhere nearby, he could understand if romance wasn't exactly on her mind. Unless the sadness he had noticed was because she preferred a different Rickner. One who was currently in custody.

Jon smiled back, his way of closing the subject until she wanted to open it again. It wasn't every day you met a woman who could keep up with the exploits of him and his brother. But then, it wasn't every day you encountered the prospect of a centuries-old treasure buried in the middle of a national historic landmark. There were bigger things afoot than romance. When they got out of this—if they got out of this—there would be plenty of time for that later.

"Where do we start looking?" Liz said. "Hundreds of people tromp through here every day. If it were obvious, it would have been found a long time ago."

"There's more to the clue."

Liz looked taken aback. "Why didn't you tell me before?"

"Because it wouldn't have done us any good before we got in here. I still don't know what all of it means."

"Fine. What's the rest of the clue?"

"Deep in the bowels of the fortress of God, in the place where daylight never touches, a chamber beneath the floor revealed— López, Menéndez, Fontainebleau, Buckingham."

"You lost me there at the end."

Jon easily conceded the point. "I have no idea, either. But as for the first part, it seems clear that the middle of the courtyard is about as far as we can get from the hiding place. We need to go deeper into the fort, somewhere that 'daylight never touches.'"

"Like a dungeon?"

He smiled. "Like a dungeon."

Jon knew the fort had a dungeon that had held a number of key historical figures throughout the centuries. Perhaps the most famous had been Chief Osceola, the leader of the Seminole tribe in Florida, who had been captured in 1837 while trying to engage in peace talks during the Second Seminole War. The Castillo had been renamed Fort Marion during the early American period, and it had been seized by the Union Army during the Civil War and used as a garrison, all that after nearly two centuries of being used by the Spanish and the British as a military fortress.

In the center of the courtyard, near the old cistern, was a sign with a diagram of the fortress, complete with a floor plan and a few historical tidbits about the Castillo. At the northeast corner was the old armory, with a small unlabeled room tucked off to one side. Jon studied the map once more, looking for another room sufficiently devoid of sunlight and tucked into the "bowels of the fortress." Nothing fit the description better.

"Here's my question," Liz whispered as they headed toward the armory. "This fort wasn't built until 1670, more than a century after Menéndez founded St. Augustine and decades after his death. How did they know where to build the armory?"

"The cross," Jon said after thinking a moment. "We, like Henry Flagler before us, see the cross as a treasure map, but for the builders of the fort, it must have been more like a blueprint. Perhaps the treasure was already buried here, and they just built the fort around it. Or perhaps trusted representatives from the mission and the admiralty moved the treasure here afterward. Regardless, it could work."

"Then why didn't they take it with them when they turned the fort over to the British? Or later on, when the Americans took over?"

Jon shrugged. "Maybe they had forgotten it existed. Nearly a century passed between the Castillo's construction and the British takeover. Everyone involved in the construction of the treasury would have been dead. Plus, maybe the Spanish saw the writing on the wall when it came to the British colonies in America. Within a decade, the Castillo would return to Spanish hands, and then by the time the United States took possession in 1821, more than one hundred and fifty years had passed since the treasury's construction."

"So it was simply forgotten."

"It would seem so. Or else we're doing all of this for nothing."

Liz winced. Jon knew the feeling. Even though this morning neither of them knew a thing about this treasury, after all they had been through, finding out it had been all for naught would have been a gut shot. Plus, Liz had lost far too much already to this mystery. Coming up snake eyes would have been an even more devastating blow. He needed to stay optimistic. He owed her that much.

"But if it had been found, there would definitely be something about it in the records. A find of that magnitude would have been huge."

She brightened a bit. "It still will be."

"It certainly will be," Jon said with an assuring grin.

They ducked through the shadowy entrance of the armory, an array of dormant movie screens and glass display cases scattered throughout, showcasing artifacts and drawings illustrating the room's previous use. The barrel-vaulted ceiling rose high overhead, with powder kegs—long ago emptied of their explosive contents—clustered against the far wall. Jon remembered being here on his last visit, nearly a decade ago. He turned to his left, where the extra room should have been. Deep in the far corner was a narrow passage just a few feet in height. He and Michael had crawled through that hole into a tiny room, isolated from the world. Jon wasn't a big fan of enclosed places, but being in that ancient chamber, cut off from the sights and sounds of the world with his big brother, was an intriguing feeling. It felt like their dominion. Little did he realize that beneath their feet might have rested a vast treasure beyond their wildest imaginations. Now he was going to find out just how deep their make-believe kingdom went.

"Through here," he said as he got on his hands and knees in front of the hole. Unlike during the day, the room beyond was pitch-black, the lights turned off once the last employee had left for the night. He would rectify that once he got through, but maneuvering the tiny passageway would be even more difficult while trying to wield a flashlight.

"Are you sure?" Liz said from behind him.

"We'll find out soon enough. Come on."

The park service had added padding to the top of the tiny tunnel, helping to dampen the effects whenever visitors inevitably banged their heads on the low ceiling. Unfortunately, it also served to shrink the already tight aperture, but after a few struggling moments, Jon got through.

He used the penlight on his keychain to illuminate the small room. It was barrel-vaulted, perhaps twelve feet by eight with the ceiling no more than seven feet high at the apex. The room had originally been used as a dungeon, though later in its history, Jon remembered, it had been used to dump refuse. He didn't understand the benefits of moving trash into the one room with absolutely no ventilation, but then these were seventeenth-century soldiers, not modern-day scientists. They likely just wanted it out of their way, which this room certainly was. It likely also had the long-term benefit of keeping people out of the room, including the British once they had first taken over.

The treasure was here. He could feel it. He tried to brush away niggling doubts that it was just his boyhood enthusiasm returning in these familiar surroundings, choosing instead to focus on everything that had led him to this point. The Flagler hunt had been real. He had to believe the Menéndez treasury was also real.

"Wow," Liz said as she squeezed through the opening and into the room. "I'd say this fits the bill for being deep in the fortress's bowels where daylight never touches."

"No doubt about it. The question is, what to do with those last four words."

"It must be some sort of a key to open the secret chamber. But I don't see any combination locks or secret bookcases or anything."

Jon painted the floor and walls with his flashlight beam, looking for something that could be used as an access mechanism, something functional while still remaining hidden for the better part of four centuries.

And then he saw it. On the ceiling, in roughly the center of the room, what appeared to be a chessboard pattern of lighter and darker stones. To be fair, the full chamber—floor, ceiling, and the walls at both ends—was constructed of such stones. But it was the pattern in the center that drew his attention. Chessboard motifs were a popular European design element in the architecture of that time period, but this wasn't just a motif.

The grid in the center of the room was eight stones square. Exactly the same as an actual chessboard.

"It's a chessboard," he said, pointing to the ceiling. "The final words must refer to pieces on the board."

"So we have to figure out the chess pieces favored by Menéndez, López, and the rest?"

"I think its simpler than that. Think about chess pieces. The game has been evolving for more than a thousand years, but the basic rules we use today were pretty much set by the fifteenth century. The pieces as they're known today are pawn, knight, bishop, rook, queen, and king."

"Fine, but that doesn't help figure out which one means which."

Jon heard a sound outside, distant but distinct, like metal glancing off stone. Like they were about to have company. He hoped he was wrong, but they'd need to hurry regardless.

"Let's just try this. We've got four names, four pieces, right? Menéndez would likely be the knight, López the bishop."

"But there's four of each on a chessboard. Which one is the right one?"

Liz was right. Trial and error on just those two pieces would increase their potential attempts sixteenfold. And if his instincts were right and someone was trying to crash their party, they couldn't afford to trial-and-error their way in.

"They saw themselves as the good guys, so let's say they're both white ones."

"Right side or left side?"

Jon thought for a moment. "They saw themselves as being loyal king's men, if not to King Philip then at least to the King of Kings. So, king's side. Left side."

"Okay, and the last two. Fontainebleau and Buckingham. Both castles. So rooks."

"And both enemies of Spain, besieged with Protestant heresies. So they would be black pieces."

"Which one first?"

"We'll have to try them both," Jon said. "It's only two combinations. If one doesn't work, we try the other."

About a foot taller than Liz, Jon took the helm for actually pushing the stones. He pressed the starting space for the king's side white knight, then the space for the white bishop. Each stone gave slightly, registering a small click before returning to its initial position once Jon removed his hand.

He moved to the other side of the board and pressed the starting space for the king's side black rook, then the queen's side black rook.

Nothing happened.

He repeated the sequence, flipping the order of the black rooks this time. But again, nothing.

"Now what?" Liz moaned.

"We must have missed something." Then he heard it again. Metal on stone, though the sound took on a different tone this time. He hadn't imagined it after all. Someone was out there. He had to hurry.

"Maybe the castles don't refer to the castles themselves but to the royals who occupied them, kind of like how 'the White House' doing something usually refers to the current president or the administration. If Admiral Menéndez and Father López created this back in the early days of St. Augustine, the French king would have been Charles the Ninth. The British monarch would have been Queen Elizabeth."

Hope returned to Liz's countenance. "Which would completely get rid of the 'which castle first' guessing."

Jon nodded. "Black king. Black queen."

"Do it."

He pressed the stones in turn, praying that this would work. It was clear that something was hidden here, and that the chessboard was the mechanism for revealing it. But if this didn't work, he was fresh out of ideas. They were literally and figuratively at a dead end. He paused right before pressing the black queen.

"Here goes nothing," he said with a grin at Liz.

He pushed the stone.

And the floor began to move.

Chapter 54

Audrey Yang could see the change come over the young man before her the instant she finished speaking. Previously, Michael Rickner had been defiantly stubborn about his brother's whereabouts. That was long gone now.

"We need to go. Now."

"Go where, Michael?"

"I need to go with you. Trust me, this is a lot more complicated than just a police case. This goes back hundreds of years."

"Henry Flagler's treasure hunt?"

Michael shook his head, though his eyes shone with surprised recognition. "Even older. Centuries older."

"Details, Michael. I need details."

"You'll get them on the way. But my brother needs me. And he needs you. Come on, detective, you know we're the lesser of two evils here. Work with me to help me finish this. Believe me, in the next hour, these few acts of vandalism will pale in comparison to the magnitude of what my brother is probably discovering right now. Help us give it back to the people. Otherwise, Caeden Monk will steal it for good and kill my brother, and the treasure will be lost forever."

"Treasure?" Yang asked, cautiously intrigued. "Actual treasure?"

Michael smiled. "The largest treasure hoard in decades. You'll be famous."

That hit home, though she tried to conceal her reaction. Finally, perhaps she had found a way to make a name for herself, though not quite in the way she had imagined. Uncovering long-forgotten treasure wasn't exactly how she had envisioned breaking her first major case, but it would certainly do the trick. And nabbing Caeden Monk on murder and arson charges, coupled with all the outstanding Interpol warrants for him and Miriam Caan, would definitely get the FBI's attention.

But more than that, she felt it was the right thing to do. Some of her colleagues would likely fight her on the way out, but if she had listened to them instead of her instincts, they wouldn't be anywhere near solving the murder, the arson, or the vandalisms, much less what Michael said was happening right now. Her mother's voice had gone silent. Her father's reassuring presence dominated her mind. No matter what protocol said, this was the right thing to do.

"How's your leg?" she asked.

"It hurts, but the bullet went straight through. Missed all the important stuff, thank God. EMTs dressed the wounds, told me to take it easy for a while." He gave her a mischievous grin. "But I never was all that great at following directions."

"You'd better get real good at it real fast, Mr. Rickner. If we do this, you are under my supervision and you need to follow any order I give. Do you understand?"

Michael conceded, nodding solemnly. "I'm in."

"Good. Hang on a sec while I get you some crutches."

She went over to where the EMTs were packing up and requisitioned a loaner pair of crutches. On her way back to the table where Michael waited, Kyle Weiss intercepted her.

"So what did the Rickner kid give you?" he asked.

"He's about to give me the whole kit and caboodle. This thing's about to go down in spectacular fashion, so I need you and whoever else is available to be ready when I give the go-ahead."

"Yang, again, we've got cops scouring the city looking for these guys. I can't pull them all off on a hunch."

She stared him down. "None of this would have even been on their radars—or yours—if it weren't for me. I think I've earned a little benefit of the doubt here today, don't you?"

Weiss pursed his lips and nodded. "You're right. I'm sorry. I thought you were being a bad partner by running off on your own. But I should have listened more."

"All is forgiven. Just start making up for it now and be ready when I call. I'm taking Michael as a material witness."

Weiss nodded then headed across the room to begin mustering his troops. Yang went back to the table.

"Got you a little present," Yang said, holding the crutches out to Michael. "You ready for this?"

Michael took the crutches and stood, wobbling briefly as he got his balance. "Absolutely."

Chapter 55

It was beautiful. Even in the narrow beam of his penlight, Jon could see this discovery was one-of-a-kind. A treasure hoard to die for. To kill for.

The chessboard lock had released some sort of latch beneath the largest of the stones in the floor, angling it downward and allowing a sliding descent into the chamber beneath. Jon had gone down first, his feet landing on the coquina floor. The chamber was no more than seven feet in height, but it was filled to the brim with royal strongboxes and sea chests. Jon opened the chest closest to him. The clasp stuck momentarily, lightly fused by centuries of disuse, but he managed to free it and lift the lid.

The ancient container was stuffed with gold and silver doubloons, stamped with the crest of King Philip II, along with emeralds and other jewels mined from Central and South America. There had to be at least ten million dollars' worth of treasure in this chest alone. And there were dozens of them piled around the room.

Liz slid down behind him. She gasped as soon as she saw the glint of gold reflecting off his flashlight's beam.

"We did it," Jon said, grinning like an idiot. Throughout the years, he and Michael had made some fairly impressive discoveries, especially for amateur archeologists growing up under a professional's tutelage. But this undoubtedly took the cake.

He and Liz began to meander through the maze of stacked treasure chests, taking in the sheer magnitude of the wealth buried there. Jon had counted thirty chests so far. Some three hundred million dollars. But beyond the monetary value, the historical value, plus the impact that this chamber's existence would have on the historical record, was incredible.

As though to drive that point home, the next chest Jon came across was topped by a sheet of vellum. Jon crouched low to read it, trying to use indirect light from his penlight so as not to damage the old document.

It was a contract of sorts, an agreement between Admiral Menéndez and Father López to establish a treasury here in St. Augustine to be used for the promulgation of the Catholic faith throughout La Florida until Christ's return. This, more than any single coin or gem in the entirety of this chamber, was likely the most valuable treasure here from a historical standpoint. Though the contract wisely omitted any mention of the source of the funds, it wouldn't take researchers long to figure out which shipwrecked galleon these chests had been purloined from prior to setting forth on its final journey into the deep. Pedro Menéndez de Avilés, Captain-General of the Spanish Treasure Fleet and longtime respected friend and servant of King Philip II, had stolen a fortune from the crown to save his immortal soul. Yet no one in his lifetime was ever the wiser. For some reason, the treasury sat forgotten, never to be used for its purpose, lost to history and time.

Until now.

"We've got to get topside," Jon said. "Tell the ranger out there, the authorities, the press, the park service, nearby universities. This has got to be one of the biggest finds in the city's history. And it's going to belong to the world."

He heard something—grunting, shuffling—coming from above. He quickly gestured for Liz to hide before dousing his light and hiding himself.

Moments later, he saw a light up above. It grew brighter as its source, a flashlight, made its way down the entrance slope, held by a stranger. And then, once the newcomer's feet had hit the floor of the hidden chamber, he spoke.

"See, that's where you're wrong, Jon," Caeden Monk called into the darkness. "This treasure belongs to me."

Chapter 56

Miriam Caan had no intention of playing lookout for Monk. She did, however, intend to make her final play against him here at the Castillo. The treasure was here. Which meant her freedom was, too.

Once Monk was over the wall, she waited few more minutes for the park service ranger to make another pass. Then she made her move.

Monk wasn't the only one who knew how to use a grappling hook.

Hers was smaller, but the prongs were sharper, better for biting into the compressible coquina wall. Disguised in a handheld umbrella-case sleeve to hide it from an overly handsy Monk, the device required a simple button press to extend its prongs. Once she had readied it, she tossed it over the wall. The device caught the battlements and held firm.

First try, she commended herself. *Eat your heart out, Monk.*

After testing her weight and gently placing her feet against the wall to prevent their slapping against the surface and drawing the guard's attention, she began to climb. Hand over hand, feet pressing softly against the coquina surface, she ascended to the top in a matter of seconds.

Once over the wall, she crouched between a pair of cannons to survey the courtyard. Down below, she saw the briefest trace of a light coming from the armory before it was snuffed out altogether.

Monk. He must have made it into the treasury. But he wouldn't make it out.

Three steps left. Kill Monk and any witnesses. Steal the treasure. And disappear.

Forever.

Chapter 57

Jon was trapped. Monk was between him and the only exit, one only the people in this room—and hopefully Michael—knew about. But perhaps that could be remedied.

"This really is something," Monk said, his voice sending shivers down Jon's spine. "For centuries, history forgot about this hidden fortune, just waiting to be discovered beneath St. Augustine's most famous landmark. And now, I have discovered it."

This guy was nuts. What part of this did he really think was *his* discovery? Was he really that full of his own self-importance that he deluded himself into forgetting that it had been Jon, Michael, and Liz that had discovered the Edison cylinder, every piece of the cross, and Menéndez's treasure?

"Yeah, thanks so much for all your help," Jon said, shouting to his right while he edged to his left. He kept low, using the stacked sea chests as cover. Monk's flashlight beam arced overhead, scanning the room for Jon and Liz. Presumably to put a bullet in their heads.

But if Jon could throw him off his location, if he could draw him in while still keeping out of sight, perhaps Liz could escape and get the patrolling park ranger outside to call in the cavalry.

It was a long shot, but the only one he had right now.

"Remind me again of what, exactly, you did to find this?" Jon said. Monk's ego, it seemed, could be his weak point. If he could prod him into doing something stupid, it could create the opening Liz needed to escape. "Because the way I see it, of everyone in the entire world, even some kid sitting at home in Bangladesh who's never even heard of Florida, you deserve the absolute *least* credit for this find."

"You shut your mouth," Monk said, the flashlight sweeping overhead becoming more aggressive. Jon had hit a nerve. Time to press the attack.

"I mean, obviously it was me, my brother, and Liz who discovered this treasure. Meanwhile, you actively got in our way all day, threatening us at Ripley's, kidnapping Michael and Liz at Memorial Presbyterian, and trying to kill us all back in the dining hall at Flagler. Heck, if not for all your interference, this discovery would already be getting catalogued and studied. Our day in the sun as archeological heroes would be just beginning, with the press and the public hailing our incomparable contribution to scholarship and world culture. We'd have a parade in our honor, with universities across the globe wanting to give us tenured positions. The president would give us medals, and history would remember us forever."

"No," Monk said through gritted teeth. "This discovery is mine."

His voice was closer now. Jon continued creeping back, deeper into the chamber, away from the exit door that he hoped Liz was about to reach, if she hadn't already. The only light he had to go on was reflected from Monk's flashlight. He squinted into a maze of deep shadows and shifting perspectives as the light source continued to dance around overhead. He didn't know how far back this chamber went, but eventually, he would run out of space. And if Liz wasn't back with some help by the time that happened, it was all over.

"Is it?" Jon gibed. "Gosh, I must be getting forgetful in my old age. See what *I* thought happened was that Liz and I found the secret entrance and were exploring this here treasure chamber long before you ever showed up. So how's that going to play out with your big discovery when some reporter throws a microphone in front of me?"

Jon heard a click. He looked up. Just a few inches away, a gun barrel was pointed at his head. Then the flashlight beam angled down into his face and Monk's smug mug appeared over the stack of sea chests.

"I don't foresee that being a problem at all," Monk said. "Reporters don't interview dead men."

Chapter 58

Caeden Monk couldn't believe his luck. The treasury was the motherlode in every conceivable way. The monetary value of the loot hidden here had to be deep into nine figures. Even with the ridiculously extravagant lifestyle he planned to enjoy after this, he would be set for several lifetimes.

But even more impressive was what a huge find this was from a historical perspective. The king's most trusted admiral, betraying him to steal a fortune *and* destroy a perfectly good galleon? That was some ballsy treason right there, especially considering how, later in his life, Menéndez would continually entreat King Philip for the promised reward for all his efforts in Florida.

Of course, Menéndez hadn't stolen this treasure for himself. He stole it for God. But now Monk would steal it for himself.

What the Rickner kid quivering in the sights of his pistol clearly didn't realize was that it was he and his brother who were the interlopers. Monk may have slit a few throats to acquire the information that led him to St. Augustine today, but that was the cost of admission to the high-stakes table. There was a reason that this chamber had sat undiscovered for centuries, all while three of the mightiest nations on earth patrolled above, completely unaware. It had taken his ingenuity and his lack of scruples to cut through the deception to find Menéndez's secret hoard, an ill-gotten offering to the Almighty. The discovery was his. All the Rickner brothers had done was burst in at the last minute and try to destroy what he had worked for. To take the credit for what was his. Years earlier, Ted Karlsson had experienced the terrible consequences of trying to steal credit for Caeden Monk's discoveries in Turkey. Now Jonathan Rickner would be the first to die for this latest slight against Monk's superlative abilities.

After he got the treasure out of there, he would disappear. Something this big was too much to trust with anyone. Including Miriam. He would kill the Rickner brothers and Liz, then fake Miriam's suicide with the same gun. Four birds, one stone. Drawn by the stench of decomposition, investigators would eventually find an empty hidden chamber beneath the Castillo, causing the archaeological community to wonder about the new discovery. Monk would sell off most of his treasure, allowing him to live out his days in luxury, but he would keep some of it. Enough to gloat. Enough to remember.

But most important, he would document everything. Take photos of the enormity of the find, perhaps the most incredible discovery in a generation. And then, once it was all gone, he'd send the photos to Cornell and Ankara, to every university and institution that spurned him since his fall from grace. They needed to know what their hubris had wrought: the loss of a discovery of untold historic impact. And untold it would remain. Those responsible for the destruction of his academic career would learn that the greatest victim of their actions was history itself. And that would be on their heads.

They had made him suffer. Now they would reap the poisonous fruit of their actions.

But first things first. Jonathan Rickner had to die.

Gun in his scowling face, Jon slowly stood from his hiding place. Defiant to the end, even though he was visibly shaking.

Brave son of a gun, Monk would give him that. Brave, but stupid.

"You think a gunshot isn't going to be heard out there?" Jon said. "By all those tourists hanging out by the water or the ghost tours walking just outside? You shoot me and you won't get out of here alive. There are cops everywhere looking for you. One shot, and you may as well slap a GPS tracker on your wrist and send them the coordinates. It'll be over."

"Good try," Monk said with a mocking grin. "We're underground, surrounded by several feet of absorbent coquina and earth on every side. Even if someone did think they heard something like a gunshot, no one would be able to pinpoint its origin. The Castillo's closed for the night, Jon. Everyone knows that."

He started to tighten his finger on the trigger. The gun blast would be deafening, but only within the stone echo chamber. It was a necessary sacrifice, though. One hand held the flashlight, the other the pistol. At this point, any effort to add some sort of ear protection would give Jon an opportunity to bolt. And that was not an option.

He heard movement behind him an instant before he pulled the trigger. The explosion was even louder than he'd expected, the flash of light brighter than the sun.

But the pain. He hadn't expected the pain. He put his hand to the epicenter of the agony, just below his left breast. His hand came away sticky and wet.

That's not supposed to happen, Monk thought.

With a staggering, torturous step, he pivoted back toward the entrance, where the sound of movement had come from. He stumbled onto a stack of sea chests, knocking the top one to the floor in a shimmering cascade of purloined doubloons. His strength was quickly leaving him, but he was able to angle his flashlight up to see the face of his attacker.

So much hate in those eyes. Eyes he definitely recognized.

He slipped inexorably toward death, tormented to the end by the enormity of Miriam's betrayal.

Chapter 59

Jon dropped to the cold stone floor at the sound of the gun blast. He had been bluffing about someone outside hearing, but he hoped that someone had. Two stacks down from his hiding spot, a full sea chest toppled over, spilling its valuable contents on the floor with an audible splash of precious metal. Monk murmured something indecipherable from the other side of the wall of sea chests. Two more gunshots ended Monk's attempts at speech, replaced by a long groaning rasp.

A death rattle. Someone had just killed Caeden Monk.

The cop? No, she would have announced herself, doing that whole "drop your weapon or I'll drop you" bit. Seconds passed, and still the newcomer had not identified him- or herself. Footsteps, though, were drawing near, carefully snaking their way around the maze of treasure chests. Toward him.

Time to move.

Striving for a balance between speed and silence, Jon slinked farther back into the chamber, feeling his way through the dark labyrinth of forgotten loot.

It had to be the sniper from the balcony back at Flagler College. She must have double-crossed her partner, killing Monk so she could take the treasure for herself. Perhaps it was more than that, though. She had seemed especially anxious for him to reveal the final clue and hand over the collected cross pieces before Monk arrived. Maybe she was planning an end run back then, and when that failed to come together in time, she fell back on this as her Plan B. Now Jon and possibly Liz were witnesses not only to the treasure, but also to her murdering Monk. So they were likely next on her hit list. He only hoped that Liz had managed to get to the ranger outside the Castillo's walls prior to the sniper slipping in.

The intruder continued to move deeper into the chamber, though her footsteps—assuming it was the sniper who had joined their little subterranean party—were veering slightly to the right. Had she lost his scent? Or was she simply maneuvering through the maze to get to him? With a weapon and an illuminated flashlight, she had the upper hand. But if Liz showed up with the ranger in tow, that could change the odds in his favor very quickly.

"Give it up, Jon," the intruder said. "It's over. You've lost."

Jon froze. He did recognize her voice. Though he wished to God he didn't.

Against his better judgment, shocked into submission by the gravity of what had just transpired, Jon rose from his hiding place. She smiled, making the whole thing even worse. The pistol that had killed Caeden Monk was pointed at his chest, her hands remarkably steady for someone who had just murdered a man in cold blood. And that scared him all the more.

"I'm sorry it has to end this way," Liz said.

Stunned out of all his normal eloquence, all Jon could say in reply was, "Me too."

Chapter 60

Was this really how it ended? It wasn't the first time he had faced a gun in the past twelve hours. In fact, not counting the pursuing cops at Flagler College, Jon had stared down the barrel of a gun no less than five times since his first standoff with Monk at Ripley's late that morning. But this one hurt the worst. There was more than anger, vengeance, or "just business" behind this time. Liz's betrayal changed everything.

"Look, you want the treasure, take it," Jon said, getting his wits about him again. "I was just trying to help you after your uncle's murder. And you got the guy. But for the love of God, I'm on your side, Liz. Put the gun away and we can talk this though."

Liz laughed derisively. "I wish it were that simple. I really do. But I'm a murderer now, Jon. And I can't be looking over my shoulder for when your conscience gets the better of you and you send the authorities my way. This is my chance for a new life. And no matter how much I might genuinely like you, I can't let you screw this up for me."

"Liz, listen. I'm not going to tell anyone." It was an easy shot from this distance. He was half blinded by her flashlight beam, but he could still see the gun trained on him. He did his best to keep the fear out of his voice, but there was no doubt this one was shaking him worse than all the others. Every other time he'd had a gun in his face today, he'd had his friends with him. Michael had been with him at Ripley's and at Flagler, then he'd faced Monk with what he had thought had been his friend Liz. Now, not only had Liz turned against him—and apparently hidden a gun on her person all day—but he was facing her alone in a room that no one else knew existed, deep in the bowels of the earth.

There was no way out of this.

Though, maybe, putting his strongest face forward was the wrong play here. She may have fooled him some, but there was something there, some amiable bond of friendship, if only in its infancy. He had helped her out of several death-defying binds today. In all but the most sociopathic, that tended to engender some sort of loyalty in people. Even if Liz was suppressing the sentiment right now, he was sure it was there, somewhere. He just needed to draw it out.

"I... I thought we were friends, Liz," he said, allowing a slight but very real quiver into his voice. "I tried to help save your uncle's life, and ever since, I've been trying to help you honor his memory by fulfilling his last wish to stop Monk from getting this treasure."

"And I appreciate that, Jon. I really do. But she says this is how it has to be."

Jon furrowed his brow and stared past the blinding light at where he assumed Liz's face to be. "Who is 'she'?"

Liz didn't answer. She seemed as entranced as he was at the sounds coming from above the entrance a dozen yards to his left.

Please be the cavalry, please be the cavalry.

Moments later, a lithe form slid down the entry ramp. His hopes were quickly dashed as Liz's flashlight flicked over the newcomer's face.

The sniper from the balcony.

"Miriam!" Liz said. "You made it."

Chapter 61

The treasure chamber was a wonder to behold. Not just because it was the most astounding discovery Miriam Caan had ever been part of, but also because it was her ticket to freedom.

"Oh my," she said. "This is incredible."

Her sister, Esther, approached from the dark recesses of the chamber, her flashlight bobbing with her footsteps. It had been hard to send her into harm's way undercover as Bouvier's fictional niece, but she needed an edge on Monk. He had never met Esther, and he, like the Rickner brothers who had stumbled into their twisted little game, was fooled by the deception.

Miriam shone her flashlight at the ground. "You killed him already?"

"I had to. He would have shot me."

"And yet this looks like a shot from behind."

"Jon provided cover. I... I couldn't have done it without him. We'd both be dead if Jon hadn't sacrificed himself as a diversion so I could get a clear shot on Monk."

"That's sweet." Miriam's voice was faintly mocking. Then she checked herself. Esther was nearly a decade younger than she was and hadn't left a trail of bodies across five continents over the past four years. She may have just killed a man, but compared to what Miriam had done, Esther was as innocent as a newborn fawn.

Miriam smiled at her sister. "Well-done. I would have loved to have finished off the beast myself, though."

"I'm sorry."

"Don't be." Miriam looked at the body of her tormentor, the man for whom she'd thrown away her promising career in academia, then had kept her in a prison of fear and manipulation ever since.

All that was over now. But instead of keeping Esther far away from the life Miriam was trying to leave, she had only served to drag her right down into the muck with her. She had turned her sister into a vandal, a thief, a murderer.

She kicked Monk's corpse, its death grimace seeming to mock her. It felt good, but not as good as she'd hoped. She kicked him again and again, before finally falling to her knees to whale on him with her fists, growling invectives at this man who had directly and indirectly ruined not only her life, but also her sister's. Then she crumpled to one side, away from the body, breathing hard and heaving long-repressed sobs.

Esther ran to her, rubbing the space between her shoulder blades and shushing her softly. It should have been Miriam comforting her sister, not the other way around. Perhaps her baby sister was stronger than she'd given her credit for. But Miriam still needed to protect her from the ghosts she had dug up over the years. They had to disappear into a new life together. And now, with a fresh body on American soil, their time had come.

Just one final loose end to tie off.

"Did you kill Jon as well?" Miriam asked.

"Yes."

"Good. Where's his body?"

"Somewhere in that mess, I don't know. Let's just grab what we need and get out of here before the cops show up."

Miriam humphed. "The cops know nothing about this place. Once we get our treasure out, we can close that trapdoor and no one will ever know about what happened here. But you're new to this, Esther. And I hope you never have to do this again. It's the kind of life I wanted to keep you from, and now we finally can start afresh. But I need to see Jon's body. I need to make sure. A dead man won't attract any attention down here. A living one who can yell for attention and shout out the method for opening the secret entrance again would. So again, where is his body?"

Esther was silent. But her eyes said plenty.

"Esther, you forget I'm your big sister. I know when you're lying. He's not dead yet, is he?"

"No," Esther said after a brief pause.

"That's fine. You've already done more killing than I ever wanted you to, and for that, I'm deeply sorry. I can finish this."

"Please, don't. He's... he's my friend."

"You just met him this morning. How close can you really be?"

"Close enough to know he's a good person. He doesn't deserve to die."

Miriam smiled paternally at her sister. "It's not about whether or not he deserves to die. It's about what he can do to us, what he knows. Do you want to spend the rest of your life in prison? Or worse, the electric chair?"

A crack in the facade. Esther's fear started to leech through. "No, of course not."

Miriam heard shuffling deep within the chamber. Her quarry was on the move. She started toward the sound, gun at the ready.

"Then this needs to happen," she said, leading the way farther into the chamber. "In order for us to live free, Jon has to die. I'm sorry, Esther, but there's no other way."

Chapter 62

Through the windshield, the Castillo loomed like an ancient sentinel, a hulking relic perched on the hill overlooking the harbor. It was the oldest stone masonry fort in the United States, full of history, legend, and secrets. Michael couldn't get there fast enough.

Detective Yang pulled the police cruiser to the curb and helped Michael out of the back. Once he was adjusted with his crutches, they headed up the path toward the entrance to the Castillo.

He still couldn't believe what Yang had told him. Liz wasn't Liz at all. Liz Bouvier didn't exist. Tristan Bouvier's son had confirmed it after they'd contacted him as the man's next of kin. The woman they had been running around town with, the one who had convinced them not to call the police, who had initiated their wave of vandalism by ripping the first piece of the cross from the altar at Grace Methodist and finished it by smashing the priceless onyx clock, she was a fraud. Everything about her—from their chance meeting in the bookshop inferno to her sob story about her uncle and her very name—was a lie.

The woman they had known and trusted as Liz Bouvier was nothing but an impostor with her own devious agenda. Which meant Jon was absolutely alone, somewhere in the bowels of the Castillo, the only ally he thought he had likely working with the enemy. An enemy who might already be in the fort with him. Michael prayed that Monk hadn't already killed Jon. If they were too late, if he had lost his brother forever...

Yang rapped on the window of the National Park Service hut just outside the entrance to the Castillo. During the day, it served as an information booth and ticket counter for tourists visiting the fort. At night, it was the headquarters of the park ranger working night guard duty.

And, apparently, he was missing.

Another knock brought the same lack of response from within. A light illuminated the back room, but there was no other sign of life. Perhaps he was out on patrol. Still, they needed him. Now.

Yang keyed her radio. "Dispatch, I need the cell number or radio frequency for the ranger on duty at the Castillo tonight."

"Let me check on that for you," the dispatcher replied.

A moment passed before Yang radioed back. "Cancel that request for ranger contact info, dispatch."

Michael followed Yang's line of sight to the lanky young man in park-service beige rounding the corner of the Castillo. He was running.

"You got here in a hurry," he said once he was within earshot, bright eyes burning above a bushy hipster beard.

Not sure what to make of that comment, Yang introduced herself.

"Zach Latham," the ranger said in turn with a perfunctory handshake before unlocking the hut and disappearing inside. A moment later, a mechanical whirring and grinding from the Castillo signaled the drawbridge being lowered. Latham emerged from the hut with keys in hand.

"Hang on a minute," Yang said. "You were expecting us? Did a Detective Weiss call ahead?"

Latham glanced at her as he led the way toward the front gate of the fort. "No. You didn't hear the shots?"

Michael's heart dropped. Were they already too late? Had Monk or one of his cronies killed his brother?

Yang gave Michael a sideways glance. "No. We're here because we think there might be something buried underneath the Castillo. Something very valuable. And there are some murderers who are of the same mindset."

The drawbridge was taking its sweet time lowering. Normally, Michael might speculate on all the soldiers, prisoners, dignitaries, and slaves who had entered through this gate throughout the centuries. How, in ages past, the bridge would have been lowered by hand, the gate guards using pulleys to offset the enormous weight of the heavy wooden bridge, rather than the machine-powered apparatus that was now artificially delaying their entry into the fort. But right now, all he could think about was Jon. And what a horrible place the world would be if he were dead.

"Well, we'd better hurry," Latham said. "It sounds like someone's already in there. And they've found a reason to start shooting."

Chapter 63

Jon's mind raced through his options, which were few and narrowing fast. Miriam and Esther Caan were between him and the only exit, the retractable ramp four feet off the ground that led back into the Castillo's dungeon. He knew the general direction of the ramp, but in the dark, he had little hope of finding it. He still had his penlight, but using it would provide an easy target for the Caan sisters to shoot him.

Use the flashlight and die. Run for the exit, get lost in the dark, and die. Or stay put, continuing to hide, and, eventually, when they find him or when they give up and seal him inside, die.

Not his dream set of options.

He could hear their footsteps. They were moving through the maze of sea chests laden with millions upon millions in ancient booty, their flashlights sweeping across the stacks, looking for him. Daring him to peek his head above cover.

He wasn't that stupid. But they were getting closer. If he didn't make a decision soon, Esther and Miriam would make it for him.

One of their beams illuminated the top of the chest directly in front of him. He ducked down farther, his back pressed softly against the opposite stack. The sisters were still behind him, but judging by the size of the beam's core compared with its size when it hit the wall deeper into the chamber, they weren't far away. He had to make a break for it.

The trick would be to use the dim ancillary light reflected from the walls and ceiling to navigate his way through the labyrinth while avoiding the direct beams that would betray his position to the Caans. A tricky proposition, but it was the best chance he was going to get.

One of them was getting close. Slow, careful footsteps to his right. Heading straight for him.

He scurried to his left, keeping below the treasure chests blocking the sisters' lines of sight. Reaching a T-junction, he went left toward the entrance. He was making too much noise. Quiet as he was, there was no ambient noise to occlude his movements in this tomb-like, underground chamber. Even if he kept out of sight, the sisters would find him by echolocation.

As if the cosmos were trying to prove his point, one of the flashlight beams struck a chest just inches from his head. He held his breath. *Be invisible.*

A moment later, the beam moved away. Jon let loose a long, measured exhalation of relief. He wasn't going to get out of here like this. He needed a distraction.

The chest nearest him was ajar, the ghostly reflections of forgotten doubloons beckoning to him from within. As silently as possible, he plucked a handful of coins from the chest, one at a time so they wouldn't clink together. He edged up, ever so slowly, to take better inventory of where the flashlight beams were coming from. Not far enough to actually see the sisters, for that would mean that they could also see him. But far enough to roughly estimate their positions. Satisfied that his plan wouldn't backfire, he retreated back to the T-junction and tossed the coins back toward his original position. The arc was low and fast, Jon aiming to keep the reflective doubloons out of the sisters' flashlight beams. The coins hit the floor with a satisfying series of clinks.

"He's over there!" Esther shouted from deeper in the chamber. A pair of gunshots immediately followed, the blasts even more terrifyingly loud in his new predicament. But instead of allowing the fear to arrest his movement, he bolted toward the exit, using the cacophony as audio cover while still keeping his body low.

It wasn't enough.

Footsteps, running back toward the exit. Trying to intercept him. It was a race now.

Then everything went black.

They had cut their flashlight beams. They were going to flush him out under cover of darkness. Or else force him to resort to using his own flashlight.

And worse, he was still caught in the maze, several rows still separating him from the exit.

Growing up, Jon had always loved classic puzzles and codes. One of the first puzzle types he had fallen in love with was the maze, most famously popularized by the Greek legend of Perseus trapped in the labyrinth of Crete with the Minotaur. While Perseus had managed to find his way out of the labyrinth by trailing a string along his path in a less edible and more effective version of the later Hansel and Gretel's bread crumbs, Jon had learned another useful method for getting out of mazes. Putting your hand on one wall and following that wall through the maze would most always lead you to the exit, depending on the construction of the labyrinth. At the very least, it would always lead you back to the entrance, and in this instance, they were one and the same. Not to mention, he had enough of an idea of where the entrance was before the lights went out that he felt confident that, given enough time, he could find the ramp in the dark.

Of course, time was not a luxury he could count on. And, of course, there was the matter of the gun-wielding sisters pursuing him. Still, he didn't have a choice. It was, quite literally, do or die. He chose the former.

One hand tracing the stack of chests to his left, the other outstretched in front of him to keep him from running into more chests, Jon began to move. The darkness no longer being an issue, he rose to a standing hunch, prepared to make himself small again should one of the sisters turn their light back on.

He made a left turn, following the stacks as they wended their way inexorably toward the entrance. It wasn't far now. But then, neither were the footsteps that were steadily zeroing in on his position.

Jon staggered and blinked as a light appeared immediately in front of him. In a split second, he took it all in. On the other side of a stacked set of sea chests, Miriam Caan held a flashlight in one hand and a pistol in the other. Both were pointed straight in Jon's face.

Even if he ducked now, he had no cover. She was close enough to the stack that his entire row was in her direct line of sight. Which only left one option.

Jon sped up.

Running straight toward Miriam, Jon hoped his unexpected response would cause her to hesitate. It did, but only for a moment.

Miriam fired the first shot just as Jon lunged feetfirst in a dropkick. The bullet tore through the air inches from his face. She adjusted her aim for a second shot. But she never got to take it.

Jon's feet slammed into the top sea chest in the stack directly in front of Miriam. Despite the immense weight of the treasure inside the chest, the impact was enough to have the desired result. The chest slid from the stack, tilted, and fell into Miriam, knocking her to the ground in a glittering explosion of gold and emeralds.

Jon jumped to his feet and ran through the final few turns of the maze, finally reaching the ramp. He pulled himself onto the ramp and clambered up into the dungeon. But Miriam and Esther could easily follow him. And in the moonlit armory and courtyard beyond, he didn't stand a chance of avoiding their bullets. He had to neutralize them.

Finally switching on his own flashlight, he looked at the chessboard on the ceiling. If it would open the secret chamber, it would have to close it as well, he surmised. He tried pressing the original sequence, then the original sequence in reverse.

Nothing.

Jon could hear the sound of shifting doubloons from below. Miriam was digging herself out. And Esther, unhindered, would also be on him in no time.

Starting to panic, he pressed random incorrect stones, from non-starting squares to the initial places of the pawns who, continuing the logic behind the clues that opened the treasury, worked for centuries patrolling this fort without realizing the priceless wonders that filled the secret vault below. Nothing worked. Until a term from his earlier conversation in this dungeon with Esther, back when she was still Liz to him, flashed back in his memory.

King's men. Menéndez's white knight and López's white bishop were both on the king's side of the board because of their loyalty to King Philip and to God. They would have wanted to keep the treasury a secret from King Philip while preserving it for God. Both entailed sealing the hidden entrance. And both entities were the same chess piece.

The white king.

Jon pressed the stone. The ramp began to move, angling back upward to seal off the entrance.

He sighed in relief, then ran over to the low tunnel to the armory.

"Stop."

He turned to see the face of the girl he'd so recently admired in the moonlight outside. Esther. Once again, she was aiming a pistol at him. But this time, she was down below in the soon-to-be-sealed treasury and he was up top.

"I'm sorry it has to end this way," Jon said.

She lowered the gun and gave him a sad smile. "Me too."

Then the ramp slid back into place, locking Esther and Miriam below.

Chapter 64

Jon listened to the shouts from within the chamber beneath his feet. They were muffled through the thick stone floor, but he could hear the unbridled fury in Miriam's voice. Liz was shouting, too, but it wasn't as vengeful. It was almost as though she was resigned to this horrible consequence for her actions.

Of course, Jon had no intention of just leaving them down there. He would go alert the police, and they would be able to arrest the Caan sisters. He hated that it had come to this, but there was no choice. Without his help, they'd die in there. And though part of him wanted to leave Miriam to that fate, he couldn't do that to Esther. Deception or not, he still felt some sort of loyalty to the Liz he thought he once knew.

The voices began to calm as the sisters realized the futility of their shouts. Soon enough they'd get their wish to be topside. Just with the added caveat of handcuffs.

Jon ducked through the low tunnel back to the armory, then raced out into the courtyard.

"Jon!"

Michael was hobbling through the high stone arch leading to the drawbridge entrance. The Asian cop was with him, as was the park ranger Jon had seen patrolling outside while he scaled the Castillo wall.

Jon raised his hands in surrender. He was technically trespassing on federal land, though his brother being here seemed to indicate they knew enough about Monk's activities, the Flagler hunt, and the Menéndez treasury that he wasn't about to be shot on sight. Still, it didn't hurt to be sure.

"Where's Monk?" the cop asked, her service pistol at the ready.

"Dead."

"Seriously?" Michael said. "And the Caan sisters?"

"You knew about Liz?" Jon asked.

"As of a few minutes ago when I told him," the cop said. "Where are they?"

"Sealed in the treasure chamber. I was running to get the police to apprehend them."

"So it's real?" Michael asked. "The treasure, it's still there?"

Jon beamed. "Oh yeah. It's very real."

The cop spoke into her radio. "Where's that backup, Weiss?"

"Be there in three," came the reply.

Michael used the moment to make quick introductions between his brother and his two companions, Detective Yang and Ranger Latham.

"So where is this secret treasury?" Yang asked.

"Beneath the dungeon," Jon said. "Through the armory."

"Show me." Yang turned to Latham. "You wait here and send my backup to the dungeon when they get here."

"Yes, ma'am," Latham said.

Jon led his brother and Yang through the armory and into the dungeon. The room felt even smaller with three people, though surely many more souls had unwillingly crowded its confines during its tenure as a cell.

"I've been in here before," Yang said. "Fourth grade trip to St. Augustine, we all came to the fort. Seems like it was bigger then."

Jon knew the feeling, not only of nostalgia occluding the true details of memories but also of forgetting to play tourist in your own hometown. The exchange student in Paris who never goes up in the Eiffel Tower. The international teacher on a multiyear adventure in Dubai who continually postpones skiing in a desert megamall until it's too late. Those big to-dos you always plan on doing but never get around to. Thankfully, throughout Jon's life, he'd been moving from place to place enough to always instill a sense of immediacy in his hometown du jour, but the phenomenon had reared its head a few key times.

"Other than that, it looks perfectly normal," Yang continued. "So how do we get in?"

Jon pointed to the chessboard pattern overhead. "Right here."

Yang and Michael squinted at the mechanism, hidden in plain sight for centuries.

"So they were chess pieces," Michael said. "Clever."

"Bishop, knight, king, and queen," Jon said as he pressed the first three stones in turn. Before he pressed the fourth, though, Yang put a hand on his arm.

"Hang on a sec. I hear my backup now."

Moments later, another detective, who introduced himself as Weiss, crawled into the increasingly cramped dungeon, with two patrol officers in tow.

"Now it's a party," Weiss said, eliciting a glare from his partner.

"Two suspects sealed below," Yang informed them. "Both armed and dangerous. Lethal force authorized if necessary, but shoot only to protect yourselves. We've got the only entrance covered here, so it's not like they're going anywhere."

After receiving affirmation from the other three cops, she nodded to Jon. With all four officers pointing their standard-issue Glocks at the floor panel he had pointed out, Jon pressed the final stone overhead.

The cops all started a bit when the floor began to move. For them, it was like something out of an Indiana Jones movie. For Jon and Michael, it wasn't the first time they'd uncovered a hidden passage or a secret entrance. But what lay on the other side was both far more valuable and far more deadly than was par for their course.

Jon half expected the Caans to start shooting from below once the entrance stone began to lower, killing their rescuers before they could be apprehended. But there was nothing. No shooting on either side. The sisters must have been hunkered down somewhere, looking for an opportunity to make their move and escape, just like Jon had been minutes earlier.

After identifying herself and her team as police officers to whoever might be listening downstairs, Yang led the charge into the treasure chamber below, followed by Weiss and one of the patrol cops. The other officer stayed topside, his weapon continually aimed at the secret entrance in case one or both of the Caan sisters should circumvent the three cops downstairs and try to make a break for it. He had instructed Jon and Michael to stand behind him, an order Jon reluctantly obeyed. He wanted to see what was going on, the climax to the day's adventures, finally apprehending the last living culprits in the death of the Rickners' family friend and the near-theft of perhaps the greatest conquistador treasures ever discovered.

Seconds dragged into minutes. No shots rang out from below, nor were any orders or threats shouted by cop or Caan. Had the sisters surrendered without a fight? Were they still hiding somewhere in the maze of treasure chests? Or, confronted with the possibility of a slow death by starvation and dehydration, had they resolved to hurry things along with a quick suicide pact?

"Don't shoot, Reilly," came a voice from below. "It's Yang. Coming up. The scene is secure."

Officer Reilly kept his weapon trained on the opening he confirmed that it was Detective Yang crawling the entrance ramp.

"Well?" Jon asked, ignoring Reilly's previous order and pushing ahead to Yang.

"You were right. Absolutely incredible. All that treasure, hidden away for all these years. The National Park Service, the Smithsonian, everyone's going to have a field day with this."

"What about the Caan sisters?"

Yang's face darkened, her lips pressed together. "They're gone."

Chapter 65

The sun was still hours from gracing the eastern horizon, yet Menéndez's long-forgotten treasury was abuzz with activity. Archeologists, historians, and preservationists from nearby universities, institutions, and the National Park Service had been roused from their homes, excitedly making this unexpected pilgrimage into the heart of the nation's oldest city. Crime-scene analysts had documented the relevant areas of the chamber before extracting the body of Caeden Monk, giving way to the crush of enthusiastic researchers diving into a virgin site of career-making historical importance.

And they were all there because of Jon and his brother. Jon was still taking it all in. Not only had they managed to discover one of the greatest treasures—literally and figuratively—in American history, but they had also prevented Caeden Monk and his cohorts from secreting it away from the world, chopping it up, and selling to the highest bidder. Now, the treasure would not only help shed new light on the earliest days of European settlements in North America, but it could also provide a beacon of inspiration for a generation so caught up in technology that it had lost sight of the allure of the past. Jon considered himself lucky that the mysteries of bygone eras had always fascinated him, owing largely to the unique circumstances of his parentage and upbringing. Hopefully this discovery would provide that same inspiration to innumerable more young people.

"It's incredible," Michael said. The Rickner brothers were standing to one side of the underground chamber, watching the hustle and bustle of leading experts rewriting history. "All this, hidden for centuries, right under the noses of the Spanish, British, and American militaries, countless tourists, and the National Park Service. All undiscovered. Until now."

"Flagler figured it out," Jon said. "Or at least enough of it to realize there was some very real treasure buried in the city he had just staked his reputation and fortune on transforming. News like that getting out could bring a very different demographic to his Deep South Riviera, set not on spending money at his hotels but on digging up his investments with pick and shovel."

"Makes sense. A shame, but still, the insanity of the gold rush was still fresh in Flagler's mind, as was the collapse of many a ghost town shortly thereafter. Repressing this would have been the logical thing for him to do to protect his interests."

Jon smiled at his brother. "And it gave us the opportunity to uncover it, all these years later."

Michael returned the expression. "It did indeed."

Detective Yang walked over from the chamber's entrance where she was leading the security team—keeping unauthorized people out, and keeping people who had access to the treasury from leaving with a pocket full of purloined doubloons and jewels.

"It's really something, isn't it?"

Jon drank in the moment. "It sure is."

"How are you holding up?"

"All right, all things considered. Is anyone going to press charges against us?"

"I've talked to representatives at Grace Methodist, Memorial Presbyterian, the Lightner, and Flagler College. Taking into account your motives and the enormity of the find, they were convinced not to pursue charges. There's even talk of using a small portion of the proceeds from this to help restore the damaged works, which could be your restitution. Besides, considering the media storm that's going to swoop down on the Castillo come morning, I doubt anyone is going to make waves for themselves by chasing after the men of the hour."

Jon tried not to beam at that last bit. More than anything, he was grateful that he and his brother wouldn't be facing charges. Legal issues and incarceration would be anathema to future adventures, and after the day's successful treasure hunt, he felt certain that there would be plenty more ahead.

Yang nodded at Michael's leg. "Docs fix you up all right?"

Michael patted his hamstring. "Stitched me up fine. They say I'll make a full recovery. Just gotta deal with these darn crutches for the next few weeks."

"Well, if you've got enough in your tank to take a little walk, I've got something you might be interested in seeing."

Jon and Michael followed her toward the rear of the chamber, stopping at an unassuming section of coquina wall.

"Press those stones at the same time," she said, pointing at a pair of coquina bricks flanking a larger one. Jon pressed one, while his brother pushed the other.

With a hollow scraping sound, the stone in the center hinged inward.

"A secret exit," Jon said.

"Of course." Michael shook his head. "The builders would have wanted some sort of emergency exit in case they accidentally got sealed in."

"It comes out in the moat," Yang said. "Near the shot furnace. The door is completely invisible and inaccessible from the outside."

"So that's how they got out," Michael said.

Jon shook his head. "Likely long gone by now."

"It appears that Miriam rented a boat under a false name early yesterday morning, ready to beat a hasty escape after sneaking some treasure out the passage and over the sea wall. We're still looking, but they may well have left the country by now."

With all this treasure still here, what Miriam had called their ticket to a new life, Jon doubted they would have gone far. The escape passage was scarcely wide enough to squeeze a single sea chest through, but as fully laden as they were, it wouldn't have made for a hasty retreat. If they had absconded with any of the treasure during their egress, it couldn't have been more than a handful or two. A decent start, but hardly the vast fortune the sisters had been planning on.

"What was their story?" Jon asked. "Miriam was saying something about starting a new life together."

"We've had a couple of people on it for the past few hours," Yang said. "Best we can figure, Miriam had thrown away a promising academic career when she cast her lot with

Monk a few years ago. Along the way, she racked up a number of warrants for theft, breaking and entering, and assault, among others. She was Monk's right hand, but a hospital report in Johannesburg about a year ago indicates he was abusive in more ways than one. Meanwhile, Esther had been passed from one foster family to another since her mother died, just weeks before Miriam disappeared into a black hole with Monk after his ignominious ouster from Cornell. Perhaps Miriam felt that this big treasure would finally give her and Esther another chance to be a family, free from the mistakes she committed with Monk—and from Monk himself."

"Well, it looks like they're free of him, and they've got each other," Jon said. "That's got to count for something."

"Aren't you worried?" Michael asked. "They tried to kill you."

"No, Miriam tried to kill me. Esther had every chance to kill me, but she chose not to. And the only reason Miriam wanted me dead was to conceal the discovery of the treasury so they could raid it and because I was a witness to Monk's murder. I'd say both of those ships have sailed now."

"So we're free to go?" Michael asked Yang. "No charges are going to be filed against either of us for anything we've done today?"

"You in that much of a hurry to get out of here?" Yang asked.

"Hardly. But it has been a big day, and I think the leg and I could use a little rest."

"I totally understand. I'll have one of the officers topside give you a lift back to your hotel. As for your question, I think you are both safe from prosecution. As far as I'm concerned, and I think most of the people in this room would agree, you two are heroes."

Michael grabbed Jon in a one-armed, over-the shoulder hug. "You hear that, bro? We're heroes."

Jon smiled. A successful treasure hunt. A historical mystery solved. And through every adventure, his brother right by his side.

Mr. Bouvier had been right. It was just like old times.

Epilogue
Anastasia Island, Florida
The next morning

Jon had been unable to sleep. After lying in bed fruitlessly for several hours, he roused his brother from his slumber, telling him to get dressed. Ten minutes later, they were again prowling the streets of St. Augustine, this time seeking a far more ancient wonder, one relished by humanity all the way back to Adam and Eve. Jon placed a call to Detective Yang, who promptly called the one person who could make the Rickners' morning dream a reality. Reluctantly, the man complied.

Which was how Jon and Michael found themselves climbing the spiral staircase that wound through the center of the St. Augustine Lighthouse. Though the current lighthouse only dated back to 1874, the location had been used since the earliest days of the city. When Sir Francis Drake attacked the city in the sixteenth century, he recorded the presence of a wooden watchtower "beacon" on the island in roughly the same spot, overlooking the Atlantic. In 1737, the Spanish would establish a new square-towered coquina lighthouse. That would be refurbished in 1824, when the United States government chose St. Augustine to be the site of the first lighthouse project in its newly acquired Florida territory, the old tower later playing witness to the Second and Third Seminole Wars as well as the American Civil War. Shortly after the Union was restored, beach erosion was discovered to be undermining the lighthouse's foundation, which led to the construction of a new, circular-towered brick lighthouse in 1874, taller and stronger than any of its predecessors, still standing nearly a century and a half later.

The lighthouse, commonly known as the St. Augustine Light, was normally closed during these early morning hours. Much of the lighthouse duties were automated in the modern era. No longer did the keeper maintain the oil flame that provided the beacon for seafaring vessels, as the advent of reliable high-powered electric lighting had supplanted the original mechanism. Windows at each landing of the interior's winding metal stairs offered views of alternating landscapes, one landing facing east toward the Atlantic, the next west toward St. Augustine proper. Darkness still cloaked the landscape, giving Jon a clear view the illuminated courtyard of the Castillo de San Marcos. He allowed himself a smile as he tackled the next part of the ascent. *We did that.*

The lighthouse keeper, a burly man in his midforties with sandy hair and a full beard to match, led the way toward the top, his flashlight illuminating the way. He wasn't happy about having to play tour guide hours before the public was supposed to show up, but Yang had promised he would be compensated for his time. A history buff, the keeper would be given an advance tour of the Menéndez treasury, an opportunity well worth the trouble of guiding a pair of like-minded enthusiasts to the top of his own historical wonder.

At the last landing before the top, Jon paused.

"What?" Michael asked.

Gripping the railing to prevent a lethal tumble down the open center of the stairwell, he peered into the darkness below. Nothing.

"I thought I heard something. Footsteps below us."

"Between all the metal and stone connected in this circular, enclosed space, this thing can become an echo chamber sometimes," the keeper said.

Maybe that was it. Jon wasn't entirely convinced it was just an echo, but the keeper was far more experienced with the sonic peculiarities of the lighthouse. He'd have to give him the benefit of the doubt.

Once they reached the top, the keeper stopped in front of a door and turned to face the brothers.

"Be careful out here," he said. "The weather may be mild down at ground level, but up here, above all the trees and buildings that break up the winds, it can get quite blustery."

"Duly noted," Michael said, giving Jon a wink. This was hardly the first time they had been atop a lighthouse. Still, that was all the more reason to heed the keeper's warning. They already knew how wild the winds could get.

His safety spiel complete, the keeper opened the door and led them outside. Just before they left the confines of the lighthouse interior, Jon thought he heard another sound from the stairwell below, but he chalked it up to more echoes wrought by the opening of the door and the rushing wind.

"You weren't lying," Jon said, surprised by the gust that hit him in the face as soon as he stepped outside.

"It gets intense," the keeper agreed. "But as long as you stay away from the edge, you should be fine." He paused, his lips twisting in thought. "Kind of late to be asking, I suppose, but neither of you are afraid of heights, are you?"

"No, we've been up in high places plenty," Michael said. "We love them."

The keeper grinned. "Good to hear." He jerked a thumb back at the door. "If you two don't mind, I've got some chores to tend to downstairs. I'll come back to walk you down after sunrise."

After he had left, Jon and Michael circumnavigated the viewing platform, taking in the full panorama of black ocean and palm trees only just beginning to reflect the faintest hint of the lightening eastern sky. Once they had seen all that the shadowed landscape had to offer at this hour, they circled back around to the eastern edge of the platform, awaiting the main event.

○

Miriam Caan wiped the lighthouse keeper's blood off her knife. She had brought her pistol, but guns made noise. It would be for last resorts only. Thankfully, she hadn't needed it with the keeper. He may have been bigger than her, but the surprise of seeing an alluring stranger on the balcony in the middle of his supposedly empty lighthouse gave her the edge she needed. As she knew it would. Ironic that he was the one to discount Jon's observation of another pair of footsteps on the stairs. And now he had been the first to die.

She took no pleasure from the murder of the keeper, but it was necessary. He was simply an obstacle to her true goal.

Retribution.

After all their hard work, collectively being more responsible for the discovery of the treasure than Jon or Michael, Miriam and Esther had been hunted like animals instead of treated like the heroes they should have been. Instead of a hefty finder's fee, taken from the top long before the first archeologist showed up on the scene, they had only been able to abscond with a few pocketfuls of doubloons and jewels, hardly enough to make the new start Miriam had envisioned. Instead of redeeming her archeological cred that she had lost years before when casting her lot with her disgraced professor, she had been saddled with an active warrant for her arrest. Aside from Caeden Monk being out of her life for good, none of this had gone the way it was supposed to. And she blamed the one man who had snatched it all from her at the last minute.

Jonathan Rickner.

Killing Jon wouldn't restore her once-enviable reputation or her robust share of the treasure, but it would give her some smaller measure of peace, a karmic balancing of the universe that the one who had so gravely wronged her would be punished for his actions. She had donned a disguise and staked out their hotel from the shadows just a few hours earlier, and their predawn sojourn had led her here. As though to confirm the cosmos's agreement with her logic, Jon and Michael had decided to isolate themselves atop this lighthouse, in the dark, with no witnesses.

Too perfect.

Climbing the stairs, she reached the last platform before the final flight. She took a moment to gaze out the window. Light was beginning to bleed across the horizon as the earth turned inexorably toward dawn. Which meant she had to hurry. The more light, the more potential witnesses. Of course, the advent of day was the reason the Rickner brothers had come here. Their focus on the sunrise would provide the perfect distraction for her to make her move. With any luck, she'd be back with Esther and cruising into international waters long before the sun began to warm the cresting waves of the Matanzas.

O

"Here it comes," Jon said. He peered at the horizon through a pair of binoculars. A strap looped around his neck kept the binoculars from tumbling 150 to the ground should a gust of wind startle him off balance.

Technically, he wasn't staring at the sun. What he was doing would be a very bad idea in a minute or two, but he enjoyed seeing the distant waves catch the first glimmers of dawn around the curvature of the earth. Witnessing a reflective sunrise seconds before dawn broke where they currently stood was like time travel.

Michael stood to his left, watching the daily spectacle with his naked eye. He had a small monocular in his pocket, which he would use in a few minutes, once there was more to see of the surrounding landscape. Happy to let his brother use the binoculars, he preferred the wider perspective of daybreak. Jon would soon abandon the tool for the full panorama as well, watching the growing light crawl its way across the sea and land to ignite the world in dawn. But for a few more seconds, he watched the dawning of a new day several miles in the future.

Through the howling wind, he thought he heard something behind him, back toward the door. The keeper returning already? As loud as it was up there, it was probably nothing. More echoes. If the keeper had, in fact, come back for them, he would announce himself. Jon dared not look away from the spectacle, not until that great celestial orb finally blinked above the horizon and made the binoculars a potential accomplice for retinal burns.

"Jon, look out!" Michael shouted.

Dropping the binoculars and turning around in one motion, Jon came face-to-face with Miriam Caan. Fury stained her features as she stabbed forward with a long switchblade.

Jon weaved to the side just in time, the blade piercing the fabric of his shirt before tearing free. Miriam quickly recovered, flipping the blade around for another attack.

She never got the chance.

Michael bodychecked her, slamming her into the railing. Dazed at the unexpected attack, Miriam wobbled, trying to regain her balance. It was no use. Another gust of wind blasted her just enough to make the difference, sending her toppling over the railing. But before she disappeared over the edge, she reached out, desperately grabbing at whatever she could.

Her hand found Jon's binocular strap. Unprepared for the sudden force, Jon was yanked over the edge.

With a desperate shout, Michael held fast to the railing and grabbed Jon's wrist just before he plummeted into oblivion.

Jon screamed with pain at his arm nearly being wrenched out of its socket. His neck felt like he had been rear-ended by an eighteen-wheeler, the whiplash of his body being pulled by the canvas strap almost too much to bear. He looked up at his brother pleadingly, but it was clear that the most Michael could do at this point was not drop Jon to his death. And judging by Michael's contorted expression, he wouldn't even be able to do that for much longer.

Dangling below Jon, Miriam screamed in pain. Her switchblade had embedded itself in her shoe, claiming her foot in the process. Serves her right, Jon thought before casting aside the petty dig. Three lives still hung in the balance, including the two most important to him in the world.

Jon grasped the binocular strap, trying to pull it over his neck to free himself from his would-be murderer, but to no avail. Miriam's weight made it impossible to budge. Neither could he move the adjustment toggles, the pressure against them too great. He tried to pull at her fingers, but her grip was iron.

"Jon," Michael grunted from above.

Jon looked up, but his brother shook his head, his eyes pointing back down toward Miriam. Jon glanced down too see what Michael was trying to show him.

Miriam had unholstered a pistol, the same one she had tried to kill him with underneath the Castillo. Killing him or Michael now would surely result in her death as well, but she was clearly past the point of caring. Regardless of how much she wanted to be free of Monk's influence, his murderous philosophy on vengeance and personal slights was living on in his former partner.

She was bringing the gun to bear, which meant the three of them were likely seconds from death. Michael was powerless to do anything except drop them both and run, but he would never do that to Jon. Even if it meant sacrificing his own life for the chance to save his brother's. Which meant Jon had to do something proactive.

So he kneed her in the face. Almost immediately, a torrent of blood began to flow from her nostrils. She screamed at the pain, wincing and blinking the unbidden tears from her eyes, but she maintained her grip on both the strap tying her to Jon and on the gun. He kneed her again, then kicked at the weapon.

Upon impact, the gun fired. Still reeling from the second knee to the face, Miriam hadn't been aiming and the shot went wide, but there were plenty left in the magazine.

Jon kicked at the gun again, and this time it was too much. The weapon flew from Miriam's injured hand and tumbled to the ground below.

Michael grunted. Jon looked to see what, if anything, he was trying to communicate this time. One glance said everything. The grunt may have been unintentional, but Jon could read the meaning as clear as day. His brother's grip was slipping.

If Jon couldn't get Miriam to let go within the next few seconds, they were both as good as dead. And even though Michael would still be alive, he would never be able to forgive himself for letting his little brother die.

He looked down to see Miriam doubled over, almost in the fetal position save for the outstretched arm that maintained its death grip on the binocular strap. Had he hit her that hard? Maybe she would fall off on her own now, the pain too much to bear.

Then she straightened up again and Jon saw the cause of her contortion. The switchblade that was previously embedded in her foot was now held at the ready in her free hand.

Game over.

He could feel Michael struggling, both of their hands sweaty despite the autumn morning air. There was no more time for maneuvering. Unless...

Jon looked up at his brother. "Let me go, bro."

Michael's face twisted with more pain than effort. "Never."

"Trust me. Let me go. Now."

Michael's eyes seemed to register what Jon was thinking. It was a desperate play, but the only one he had. Otherwise, they both might be dead in a moment, Jon stabbed by Miriam, Michael plummeting to his death for his refusal to leave his brother behind. He nodded solemnly, then released Jon's hand.

Miriam was in mid-stab when they both began to fall. Jon grabbed the bottom rail ringing the floor of the viewing platform, bringing their descent to a quick halt. Miriam held on tight to the strap, her other arm continuing to sweep forward with the blade.

At the last second, Jon twisted his body to the side, angling the taut strap to just the right spot.

Miriam's blade missed Jon. But it sliced clean through the binocular strap.

Whether through shock at being bested, anger at her unfinished mission, or resignation at the last of her long line of bad decisions, Miriam was silent as she plummeted fifteen stories to the grass below. The sound of her fatal landing was thankfully obscured by the howling wind and the pounding of blood in his ears.

Jon felt his wrists grabbed anew. He looked up into the relieved face of his brother as Michael pulled him back up and helped him over the railing.

"Thanks," he said between huffs once his feet were back on solid ground. The sun had finally crested the horizon, casting out shadows with blazes of yellow and orange as it climbed higher from its nightly exile. Although Jon had missed the anticipated breaking of dawn, he couldn't remember the last time he'd seen a sunrise so beautiful as the one he now beheld.

"I thought I'd lost you there for a minute," Michael said, drawing him into a hug.

"Never."

Below them, on the coast, Jon noticed a little speedboat roar to life.

"Let me see your monocular," Jon said. Reading Jon's line of sight to the boat bobbing in the waves, Michael handed it over.

Putting the miniature spyglass to his eye in much the same way that St. Augustine's protectors would have from this very spot for the past four centuries, Jon adjusted the device until the boat's sole occupant came into focus.

Esther Caan sat staring back at him, looking immeasurably sad yet somewhat resigned. She must have just witnessed her sister's death, powerless to stop it yet seemingly unsurprised that Miriam's attempt at redemption had fallen short, acquiescing to the vengeful spirit cultivated by long-term proximity to the narcissistic evils of Caeden Monk. Esther looked incredibly lost, broken by the loss of the one piece of hope she had left in the world. She sighed, a deep, slow breath that raised and lowered her shoulders, perhaps trying to process her sister's death, perhaps trying to expel the ghosts of her own haunted past. Bowing her head, she goosed the throttle and puttered out of the shallows before opening it up and plowing through the sprawling waters of the Atlantic.

A lost young woman, suddenly alone in the world, seeking some measure of peace and happiness in the vast ocean of pain that life had dealt her.

Jon hoped she found what she was looking for.

Author's Note

St. Augustine has been near and dear to my heart for as long as I can remember. Growing up just a few hours away, living in a county named after one 16th-century Spanish explorer and attending a school named after another, the Spanish colonial history of my home state was present in my mind from my earliest days. But it was my first visits to St. Augustine that truly impressed upon me how awesome that history really was. While my parents were fans of the historic city years before I was born, even spending their honeymoon there, they helped introduce my sister and me to the city's charms and wonders on numerous family trips. In fact, by the time my fourth-grade class took its overnight trip to St. Augustine, I already felt like an old pro navigating the country's oldest city. As with all of my books, site research was paramount in my writing process for *The Flagler Hunt*. I have probably visited St. Augustine a few dozen times over the past thirty years, but I made a pair of special trips to the key locations in the book to ensure I had them as right as I could. Plus, let's be honest, the city is incredibly inspirational, transporting visitors to another place and time like few other places in the country.

After getting so much fan feedback that they loved Jon's relationship with his brother Michael after it was a driving factor in the events of my debut novel, *From the Ashes*, I knew I needed to visit that in a prequel that showcased one of the adventures that cemented their bond. And where better for them to explore than my old stomping grounds of St. Augustine?

The Flagler Hunt is chock-full of real history and locations. Now this is the part of the book where I get to share what is real and what is fiction.

The historical prologue is based largely in fact. A hurricane did obscure Menéndez's overland assault on Fort Caroline while also shipwrecking Jean Ribault's men during their attempt to attack the new settlement of St. Augustine. The two massacres of the French perpetrated by Admiral Menéndez and his men really happened as described. The events were so gruesome and yet integral to the future of St. Augustine (and indeed all of Florida's future) that the Matanzas was in fact named after the bloody incidents. The treasonous deal struck between Father López and Admiral Menéndez in the massacres' wake, however, is my invention.

Emerson Kirkheimer's misadventure on Mount Mansfield is based loosely on one that Meredith and I experienced several years back. While there wasn't a killer on our tails, we were ill equipped to make the journey and set off far too late in the day. The last hour or so was a desperate race up the aptly named Profanity Trail to the summit, then clambering across the treacherous Cliff Trail to catch the last gondola back to civilization before the late October sun disappeared behind the mountain, stranding us on Vermont's highest peak without water, shelter, or a light source through a cold October night. Thankfully, we survived, but it was such a harrowing (and at times otherworldly) experience, I had to use it here.

The history behind St. Augustine's founding is described as accurately as possible throughout the narrative, as is its tumultuous history in the centuries since. I also tried to adhere to the general layout, including street names, landmarks, and public squares, as much as possible, so visitors to St. Augustine should be able to retrace the characters' steps (albeit without the trespassing, vandalism, and other felonies) with a copy of the book in hand.

St. George Street and Aviles Street are some of the oldest streets in the city, both retaining the cobblestone paths that harken back to their earlier days. While St. George Street has become decidedly more commercialized in recent years, Aviles Street is far more quiet and laid back. Ancient City Antiques is, of course, fictional, though it was loosely inspired by real shops in the city I've had the pleasure of patronizing over the past decade or so.

The Old City Gates that Caeden Monk walks through at the beginning and end of the book have stood sentinel over the city's northern boundary since 1808. The gates and the surrounding walls are the last remaining portion of the

Cubo Line fortifications built to protect the city from invaders more than three centuries ago.

The Plaza de la Constitucion is one of the largest and oldest parks in the city, surrounded by historic buildings like the Government House and the Cathedral Basilica of St. Augustine. The history behind the so-called old slave market is true, and the statue of Ponce de Leon—whose legend is forever tied to the site by the nearby Fountain of Youth tourist attraction—can be seen in his own park at the edge of the Plaza today.

Thomas Edison's impact on St. Augustine cannot be understated. A pioneer in numerous arenas during the late 19th century, his friendship with Henry Flagler was a big driver in bringing St. Augustine into the modern age, introducing newfangled technologies like "electricity" to the city to help draw rich tourists from up north. The phonographs used by Monk and by Jon are based on Edison's first-generation devices, as are the wax cylinders that would have been new and innovative enough to delight visitors with the wonder of recorded sound. The cylinder at the heart of the Flagler hunt, however, is fictional.

The history of the imposing Castle Warden is real. Marjorie Kinnan Rawlings did later own the building and run it as the Castle Warden Hotel, and the establishment really was patronized by the celebrities described in the narrative—Robert Ripley foremost among them. The hotel fire in 1944 happened, and the building remains a staple on the city's numerous ghost tours due to the purported specters of the two women who died in the conflagration. The exhibits described within Ripley's are also real, with the medieval torture device/vampire hunting kit room long being one of my favorites. The secret door to the employees-only section is my invention, as is my description of that area. But considering the building's rich history, I do like to think that Ripley's preserved as much of the hotel as possible behind the scenes. After all, there's no sense in unnecessarily disturbing those ghosts.

Grace United Methodist Church may be the "lesser" of the two churches built by Flagler in St. Augustine, but it remains a beauty to behold. The unique history behind the church and how the building was offered to the congregation in return for the land on which Flagler wanted to build his Hotel Alcazar is

true, and even though Flagler wasn't going to regularly attend
Grace like he would Memorial Presbyterian, he didn't skimp on
the construction, ensuring that Carrère and Hasting's work on
the church would rival that of his other projects throughout the
city. The church, including its curious width-to-depth ratio and
the placement of the altar, is described as accurately as possible.
The golden cross piece set into the altar, however, is fictional, as
are all of the pieces throughout the story, though they are based
on real artifacts from the period.

In addition to offering tantalizing free samples to passersby on St. George Street, Pizzalley's really lives up to its
name of being an alley that sells pizza. I've always enjoyed
retreating to the brick-walled cloister between Pizzalley's
two restaurants, as it felt like a nice little retreat from the
often-boisterous tourist trappings of St. George Street. The
fact that it straddles two streets was an added bonus for having Jon and company eat lunch there.

Similarly, Scarlett O'Hara's is an institution in St. Augustine. While the front porch and weathered wood exterior betray the building's origins as an 1879 home, the past
40 years as a restaurant have given it a reputation as a live-
ly place for food, drink, and nightlife. As for the original
homeowner who is said to haunt the second-floor martini
bar, I haven't yet seen him, though the restaurant's place
on haunted pub tours and other ghost-hunting excursions
mean visitors have no shortage of opportunities for their
own spectral experience.

The Hotel Alcazar is a magnificent complex, with a
unique style focusing more on the Moorish side of Spanish architecture. The courtyards and plazas are all real, but
the meat of the experience is in the core of the hotel, now
the Lightner Museum. The Alcazar was renowned for its
health-conscious offerings, from Turkish and Russian baths
to the then-largest indoor swimming pool in the world to a
full-featured gymnasium and an array of outdoor activities
to numerous high-tech devices aimed at providing healing
influences. The Morton-Wimshurst-Holtz Influence Machine was one such device the Alcazar offered its guests, and
it can still be seen on display in the Lightner Museum today
(assuming they've repaired the glass case Liz/Esther broke).
The third-story door through which Jon's group make their

escape is real, as is the rooftop walkway from which they jump to the ground.

Memorial Presbyterian Church is rightly recognized as one of the most beautiful churches in the country. Strongly influenced by Venice's iconic St. Mark's Basilica, Flagler built the church quite literally in memory of his daughter, who had died from complications from childbirth while it was being built. The gated mausoleum was built for his daughter, the granddaughter who she had borne, and his first wife, who had died in 1881.

The heavenly ceiling and frequent organ music Jon describes are real, as is Flagler's pew, which he used whenever he was in town. In my earliest drafts of *From the Ashes* more than a decade ago, I created a secret-compartment-under-a-pew hiding place for the St. Patrick's Cathedral clue, but ultimately decided on a better option for that story. Here, it seemed to fit much better, though the secret compartment is, of course, fictional.

Hotel Ponce de Leon was Flagler's architectural magnum opus in St. Augustine, outshined only by his Breakers hotel later built in Palm Beach (and even that's debatable). Encompassing open-air courtyards, luxurious accommodations, and an atmosphere of idealized Old World Spain, the palatial complex was the epitome of Flagler's St. Augustine, a fanciful fusion of a romanticized past and a brave new future, replete with the sort of furnishings and features that could rival the finest hotels New York or Boston had to offer. Today, the hotel is the bustling heart of Flagler College, though visitors are welcome and official tours are conducted.

The Ponce de Leon's sundial fountain, hand-carved lobby sculptures, and dining room (complete with Miriam's balcony and the constellation-strewn ceiling) are all real. So too is the Flagler Room, including its history as a women's parlor during the hotel's heyday. The clock hiding the fourth piece of the cross did stop back in 1968, with decades of engineers since unable to fix it. The clock face really is the largest piece of white onyx in the Western Hemisphere, and its value is perhaps the primary reason why more drastic attempts haven't been made to get the clock running again.

Mission Nombre de Dios long served as a Catholic mission to the indigenous peoples of northeast Florida. Situated at the site of Father López's 1565 Thanksgiving mass, the mission today hosts several shrines, a church, a bell tower, a historic cemetery, and archeological dig sites, among other features. The statue of Father López on the grounds is a testament to the impact the Franciscan priest had on the people of the land—both Spaniards and natives alike. Meanwhile, the stainless steel Great Cross stretches more than 200 feet heavenward and can be seen for miles around.

The current St. Augustine Lighthouse has watched over the Matanzas and the nation's oldest city for well over a century, but the site has played host to a beacon for seafarers since the sixteenth century. The metal stairs snaking up the inside of the stone lighthouse are as described, and the viewing platform at the top can get quite windy indeed. But the views—of the Atlantic to the east and of St. Augustine to the west—are more than worth the climb.

Of all the historic features of St. Augustine, none of them come close to being as iconic or as important as the Castillo de San Marcos. While the Castillo's walls are pocked with the impacts of artillery fire, the fortress was never taken by force and its presence helped to defend St. Augustine from foreign navies, hostile tribesmen, and infamous pirates. The history of the fort's construction, as well as its role in the Seminole Wars and the Civil War, is also real.

With the cannons perched on the parapets (some of which are still fired every weekend to the delight of visitors), corner watchtowers with a clear view of vessels sailing through the Matanzas, guides and actors dressed in period military garb, and a host of stone chambers filled with history and mystery, it was hard not to lose myself in imaginary adventures every time I visited the fort as a boy. While I have fond memories of many of the rooms in the Castillo, the dungeon—with its complete lack of sunlight and crawlspace entrance—was always my favorite. Between evolving scholarship and the fort's changing hands between nations three times (five if you include the shift to and from the Confederacy at the beginning and end of the Civil War), another room was also identified as possibly serving as a dungeon of sorts at one point in its history, but the tiny, isolated, barrel-vaulted room I grew up knowing as the dungeon was the perfect place to bring Flagler's hunt to its unlikely conclusion. But while and array of stones cover the room's ceiling and floor, the chessboard puzzle, secret floor mechanism, and hidden treasury are my inventions.

At its heart, the historical conceit behind *The Flagler Hunt* is centered on two men who made an indelible mark on St. Augustine and, as a result, on Florida as a whole. Two men who, despite the centuries separating them, were bound by a shared secret that could undermine their careers and reputations. While Menéndez's secret treasury and Flagler's abandoned treasure hunt are my inventions, they are framed in real history and are based on the larger-than-life characters of both men.

Don Pedro Menéndez de Aviles was a man of great skill and courage. The descriptions of his derring-do and bold maneuvers in the narrative scarcely do him justice, and his achievements quickly gained him the favor and friendship of King Philip II, who made him admiral-general of Spain's treasure fleet and the first governor of Spanish Florida. The *San Miguel*, the treasure ship Menéndez conspired to sack to fill the secret treasury and then sink at sea, is fictional but is based on a number of galleons laden with precious metals and gems from South and Central America that were lost at sea during the period. Many still have not been found.

While the conspiracy that López devised to help spread the Gospel to the native peoples of Spanish Florida is my own invention, Menéndez's own life shows his unparalleled dedication to evangelizing this corner of the New World. In the years after he founded St. Augustine, he would travel through the dense inhospitable swamplands of Central and South Florida, befriending a number of tribes and proselytizing to them. He converted numerous natives to Catholicism, even marrying the sister of the Calusa chief at one point to gain that tribe's trust. And despite his apparent unwavering service to the crown, King Philip never did give Menéndez the financial reward he had been promised, despite numerous entreaties from the admiral. Why that was remains a mystery to this day.

Though Admiral Menéndez may have founded St. Augustine, it was Henry Flagler who transformed it into the city it is today. Armed with an unparalleled fortune in oil money and looking to expand his railroad empire, he fell in love with the mystique of St. Augustine almost as soon as he arrived. By bringing in electric generators, building countless hotels, churches, and civic projects, and infusing the city with massive amounts of tourist dollars, Flagler helped catapult the city into the modern age while preserving—and in many ways, reimagining—the city's unique past.

The treasure hunt I have him create and abandon in the narrative is my invention, but something like it wouldn't have been outside the bounds of possibility. The hunt was essentially devised as a city-wide parlor game, tying together the popularity of *Treasure Island*, St. Augustine's authentic historical past, and the beautiful new landmarks Flagler had built in the city. A gimmick like that could have been just the thing he needed to drive an offseason wave of tourism to his resorts.

Flagler would eventually move further south down his railroad line to tackle new real estate challenges in Palm Beach and Miami, eventually being honored as the father of both cities. His Florida East Coast Railroad and unparalleled real estate empire along the state's Atlantic coast was instrumental in establishing Florida as a tourist destination. Without Flagler laying the groundwork, Walt Disney never would have taken the chance on Florida for his Disney World project decades later. Without his pioneering ingenuity and investment, my home state's biggest industry might be citrus instead of tourism. Florida's role as a premier tourist destination for travelers across the world owes a tremendous debt to what Henry Flagler started in St. Augustine more than a century ago.

In 1917, four years after his death, a new county would be carved out directly south of St. Augustine and named after him. And while the last two decades of his life would see him spending more time focused on his newer resorts in further south Palm Beach and Miami, he chose to be buried in St. Augustine, joining his loved ones in the Memorial Presbyterian mausoleum. Despite all his accomplishments across numerous states, cities, and industries, it was St. Augustine that had ultimately captured his heart.

I know exactly how he must have felt.

Acknowledgements

This was a fun book to write, and a lot of that is thanks to the support I had from a number of people in writing it.

Thanks to the great people of St. Augustine and especially the tour guides and staffers of the churches, museums, and other historic sites at the heart of this book. While I've always loved the rich history of St. Augustine, researching this book has helped me to gain a whole new level of appreciation for the city, and much of that is due to your tremendous insight and hospitality.

Thanks also to the rangers and gondola staffers on Mount Mansfield, Vermont who kept the gondola station open for one last trip down the mountain one late autumn evening to make sure Meredith and I didn't end up meeting the sort of fate Emerson Kirkheimer feared.

Thanks to Travis Lafitte, my lifelong friend who reintroduced me to St. Augustine as an adult and shared more than a few memorable adventures in the city with me.

Thanks to my amazing wife Meredith, who not only supported me in all the hours I spent writing and editing this book but also helped me on several research trips to the city (and, of course, on that fateful misadventure on Mount Mansfield). None of this would be possible without you, and I'm so excited to see where this takes us.

Thanks to my son Graham who was born shortly after I initially finished this book a few years ago. You're everything I could want in a son and so much more. With you, every day's an adventure in all the best ways.

Thanks to my parents, my sister Becca, and Travis for reading through the manuscript and offering some helpful hints.

Also thanks to my parents for introducing me at such an early age to how exciting history can be in a place like St. Augustine.

Thanks to my awesome agent Pam Ahearn and my incredible editor Lou Aronica for helping to polish the rough edges out of the book and mold it into the story it needed to be.

And finally, thanks to all of you, my readers. An extra special thank you to everyone who read *From the Ashes* and left a review or sent me a note letting me know how much you enjoyed Jon as a character and wanted to see more of his relationship with his brother. Find me on social media or on my website and let me know what you thought of their adventure together.

Until the next time, my friends (which will be very soon indeed...)!

About the Author

Jeremy Burns is the nationally bestselling author of *The Dubai Betrayal*, *From the Ashes*, and the upcoming *The Founding Treason*. He is a lifelong storyteller and explorer whose travels have taken him to more than twenty countries across four continents. He has gained some unique professional experiences alongside his writing career, including working as an international educator in Dubai, a law enforcement consultant, a Walt Disney World cast member, and a journalist, writing for a number of award-winning publications on topics ranging from global terrorism to haunted asylums to end-time prophecies. He holds degrees in history, business, and computer science, and has far more interests than can possibly be healthy. He lives in Florida with his wife, son, and two dogs, where he is working on his next book.

Also by Jeremy Burns

FROM THE ASHES

A DEADLY CONSPIRACY

Graduate students Jonathan and Michael Rickner, sons of
eminent archaeologist Sir William Rickner, are no strangers
to historical mysteries and archaeological adventures. But
when Michael is discovered dead in his Washington, D.C.
apartment, Jon refuses to believe the official ruling of suicide. Digging deeper into his brother's work, he discovers
evidence that Michael was murdered to keep his dissertation
research buried.

A DEVASTATING NATIONAL SECRET

Joined by Michael's fiancée Mara Ellison, Jon travels to New
York where he uncovers the threads of a deadly Depres-
sion-era conspiracy - one entangling the Hoover Administration, the Rockefellers, and the rise of Nazi Germany - and
the elite cadre of assassins that still guard its unspeakable
secret.

THE LABYRINTHINE PATH TO THE TRUTH

Finding themselves in the crosshairs of the same men who
killed Michael, Jon and Mara must navigate a complex web
of historical cover-ups and modern-day subterfuge, outwit-
ting and outrunning their all-powerful pursuers as they race
through the monuments and museums of Manhattan in a
labyrinthine treasure hunt to discover the last secret of John
D. Rockefeller, Jr., before their enemies can bury the truth -
and them - forever.

Read an excerpt on the next page.

Roger turned east and began ascending the pedestrian section of the Brooklyn Bridge. An American icon, its strong steel cables and massive stone arches standing as a monument of a bygone era. A beacon of ingenuity and bravado, of innovation and work ethic. Everything like the America that stood up to Hitler, to Stalin, to despots and injustice worldwide, the great bastion of freedom she publicly considered herself to be. And nothing like the America he knew. At least, not anymore.

His footfalls echoed in the cold, dry air. It was quiet, but then, at this hour of the night, it should be. His breath came in short bursts, visible as puffs of smoke in the icy air. A haunting pair of sad brown eyes appeared in the mist and stared longingly at the breaths. Trudging onward, he tried to put it out of his mind. But failed.

Billy Yates was dead. The Division would ensure that his nameless friend would meet a similar fate, fixing Roger's mistake, his breach of conscience. They were perfect at what they did, if not as individuals, then as a unit, killing off any whispers of the truth behind the Operation. Billy and his friend had known enough of the truth to make them a liability. Never mind their age. Never mind their innocence. They had to die. And die Billy had. And die his friend would. But the face of Billy as he'd choked his last, the eyes that had locked with Roger's, opened the floodgates of the agent's mind, releasing an onslaught of the faces of the nameless dead, the Division's *traitors*, Roger's *victims*.

Officially, Roger's mistake had been leaving evidence, not disposing of the body, not killing the friend. The more faces rushed back into his memory, though, the more he began to wonder exactly what – and when – his biggest mistake really was.

Upon reaching the center of the bridge, the point with the greatest distance between the bridge above and the river below, he stopped and surveyed the area. A series of iron girders extended across the space between the central pedestrian bridge and the sides of the bridge itself. One of these led to a platform that jutted over the river. The intersection of two crossbeams in the vicinity completed the package.

The perfect spot.

Roger swung his body over the rail and onto the girder leading to the platform. He grabbed the briefcase and lugged it over the rail as well, careful not to let its weight throw off his balance and send him tumbling to the automobile section of the bridge some twenty feet below. He went through the motions emotionlessly, thoughtlessly. He was in mission mode, just as he always was before he made a kill.

He clambered across the girder and onto the platform, setting the briefcase down as soon as he got to its relative safety. From the briefcase he withdrew a length of steel cable, a loop at each end. Each loop was held by an apparatus bolted to each end that allowed the loop to loosen or tighten when the catch was released, but only to tighten when it was locked. He tied one loop around one of the supports of the bridge, threading the cable through the hole and pulling the knot tight, the catch set to secure the binding. The other loop he placed around his neck.

He hefted the cable in his hands. Heavy. Thirty-two feet of cable. Thirty-two. A symbolically fitting message, he felt. Thirty-two was where it began. Thirty-two was where it would end.

His suit jacket flapped in the brisk wind, his perfectly shined black shoes catching the light of the full moon above, that watchful orb that condemned him even now, as he stood on his self-prescribed gallows. He stared downriver, the lights of the Lower Manhattan harbors twinkling in the distance, the black expanse of the bay opening up beyond. And beneath him, the icy waters of the East River glimmered in the moonlight, beckoning him downward, calling him toward a descent that he would only be able to make partway. The cable would hold him back from completing the journey into oblivion, just as some uncrushed fragment of his humanity, lying dormant for so many years, numbed into nothingness by training and necessity, had prevented him from continuing his descent into depravity in the name of duty and patriotism. The icy wind bit at the exposed skin on his face, his hands, his steel-encircled neck, the flesh growing numb with the pain that Roger's occupied mind was already dead to.

The loop around Roger's neck was not a proper noose. A proper noose would have snapped Roger's neck the moment it drew tight: a merciful death. And Roger had decided that the monster he had become deserved no mercy. But although his noose would normally lend itself to a slow death by strangulation, in all likelihood, the speed his body would reach by the end of a thirty-foot free fall would more than provide the required force to break his neck. But the cable's thirty-two feet had more than just a symbolic purpose: that length would also ensure maximum visibility of his body from the city and from the river. Much shorter, and the underside of the bridge would obscure his body from many vantage points. Much longer, and the force of the noose stopping his free fall might decapitate him, his head and body plummeting to the inky depths below, being swept out to sea instead of remaining suspended from the East Coast's most famous bridge. A ghost dangling from an icon by a symbol. The importance of which most people would never fully grasp. But hopefully someone would. Someday.

A memory came to him as he stood on the precipice, ready to take the final plunge. As a boy, he had attended a Baptist church every Sunday with his family. He remembered Mrs. Booth, the bespectacled, grandmotherly Sunday school teacher who had taught the children about a "new life" in Jesus; a "second birth," as Christ Himself had put it. The irony was overwhelming. For Roger was not looking at a second birth, but a second death: the killing of a man already six years dead, buried in an unmarked grave in a country seven-thousand miles away. Maybe this would send ripples through someone's pond. Maybe this would rattle some cages.

That was part of the beauty of the whole operation: they didn't exist. Not as individuals, not as an organization. They were naught but shadows glimpsed from the corner of one's eye, ghosts that existed solely in dreamscapes. Dead men begetting more dead men.

Someday, the truth would come out, but not today. Not with the Cold War, as some were starting to call the tensions between the United States and the Soviet Union, escalating as it was. Just days earlier, the Soviets had launched a man-made satellite into space, broadcasting its ominous beeping as it traced a terrifying line across the night sky. No, the secret he guarded could not be revealed in this day. But by the same token, it would no longer be guarded by his hand.

His story, his secret, a secret that even his superiors would kill for, was in a safe place, even if its caretaker was unaware of its importance and potential implications for the nation, for the world. All of his loose ends in this life were tied up. All of them save one.

Roger gripped the cable in his hands, drawing the noose tight around his neck like a businessman tying his tie in the morning before going off to work. He was already dead, he told himself. He was just finishing what the Division had already done to him. What he had done to so many others in the name of freedom.

He took a deep breath, raised his eyes skyward in a last-minute plea for redemption, and, gripping the cable around his neck with both hands, stepped from the girder into nothingness. Three seconds and thirty-two feet later, the cord drew tight around his neck, lacerating the skin and muscle but leaving the head attached to its body. The eyes rolled back as the head lolled forward. A left shoe plummeting to the dark waters below, the body danced its brief fandango, a lifeless marionette held aloft by one fatal string.

On display for the city to see, a man six years dead was just growing cold. The Division had claimed its latest victim. One of its own.

THE DUBAI BETRAYAL

During a desperate attempt to rally support for a controversial Middle Eastern peace summit, U.S. Ambassador Christine Needham is kidnapped on an unauthorized visit to Dubai. Forced to walk a thin line between diplomacy and effectiveness, President James Talquin assembles a new covert team, helmed by black ops veteran Wayne Wilkins, to rescue the ambassador before she is executed by terrorists. But the ambassador is in possession of a dangerous secret, one that, if not recovered in time, could lead to the most devastating terror attack in history.

Now Wayne and his team are on a collision course with unseen forces that seem to be manipulating world powers toward a devastating conclusion. With a nuclear apocalypse just hours away, the operatives must confront a new kind of jihad, one that breaks all the rules of warfare and terrorism.

But all of the players may not be what they seem, and with no one left to trust, the newly founded team must lean on each other to navigate the glittering heights and hidden depths of one of the world's most fascinating cities and infiltrate a centuries-old shadow war raging within Islam itself. As the twists and betrayals mount, it soon becomes clear that unless Wayne and his men can recover the ambassador and the secret she holds in time, the terrorists' enigmatic paymaster may get exactly what he wants: an all-consuming world war from which America and her allies would never recover.

Read an excerpt here:

Seconds after her chartered flight touched down at Dubai International Airport, Christine Needham dashed to the door, anxious for the pilot to give the all clear and to lower the air stairs. She had Dan contact the US Consulate in Dubai while en route, and they would be sending an SUV to pick her up on the tarmac and take her straight to the consulate. She wanted to tell them what she had discovered, but she couldn't trust a revelation of this magnitude over an unsecured line. They had secure lines at the consulate, and it was there that she would place the call to the president.

The most important phone call of her career.

As ambassador to the most beleaguered and controversial region in the world, Christine was no stranger to feeling the pressure of the world on her shoulders. But this was something else altogether. Even lobbying Sheikh Khalid for his support on the peace summit on the issue of Israel and Palestine didn't come close. What she had discovered on the memory card was even worse than the accompanying note had portended. This was instantly and irrevocably world-changing.

The most devastating conflict the world had seen in generations was looming. And only she had the key to stopping it.

She had been in high-pressure situations before, when economies hung in the balance, and had come out on top. Still, without her surging adrenaline, she might have had a panic attack. If she were completely honest, she'd have to admit she was terrified for her nation and for her diplomatic charge.

Despite her role as arbiter for the United States across the region, she couldn't deny that she harbored a particular affinity for Israel. Her maternal grandmother had immigrated to the United States from Nazi-controlled Germany before the borders were closed to Jews, so she felt a passion for the tiny nation that always seemed to be in the world's crosshairs. At the same time, she was a pragmatist and realized that within a decade, and without some sort of course correction, there might not be an Israel anymore. America's influence in the region was waning, and sentiments at home and across the Western world were shifting toward the Palestinians' cause. The recent refusal of the West to stand up to ISIS or the Iranian nuclear program in any meaningful way had emboldened Hamas and Hezbollah, and conflict in the region seemed to be moving to a point where Israel's own potent military capabilities might not be sufficient to stave off a massive multi-nation attack on its own. The possibility of losing the homeland her forefathers had been denied for nearly nineteen centuries was unthinkable.

The package she had received in Cairo changed all of that. It changed everything. Peace—in Israel, in the Middle East, and even across the globe—might never again be attainable if she couldn't get this information to the president before it was too late.

As soon as she reached the stairs, she could see something was terribly wrong. Not one SUV waited outside, but three. And the men getting out of the vehicles were not diplomatic staffers holding agendas and sat phones.

They were jihadists. Guns drawn, well organized, no official uniforms, and very much where they shouldn't have been. They had come for her.

Christine froze atop the first step and tumbled back into the cabin, rolling away from the open door. She heard shouts from outside, some in Arabic, others in English.

Rick looked at Christine on the ground, and then at the men outside, and also dove out of the doorway. Ben rushed to her side while Dan conferred with the pilots, trying to figure a way out of this mess.

The evidence! Christine thought. That had to be why the gunmen were here. She opened her briefcase and withdrew the Micro SD memory card that had been delivered to her just hours earlier. Back when the world was only marginally screwed up and Christine wasn't aware of a deadly conspiracy, nor of being actively threatened by terrorists. None of that mattered now. She had to protect the evidence at all costs.

The briefcase was not an option. Far too obvious. But she couldn't leave it either. Surely they'd either scour the plane for anything they could use to their advantage or, more likely, they'd torch it when they were done. Either way, the revelations on the card would be lost. Then where?

The answer came to her like an inspiration from heaven. She knew all too well that men like these perverted the teachings of Islam to suit their political needs, but she had to hope that they were at least observant enough of their faith's basic tenets. The fact that she was one-quarter Jewish—and thus, decidedly unclean in these fanatics' eyes—should work in her favor as well.

As if that would matter if they did manage to get their hands on her.

She took the Micro SD card between thumb and forefinger and, being careful to ensure the tiny memory stick would remain secure, placed it underneath her left breast inside her bra.

They may be terrorists, she prayed silently, but don't let them be savages.

THE FOUNDING TREASON

What if some of our nation's architects set into motion a series of acts so treasonous that we are still feeling their effects nearly two-and-a-half centuries later? That is the question at the heart of this stunning, provocative thriller.

When newly minted doctor of history Jonathan Rickner stumbles across an old film canister in the National Archives, he sets off an explosive chain of events that leaves dozens dead and himself on the run. The contents of that canister, revealing long-buried evidence about the Kennedy assassination, is just the first piece of a centuries-old puzzle stretching from the Civil War to the Constitutional Convention and back to modern day.

Joined by Chloe Harper, a conspiracy devotee desperate to clear her disgraced FBI agent father's name, Jon becomes entangled in a web of deception dating to the American Revolution. Going toe-to-toe with a powerful secret aristocracy formed by a rogue faction of Founding Fathers, Jon and Chloe are forced into a desperate race to discover the incredible truth behind a conspiracy theory older than the United States itself.

From the streets of Dallas to the colonial meeting halls of Boston to the palatial mansions of Embassy Row to a secret complex deep beneath the American heartland, through celebrated museums, forgotten chambers, and presidential tombs, Jon and Chloe must expose those responsible before it's too late. For another attack is imminent, and if they fail in their quest, America may never recover.

Propelled by puzzles and mysteries that demand to be solved and brimming with exhaustively researched details from America's past, The Founding Treason is a singularly immersive thriller, one that will leave you questioning who is really calling the shots.

Read an excerpt here:

February 1865
Philadelphia, Pennsylvania

Nicholas Longworth Anderson held tight to the reins, praying his hired horse wouldn't be spooked by the latest flash of lightning. The horse raced on, tensing at every boom of thunder, beating through the empty streets and splashing puddles in all directions as its master urged him onward. Why this meeting couldn't wait until more favorable weather was beyond Anderson's understanding. But Powell had been adamant. The future of the Union was at stake. So he raced on.

Minutes later, the home of Hiram Powell materialized through the haze of rain-soaked night. The three-story mansion was dark save for a light that burned in a second-story window. Powell's den. Anderson handed the reins of his horse to the stable boy, then rushed to the door. He used the knocker to rap the agreed-upon pattern, then checked his pocket watch. Ten minutes late. Considering the weather and how far he had come, surely the others would understand.

A Negro servant answered the door and took Anderson's coat and hat. Anderson knew the way to the den. He also knew that whatever was going on in there was for members' ears only. Powell wouldn't trust anyone outside the circle—not even his own wife—with their secret business. So Anderson saw himself up.

Arriving at the entrance to the den, he paused. He could hear indistinct voices through the heavy oaken door. A heated argument. Something big was indeed going down. He brushed in vain at the water soaking his trousers and shirt, then rapped the secret tattoo upon the wood. The voices stopped immediately. Moments later, the door creaked open and the broad face of his friend Jeremiah Burkett greeted him.

"Come in, Nicholas, quickly."

Immediately, Anderson knew something was amiss. There were far more brothers here than he had expected, including a number he had never seen before. They must have come from another chapter of the society, which made the urgent business Powell had called the meeting for all the more mysterious. The room was charged with a curious energy, not unlike the air shortly before a storm struck. Burkett's normally jovial face was pinched with worry. Anderson surveyed the expressions of his fellow brothers as he took his seat. An array of emotions bedecked their countenances. None were pleasant. Anger, frustration, and disbelief made multiple appearances. But most prominent of all, an underlying emotion seemingly present on most of the faces here, was a fatalistic resignation.

"Nicholas, so nice of you to join us," Powell said. Anderson was about to reply with an excuse about the weather, but Powell didn't give him the chance.

"Gentlemen, the path forward is clear. The only question is, do we have the courage to take it?"

"What you're proposing is treason!" countered a thin man with a New England accent.

"We were born in treason," Powell countered. "We had to defend against allegations of further treason throughout our early years. And yet, we remained stalwart. Our forefathers made the difficult decisions necessary to defend our nation. Shall we cast off their sacrifice and disgrace their legacy, in this, our nation's hour of need?"

Most of the room shouted "no!" But a few dissenters remained. Anderson, for his part, remained silent, unsure what Powell was proposing. "How do we know this won't make things worse?" asked a whitehaired man with a bushy mustache and an aristocratic South Carolina accent. Anderson blinked in confusion. A Confederate brother? Had Powell actually managed to get brothers from Confederate-held chapters to attend his secret meeting? How big was this plan of his?

"The war is drawing to a close, but there are those who remain dedicated to rebellion at all costs. When the time comes, my plan will be the only thing that can prevent the Union from dissolving again. The successor has his issues, but he is from Tennessee and will be much more palatable to those who would tear us apart again. And need I remind you that the election four years ago was what spurred your great state to turn its back on our nation in secession?"

The man from South Carolina assented under his breath. In a group whose founding had been built upon a series of treasonous acts, the reminder of a more recent treason against everything their forefathers had built was more than enough to silence him.

"You know Hamilton Fish won't stand for this," argued a brother from Maryland.

"He doesn't have to. Gentlemen, I called each of you for a reason. All of you are powerful men of finance and influence, chosen from each of our thirteen chapters. If it comes to it, those of us in this room—and our sons in the years to come—can stand alone. Our forefathers fought valiantly to create our nation. Now we must become the vanguard to defend it from the enemies lurking within our very borders."

A murmur grew among the members as they debated Powell's points. In the lamplight, their faces appeared curiously contorted, deepened shadows flickering until obliterated by the occasional blaze of lightning from the windows. Anderson took the opportunity to whisper to his friend.

"Jeremiah, what is Powell talking about?" Burkett leaned toward him and opened his mouth to speak, but

Powell's booming voice cut through the discussion before he could answer.

"I propose we put it to a vote," Powell said, raising his hand. "All in favor of proceeding with my plan to defend our nation and the legacy of our forefathers, raise your right hand."

One by one, hands went up across the room. Anderson, still ignorant of the plan Powell was proposing, saw Burkett's hand raised and realized that only one hand was not raised. Slowly, Anderson lifted his hand, trusting that a unanimous vote in spite of the contentious discussion had to signify the plan was the right decision.

Powell looked from brother to brother, letting the gravity of their decision sink in. Moments later, he finally spoke.

"Then it's decided, my brothers. History shall never know of our actions, but our nation will survive because of your boldness. May it ever be so. In order for the United States to survive, President Lincoln must die."